Advance Praise for Bride of ISIS

"Fascinating and brilliantly written, Anne Speckhard's fictionalized, true-life tale is as compelling as it is shocking." —**U.S. Ambassador Alberto Fernandez (Ret.)**, Former Coordinator for Strategic Counterterrorism Communications (CSCC), U.S. State Department, Vice President Middle East Media Research Institute (MEMRI)

"As the US government insists on keeping real facts classified on terrorism cases, we must turn to fiction to try to peek into the minds of the new crop of teenager terrorists. Speckhard's thinly fictionalized tale of a real case peels back some layers of this chilling darkness." —**Marc Sageman**, Former CIA case officer and author of *Understanding Terror Networks and Leaderless Jihad*

"I have had the honor to know and work with Anne Speckhard over many years, and find her work and books prolific and of great use to anyone that wants to understand terrorism by khawarej (zealots hiding behind religion) and their manipulation of women." –**Major General HRH Princess Aisha Bint Al Hussein** of Jordan

"Some of the most illuminating discussions of terrorism have been works of fiction by eminent authors like Albert Camus, *The Just Assassins;* Joseph Conrad, *The Secret Agent;* Fyodor Dostoyevsky, *The Possessed;* etc. works I used in the terrorism courses I taught in late 1960s before the subject interested academics. Anne Speckhard, a psychologist, who has spent considerable time interviewing terrorists, has decided to use her talent and experience to produce a novel on how one becomes a terrorist today. My students always found the great fictional works generated more valuable and exciting discussions than the academic works assigned, and *Bride of ISIS* will have the same effect." –**David C. Rapoport**, Founding and Chief Editor of *Terrorism and Political Violence*, Author of *Four Waves of Modern Terror*

"People often ask me the question: what brings people to join violent groups like ISIS? If you really want to know, there is only one advice: read Anne Speckhard. She did the most obvious thing that very few others seem to have the courage for. She spoke to them. Those who joined. Re-humanizing what so many others have demonized. It is the only way to understand motives. It is also the only way to begin to find the road to the solution. Anne Speckhard has (once more) written a book that all those who develop counter terrorism policies and approaches should read." —**Peter Knoope**, Former Director of the International Centre for Counter Terrorism - The Hague

"Drawing on her more than four hundred interviews with terrorists and their associates, Anne Speckhard skillfully leads us into the inner world of the traumatized youth who have been adroitly manipulated to join the virtual community of hatred. The novelization of politics, psychology, and culture is a splendid route to understanding that persuasively conveys the passage from lost adolescent to the power of using her own body as a weapon. The implications as ISIS draws successfully on Western youth to magnify their ranks are quite frightening." —**Jerrold M. Post, M.D.**, Director of the Political Psychology Program, The George Washington University and author of _The Mind of the Terrorist_

"Anne Speckhard's _Bride of ISIS_ should be mandatory reading for people working in counter terrorism operations and national security policy. Fictional, but grounded in cases and trends that governments, communities and academics around the world are trying to get a handle on." —**Laurence Brooks**, Director General (ret) Canadian Security Intelligence Service (CSIS)

"Dr. Anne Speckhard is a true expert in what makes terrorists tick, the men, and especially the women. This book is the first of its kind to discuss the shocking cases of young women lured by ISIS and the deep psychological undercurrents that hypnotize young girls to traverse borders thousands of miles away in search of romance amidst a raging battle of identity, sense of meaning and belonging. This book will become required reading in various genres." —**Mubin Shaikh**, Islamic Radicalization and Counter-terrorism Expert, coauthor of *Undercover Jihadi: Inside the Toronto 18*

"From an esteemed author who has interviewed over four hundred terrorists and their associates, *Bride of ISIS* shows us how a young American girl could be seduced into extremist thinking and give up everything in search of what she falsely believes will be meaning, adventure, romance and a new identity inside a terrorist group. A spellbinding and captivating read!" —**Rita Cosby**, Emmy-Winning TV/Radio Host and Best Selling Author of *Quiet Hero: Secrets From My Father's Past*

"In *Bride of ISIS* Anne Speckhard draws on her unrivaled research experience to produce a compelling story that sheds important light on a real and urgent problem. The case of Sophie Lindsay may be fictional but it is based on a present reality that will be better understood by reading this riveting book." —**Robert Lambert**, Ph.D., Lecturer, Handa Centre for the Study of Terrorism and Political Violence, School of International Relations, University of St. Andrews, UK

"An amazing piece of fiction based on the real world! A must read to understand and fight the contemporary wave of terrorism and extremism! Anne Speckhard's work is informed by years of interviews with terrorists, supporters and their families!" —**Rohan Gunaratna**, Professor Security Studies, Head, International Centre for Political Violence and Terrorism Research, Singapore, Author, *Inside al Qaeda: Global Network of Terror* Columbia University Press

"*Bride of ISIS* is every parent's worst nightmare and too many kids' fantasies come true. Anne Speckhard is uniquely qualified to tell this painful story of a disenfranchised teen who becomes obsessed with radical Islamic ideas.

Dr. Speckhard's in-depth research into the psychology of terrorists gives this book an authenticity that makes it a valuable read for anyone interested in the process that can transform an all American teenager into a would-be terrorist." —**Amanda Ohlke**, Adult Education Director, International Spy Museum

"A fascinating look at the trajectory from trauma to radicalization from the viewpoint of a young American woman. Only Anne Speckhard could tell this tale, drawing upon her unique, extensive experience and hundreds of interviews delving into both trauma and terrorism. A complete page-turner, you may never sleep well again..." —**Laurie Fenstermacher**, U.S. Air Force Research Laboratory

"After her last exciting nonfiction book, *Undercover Jihadi*, in which Anne Speckhard traces the emotional stages of a jihadi who eventually does a full turnaround and becomes an informer - *Bride of ISIS*, in her usual vibrant style, tells the story of a young woman who becomes enmeshed in the same web of lies and deception about jihad, revealing a stark truth—that terrorists twist the interpretation of the Koran to persuade the weak and vulnerable to join their cause. Another of her books that you won't be able to put down." —**Joe Charlaff**, Middle East Correspondent for *Homeland Security Today*

"Sometimes, the most nuanced understandings of critical issues are found in works of fiction. *Bride of ISIS* gives us a deeply insightful—and important— look into the personal transformation process of a fiction-based-on-fact individual who is radicalized emotionally as much as intellectually, and chooses to join the murderous jihadist movement, ISIS. Anne Speckhard has a uniquely well-informed, carefully researched knowledge of terrorism and terrorists at the individual psychological and emotional level, and she has drawn on this knowledge to provide a powerful and valuable look at one individual on this journey into violence." —**Dr. Alistair D. Edgar**, Executive Director, Academic Council on the UN System, Associate Professor of

Political Science, Wilfrid Laurier University

"Anne Speckhard is one of the leading experts on the intersection between psychology and terrorism studies. In *Bride of ISIS*, she masterfully combines the two disciplines to take the reader into the mind of a suburban Denver teenager who sought to join the world's most violent terrorist organization." — **Dr. Lorenzo Vidino**, Director, Program on Extremism, George Washington University

"Dr. Anne Speckhard brings an extraordinary understanding of human and terrorist psychology to her latest novel, a page-turner about the radicalization of the girl next door. Speckhard draws on extensive research over many years, including more than four hundred interviews with terrorists and their associates. The result is a captivating and cautionary tale of a tragic progression that is becoming all too common in the real world." —**Carol Rollie Flynn**, Former CIA Senior Executive

"Female terrorists are growing in number and increasing in sophistication, and yet they rarely make the headlines. In this much-needed book, Anne Speckhard provides valuable insight and intelligence into the radicalization of a disenfranchised young woman and tackles the subject with the same skill and sensitivity shown in her earlier work, *Undercover Jihadi*. The novelization route strikes right at the reader's heart and enhances understanding of the practical and psychological process of radicalization." —**Kylie Bull**, Managing Editor, *Homeland Security Today*

"In *Bride of ISIS*, Anne Speckhard has given us one of the smartest terrorism books of the year. In this troubling story of Sophie Lindsay—inspired by a real case—we see how manipulative terrorists, in groups such as ISIS, seduce young girls via the Internet and lure them into self-destruction. A compelling, must-read book for understanding the role of females in terrorist groups." —**Max Abrahms**, Professor of Political Science at Northeastern University,

Member at the Council on Foreign Relations

"Anne Speckhard is something of a marvel. She knows violent jihad not only from deep study but from face-to-face field research among hundreds of jihadists and their families. She understands from close-up the thinking and methods of counter-terrorism. And she commands a prose style that is vivid and clear. Now she has produced a novel that incorporates all these resources, creates credible characters, voices and motives, educates the reader in arcane but vital areas and keeps him or her turning the pages in suspense." —**Robert S. Leiken**, author of *Europe's Angry Muslims* (Oxford)

"Anne Speckhard draws on her wide knowledge of extremists and extremism in this fictional, but all too real, account of how a young woman can be drawn into the cult of terrorism." —**Richard Barrett**, Senior VP at the Soufan Group

"A profound psychological look at forces that propel individuals to militant fanaticism. It depicts the intriguing "sinners to saints" road that so many disaffected youngsters traverse these days, and that leads to mayhem masquerading as martyrdom. Another masterpiece from this insightful author!"—**Arie W. Kruglanski**, Distinguished University Professor, University of Maryland, College Park

"Dr. Speckhard never shies away from the path least taken to shine a bright light through extraordinarily complex issues that are on the whole, misunderstood. This work demands focused and candid conversations in both the public and private sectors and a widening of the apertures in each." —**Dr. Kathleen Kiernan**, Johns Hopkins University, School of Education

"Smartly written, intriguing, eminently readable and like all of Speckhard's work *Bride of ISIS* vibrates the pulse of history." —**Halli Casser-Jayne**, host of *The Halli Casser-Jayne Show Podcast*

To Jessica,
all my best!
Anne

Bride of ISIS

One Young Woman's Path
into Homegrown
Terrorism

Anne Speckhard, Ph.D.

First published 2015
By Advances Press, LLC
McLean, VA

Developmental Editor - Jilly Prather, www.jillyprather.com
Consulting Editor - Maya Sloan
Copy Editor - Vanessa Veazie
Cover Design by Jessica Speckhard, www.SpeckhardSavc.com
Cover Model – Madison Campe, www.facebook.com/madisoncampemodel
Book Publicist – Ellin Sanger, www.sangerblackmanmedia.com

Bride of ISIS is a work of fiction inspired by real events. Except where endnotes indicate the events are based upon actual terrorist cases and real events involving public figures; the names, characters, businesses, places, events and incidents in this book are either the products of the author's imagination or used in a fictitious manner. Any resemblance to actual persons, living or dead, or actual events, other than where clearly referenced, is coincidental. While *Bride of ISIS* was inspired by real cases (that are indicated throughout with endnotes), this is *not* a biographical work of any real person or persons, and it is purely, one hundred percent fictional.

Every effort has been made to contact and acknowledge copyright owners, but the author and publisher would be pleased to have any errors or omissions brought to their attention so that corrections may be published at a later printing.

Library of Congress Control Number: 2015902857

ISBN 978-1-935866-62-6 –Bride of ISIS – Hardcover
ISBN 978-1-935866-63-3 – Bride of ISIS – Paperback
ISBN 978-1-935866-64-0 – Bride of ISIS – e-pub

Dedication

To Daniel, my support and foundation. Thank you for being the wind beneath my wings.

Table of Contents

Stealing Innocence

"**W**here is everyone?" Sophie Lindsay muttered to herself as she stumbled on the dimly lit grey concrete steps leading from the ladies room back to the dance floor. Pushing her long, blonde hair back over her shoulders, Sophie stood perched unsteadily on the jeweled black platform heels she'd borrowed from her girlfriend Cara, scanning the dance floor as the strobe lights flashed and the house music banged away. Her plunging black V-neck halter showed off her smooth, glitter-lotioned skin and her black skirt barely skimming her rear end highlighted her long legs poking out beneath. Her platform heels were hard enough to walk in when sober, but were now even difficult to balance on standing. She felt woozy noticing that things were a bit unfocused from all the shots.

Damn, where is she? Sophie wondered as she looked around for Cara. A small panic rose in her chest as she tasted again the sickening sweet last round of Baileys chocolate cherry shots they'd thrown back a half hour before. That, along with the colored lights swirling above, were making her feel a bit nauseous.

"Wanna drink?" a muscular thirty-something-year-old man sitting at the bar asked. Sophie stumbled over as he smiled and pulled out the worn looking bar stool next to him. "You look like you need to sit down. I'm Colin, by the way," he said smiling, as his brown eyes peered at her from beneath his wavy, dark hair.

"Hi Colin," Sophie answered as she staggered over to the seat offered. "I can't find my friends." Reaching for her purse she pulled out her phone. The swirling lights reeled overhead.

Where are you? Cara's texts screamed as Sophie scrolled down, reading them one after the other. I looked everywhere! Did u go home? Sorry I'm leaving. Sophie squinted to see the time it was sent.

"What do they look like?" Colin asked as he took a swig of his whiskey. Sophie took in his crisp white business shirt and blue creased khaki pants. *Looks like he's coming from an office job,* she reflected. He was tall, fit and had a nice smile.

"They're gone," Sophie answered, her heart sinking as she looked absent-mindedly around her. *Now, how am I going to get home?*

"It's okay, I've got a car," Colin offered, reading her thoughts. "I can take you home."

"Oh no. That's okay," Sophie quickly answered, her stomach constricting in a sudden visceral warning of caution.

"There's always taxis," Colin suggested, apparently unperturbed by her refusal. He seemed to understand her concern about taking a ride from a stranger.

Nodding, Sophie thought that sounded like a good idea until an inner, still sober voice screamed, *I'm out of cash! You spent it all on the last round of shots!* It prompted Sophie to recall in a haze of memory forking over her last dollars to buy the final round of shots. She'd accepted so many free ones. It was her time to pay up.

Can you come back and pick me up? Sophie texted her girlfriend Cara. Truth was she wondered how Cara had driven home so drunk to begin with.

No answer flashed back on the screen as Sophie stared at it, willing Cara to answer, knowing the most likely thing was Cara was already passed out sleeping on their sofa bed.

"Drink for the road?" Colin asked, interrupting her thoughts.

"Sure," Cara answered glad to have a distraction from trying to figure out how to get home safely. *What's one more anyway?*

Sophie was sixteen. It was her first night out dancing at Solar. Cara had shown her how to get a fake ID and it had worked. "We're old enough to pass now," Cara had said after they both turned sixteen. "It's time to start partying! We need to get ready for college, Sophie. Hell, maybe we'll meet some college guys!"

Sophie had been a reluctant co-conspirator at first. She didn't think she could get around her strict father until Cara convinced her to tell him she was on a sleepover. It had sounded fun at the time and up to now, it had been.

Despite her fears of getting caught it had all gone well. When they'd arrived at the bar, the bouncer hadn't even looked twice at Sophie's fake ID. That, the extra layers of makeup and hot clothes borrowed from Cara made her look older and had gained her a lot of attention from the young guys at the bar as well. They'd been dancing up a storm in between drinking shots, laughing and having a great time, but now she was here, alone—except for Colin. The guys they'd been partying with had left before she'd gone to the bathroom and now Cara was also gone.

It wasn't supposed to work out this way.

A brief tweak of guilt tugged at Sophie's heart as she thought about calling her parents to pick her up. *No that's out of the question,* she immediately realized. Her parents didn't know she was here. She'd told them she was sleeping over at Cara's—not going out drinking and dancing. Sophie's Dad, Jake would kill her if he knew. Cara's parents were pretty relaxed. Sophie's weren't—especially her Dad. He'd be livid if he found out she'd been out at a bar dancing and drinking.

"You work around here?" Colin asked, interrupting her thoughts as Sophie looked up at him from her phone. Smiling he pushed the drink she'd just been served closer down the bar as he picked his up and took a sip.

He thinks I'm older too, Sophie thought as she smiled back at him, satisfaction at having "passed" making her face light up with pleasure. She flipped her blonde hair forward over one shoulder as she answered, "No, I'm a student," while hoping he wouldn't ask too many questions to blow that cover.

"What are you studying?" Colin asked.

"Business," Sophie blurted out unsure why that major came to mind—maybe his business attire?

"Oh, that was my major too," Colin said, his eyes lighting up. "But I've been out working for awhile. I miss the old college days," he added wistfully. Sophie looked at his wavy brown hair framing his handsome face, and his long lean figure. He looked like the type that probably had made a lot of good college memories.

Glancing down at her phone Sophie saw Cara's answer: I'm too drunk to drive now. I've got the bed spins, LOL. Taxi? Sophie frowned as she imagined Cara lying drunk on the sofa bed while her mind raced ahead about how to get home.

"I'm going to crash soon," Colin said disrupting her thoughts again. "You sure you don't want a lift home?"

Sophie took in his sincere brown eyes, handsome build and kind smile. *What's to lose?* she thought as she nodded and slipped down from the bar stool to accept his offer. He seemed like a nice enough guy.

***

For some reason Sophie's mind drifted home as they sped along the highway in Colin's silver Ford Taurus toward Cara's house. Colin had flipped on a radio station playing soft rock, turning the volume up high. *He's even got handsome hands,* Sophie thought as the soft music moved through her body. It was soothing and she suddenly felt protected being in the car with him heading back to Cara's place. It all felt so grown-up. Maybe that's why her mind drifted back to her father and their recent argument.

"You're not going," Jake shouted, adamant as he stood in the kitchen, his hands firmly on his hips. "I don't care who else is going, *you* are not."

"But Dad, it's the senior send-off party. *Everyone* is going to be there," Sophie argued, her eyes ablaze as they bored into him.

"I don't care if it's your Geometry teacher's fiftieth birthday party," Jake stormed. "There's sure to be alcohol there and you're too young for that."

"No, Dad I'm not," Sophie stormed back, her anger like a stray bullet ricocheting inside the walls of her skull. "It's only a year until I go to college and then I'll be exposed to everything—drinking, sex, drugs. Don't you think I need to grow up a bit *now*? Not live this crazy sheltered life you think is so safe for me? I need to understand the world if I'm going to join it."

"Nice try," Jake said suppressing a smile, "but no, you're not going."

They'd argued for a long time, but Jake held firm. Remembering it, Sophie felt the anger she had felt then rising again in her chest. *He thinks I'm such a baby, why can't he get it that I'm grown-up already!* That was when she'd decided to defy him and his strict old-fashioned rules about what was appropriate for a sixteen-year-old. Cara had offered the fake ID possibility only a week later and now here she was out on the town without her father having any idea—and it was all working out fine. *So take that Dad!* Sophie thought crossing her arms in defiance.

"So you're not really in college?" Colin asked interrupting her thoughts.

"No, not yet," Sophie answered, deciding to come clean. No sense starting out a relationship with lies, and he seemed into her. She'd seen him checking out her cleavage when they got in the car and sneaking a peek or two at her long naked legs now and then. Looking over at him she noticed he didn't seem surprised by her admission. Maybe her "adult" get up wasn't so convincing after all.

"Let me guess, you are on a sleepover at your friend's house and you two are here all alone—no parents?" Colin asked as they drove up to Cara's two-story suburban brick house, chuckling as he put the car in park.

"Yeah," Sophie answered as she giggled drunkenly. "Cara figured out how to get the fake IDs, her parents are out of town and mine think I've been watching movies at Cara's house," Sophie admitted. "But I'll be in college in a year and I may even major in Business though," she added as she opened her door to exit.

"Hey, not so fast," Colin said, as he also jumped out of the car. "Let's go sit in the backyard and talk," he offered coming to stand alongside Sophie.

"I should probably go check on my friend," Sophie replied, hesitating. *He smells good,* she thought as he sidled up to her, sliding his arm firmly around her waist. She could smell the starch in his shirt and his cologne as he steered her toward the back patio.

"Let's just hang out back for a little while—we can talk," he offered. Sophie liked his arm around her. He felt strong and protective. She'd had lots of crushes, but this guy was way smoother than any of the high school guys she'd been into. Not that her father had let her date any of them anyway.

"Okay," Sophie consented, a little uncertain what there was to talk about. *He feels muscular,* she thought as they crossed into the darkness of Cara's backyard as she felt his body pressed next to hers. The late May air was balmy as Sophie headed for the patio swing when Colin suddenly steered her over to one of the chaise lounges hidden in the even darker shadows. The house was dark Sophie noticed. *Cara must be sleeping,* Sophie thought as she felt a tingling of excitement course through her body.

Colin turned to face her and suddenly with his strong arms wrapped around her body began kissing her, thrusting his tongue deep into her mouth as one of his other hands ran up inside her shirt searching for the clasp of her bra. Sophie let him kiss her but pushed his groping hand back down around her waist.

"What's wrong? Colin asked suddenly as he suddenly stopped kissing her and Sophie continued to push his hand back down.

"I'm not ready for that yet," Sophie said, blushing deeply. "We just met!"

"I thought you wanted to be all grown-up," Colin chided and began kissing her again, this time lifting her shirt and somehow managing to unclasp her bra. Now his free hand was cupping her breast and he bent down and began sucking at one of her nipples.

"No," Sophie said, excitement and fear tingling through her body. "I need to stop now," she said pushing Colin's face away from her chest. "I'm not ready," but Colin was already groping inside her skirt, trying to lift it up her hips. He was grabbing for her underwear.

"Stop!" Sophie argued trying to pull away from him.

"You think I could get a decent thank you for the drink and the ride home?" Colin asked, his voice suddenly turning harsh as he pushed Sophie down onto one of the chaise lounges.

"What?" Sophie asked, her eyes widening in shock. "What do you mean?"

"It's time to grow up," Colin sneered, his voice husky and deep as he unzipped his jeans and shoved her back again hard against the chair. "You dressed like you were ready for this—so don't pretend to be all innocent now," he growled. Suddenly Colin was on top of her, pinning her to the lounge chair. Meanwhile, his legs forced hers open as the black outlines of the trees above her begin to spin.

"No, don't do this," Sophie started to say but Colin's hand quickly clamped over her mouth preventing her from screaming.

"You need to shut up," Colin growled, holding his hand firmly over her mouth.

Sophie could feel one of the wooden arms of the chair digging painfully into her flesh, but even worse she felt Colin's hands groping inside her short skirt, pulling at her panties.

Wide-eyed Sophie watched his face as he used his free hand to pull his jeans open and pressed his body down upon hers. He was fumbling with himself between her legs as Sophie's mind raced and her breath became shallow.

"No!" she tried to scream, but nothing but a stifled sound emerged. *That hurts. I don't like this...* "You're hurting me please stop it. Please don't hurt me!" Sophie gurgled into his hand, as tears slipped down her reddened cheeks. "Why are you hurting me? What have I done to you?"

Feeling him between her legs, her heart pounded furiously. No one had ever touched her there before. She'd barely been kissed. As Colin groped between her legs Sophie tried to twist away and wriggle free but he was far too strong—his arms and legs held her firmly. Suddenly the pain was overwhelming as he ripped into her and then it worsened as he pounded away. The dry, tearing flesh inside her felt raw as he pushed himself again and again deep inside, soiling her with his sick desire.

The pain was overwhelming. It seemed like the patio started spinning underneath her and it felt as if the trees were closing in—creating a dark abyss into which Sophie feared she might disappear, sucked downward by some sort of gravitational force of evil incarnate. Sophie's grip on time and place surrendered as she felt her mind dematerialize into a swirling kaleidoscope of confused shades—grey and darkness mixed into one. Suddenly she felt she was no longer in her body but floating far above it, away from here, and what Colin was doing to the body she no longer inhabited.

When it seemed it would never end, Colin finally finished. He knelt over her breathing as if he'd run a marathon. Coming back to awareness, Sophie stared at him with fear and hatred in her eyes. Colin seemed unaware. He brushed her hair from her forehead as he said. "I trust you won't tell anyone about our little tryst. If you do, I'll find you and this will happen again—only much, much worse." Then he stood and zipped his pants and walked back to the street where he'd left his car. In the street she heard his car start and drive away.

Coming back slowly into her body, Sophie thought about screaming—but knew it would bring nothing but trouble. Feeling around with her hands she ascertained that her skirt was pushed up to her chest and her panties were torn open exposing the slash of her bottom that he'd just assaulted. Sophie reached for her skirt, pulling it back down around her and then tried to pull her panties back into place. Her hand recoiled in horror when she felt the slimy wetness he'd left there.

Sophie rolled over onto her side and sobbed silently for a while. She wasn't supposed to be drunk. She wasn't supposed to have gone to a club. She wasn't supposed to have taken a ride from a stranger. Her father's voice from times before this, when she had screwed up, was ringing in her ears—*there's no one to blame for this but you, Sophie.* How many times had he told her, "You have no idea what guys are like, what they can do to you and how they can make you into something you don't wish to become. You're naïve and innocent, and should stay that way."

Sophie rolled into a little ball sobbing on the lounge trying to make it not real—what he'd done to her—but nothing could undo the shame and pain that now throbbed between her legs. Finally, chilled by the cold night air she stood unsteadily and stumbled to the patio door. It was unlocked. Opening it, she lurched into the family room where Cara was snoring loudly on the sofa bed where they always held their sleepovers. Sophie thought of waking her, but decided it was useless to trouble her.

What would I tell her? Sophie thought as tears streamed down her face. *I should have never accepted a ride from that dickhead and I shouldn't have been at that bar in the first place.* Drunk, exhausted and filled with remorse and disgust for what had just happened, Sophie fell into bed beside Cara and briefly fell unconscious.

Fusion Center

"**D**id you see the latest from al-Baghdadi?" Ken asked as he crushed out his cigarette and pulled the glass door of the Denver, Colorado Fusion Center open for his coworker, Cathy Chambers. Inside, the offices were set up open style with sleek, polished silver steel and glass cubicles, beige government-issue carpet, and offices ringing the perimeter for those lucky few who were allotted private space. Ken Follett was a thirty-one-year-old security analyst assigned to work here from the United States Department of Homeland Security. He was dressed in brown khakis and a blue, cotton, button-down shirt. His light blue eyes matched his shirt and they were lit up now as he gazed at her. Cathy was twenty-nine years old—slim and wearing a navy pantsuit and matching low-heeled pumps. Her dark, wavy red hair was piled up in a tortoise shell hair clip on the back of her head, although a few wavy tendrils had escaped to frame her face. She was from the FBI. The Fusion Center in Denver was made up of a mix of local and federal law enforcement agents working together to share information and proactively identify and stop threats before they occurred.

Shaking her head *no*, in answer to Ken's question, Cathy stepped through the door into the building, the cold air conditioning hitting her like an Artic blast compared to the summer heat outside the building.

"He's declared a Caliphate," Ken announced. "It goes against all Islamic teachings, as there's no living Caliph. But al-Baghdadi solved that problem easily enough—by declaring *himself* the Caliph.[1] So now we have a Caliphate and a flipping Caliph as well—isn't that just great?" Ken asked, running his hand through his wavy, sandy brown hair.

Ken was unnerved by this turn of events. Ever since he'd been young, he'd been wary of those unilaterally declaring themselves leaders. How many times had he seen the school bullies take over pick-up games in his youth just to make all the fun disintegrate into shouting and fighting? Now a world bully, al-Baghdadi was not only declaring himself Caliph, but also doing so in a part of the world that many Muslims already believed would someday usher in the final Caliphate that was prophesied to rise up in the End Times. It was a worrying sign in an already volatile area that seemed to easily garner the world's attention.

"Does it really matter?" Cathy asked as she made her way with Ken, past all the cubicles and computer stations to the break room and the coffee pot. Cathy was the new Special Agent, just out of the FBI Academy six months ago. She'd been a decorated cop with the Denver Police Force before that.

"Yeah, for sure," Ken answered, his blue eyes catching hers as he reached into the grey steel, overhead cabinet to pull down a coffee mug for each of them. It was their daily morning chat. Ken was the Islamic terrorism expert assigned from the U.S. Department of Homeland Security to the CIAC (the Colorado Information Analysis Center) in Denver. He was the academic. Cathy wore the gun.

Ken found Cathy to be an anomaly among the FBI agents. She was weapons trained and could take him down in hand-to-hand combat, but she was also smart like him. He found that an attractive combination.

"Now we will see a steady stream of youth—both born into and newly converted Muslims, along with the unhappy, disillusioned, and maybe even the mentally ill, dying to get to Syria and Iraq to become part of this newly declared Caliphate and to join the Great Jihad," Ken explained as he handed a blue ceramic coffee mug over to Cathy.[2]

Cathy nodded, happy that Ken took the time to invest in her. Maybe he saw her hunger to master the academic as well as the kinetic part of her job, she told herself, pushing away the more obvious, yet less interesting alternative: that he just wanted to get her into bed. Either way, she took in everything he said. She may not have his education, but she was a quick learner and she was dedicated to climbing the ranks at the FBI. Cathy wasn't going to let being a woman, or less educated than some of the others, stop her.

While Ken had a Master's degree in Security Studies with a concentration in Islamic studies, Cathy had worked and paid her own way through college and had taken a job as a cop as soon as she graduated the Aurora Police Academy. She had continued on with her college coursework, taking night and weekend classes, until she graduated with her BA in criminal justice from the University of Colorado, Denver. But unlike Ken, she was more into action than books. She'd always had her eyes on joining the FBI.

The road had been rough though, with pregnancy, a failed marriage to another cop, and then divorce derailing her plans for half a dozen years. It had been a hard haul qualifying for the FBI. Cathy's Mom had taken six-year-old Daniela last spring while Cathy spent twenty-one weeks training at Quantico. Now reunited with her daughter, Cathy found it challenging balancing the demands of a rewarding career in the FBI and motherhood.

Cathy remembered how nervous she had been that first day in the Center and what a relief it had been when Ken had approached her on coffee break and started up a conversation that continued to the present. And luckily, after two weeks into the job, Cathy's FBI supervisor, Jason, had seen how well they got along and actually assigned Ken to mentor Cathy on Islamic issues—to bring her up to speed. Cathy was happy for the mentoring opportunity, particularly given that it was Ken, as she found him both attractive and smart. He'd been mentoring her for half a year now, sometimes in informal meet-ups like this at coffee, other times inviting her to sit with him in his cubicle.

Cathy's mind flickered to her recurrent desire to ask him out one of these days, in between panicking at the thought of dating again. *Maybe he's heard I'm divorced with a six-year-old,* she thought as she wondered if that would be a turn-off. It wasn't easy dating as a single mother. Everything was complicated—not like the first time around when she'd been young and carefree.

"I was reading that we've already got more than two hundred Americans who've tried to go to Syria as foreign fighters," Cathy said.[3] She was used to chasing interstate criminals and drug dealers—not terrorists. Now in this job she'd been reading furiously trying to get up to speed on the homegrown terrorists that were increasingly threatening to become a serious domestic threat. While she'd been a Denver cop no one had been overly worried about teenagers spinning up to become lethal terrorists, but now with the social media acuity of groups like ISIS, the scene was rapidly changing. Not only did teens fire up after engaging with extremists groups online and take off for Syria and Iraq but they were also becoming a threat to the homeland—and that's where Cathy's responsibility kicked in.

"That's right," Ken answered. "The kids going off as foreign fighters weren't that big of a worry when the uprising in Syria started because then if a guy went over to fight Assad, maybe he hated dictators and felt sorry for his 'Muslim brothers' over in Syria, but chances were he wasn't interested in taking any of his frustrations out on us. But now with ISIS, if the same kind of guy goes over to join, he's a goner. He's likely already been poisoned by ISIS *before* going, having drunk up their hatred for the West. And he probably believes in their utopian state they claim to be building in Syria and Iraq, and that it's the End Times—that he's joining a cosmic battle where anything goes. The people that join ISIS nowadays have become religious fanatics."

Cathy listened closely as she emptied yesterday's coffee filter, refilled it and started up the coffee maker. Almost immediately the rewarding smell of roasted coffee filled her senses, enlivening her brain even before the first sip. She still had a hard time wrapping her mind around how everyday human beings could go to such extremes. The drug dealers were ruthless and money hungry and also followed a strict code of rules but religious fanaticism was not part of their motivation. Islamic extremism was a whole new worldview that she was still struggling to get a handle on.

"They believe that migrating to the battleground to fight jihad is *fard al-ayn,* that means their duty in Islam, and that 'martyrdom' is not a problem because it delivers them directly to jannah—that's Islamic paradise," Ken explained as Cathy tried to imagine what would make a person believe dying for paradise now was better than staying alive.

Who can be so certain of an afterlife and of going to paradise after murdering innocents? she wondered. "So if these violent fanatics are all taking off for Iraq and Syria isn't that good for us?" Cathy asked. "They can go kill each other over there instead of being our problem," she added feeling a small, guilty twinge at wishing good riddance to the American riff raff who would leave home to join ISIS.

"Sure, but what about when they start sending them back over here?" Ken asked fidgeting with one of the empty mugs on the Formica countertop as they both waited for the coffee to finish brewing. "These hundred or so— it may be two hundred by now—young men and women carrying American passports returning as hardened soldiers, trained in explosives and combat can reenter under the radar—because the truth is we don't know everyone who has joined ISIS. If an American extremist travels to Europe, Turkey or elsewhere, they can enter Syria and Iraq from numerous points, join ISIS, train and then return to attack here. It's impossible to track them all."

Wow, Cathy thought imagining young "clean skins"—that is youth with no criminal records reentering the homeland trained in operating RPG's, building bombs, and terror attacks. *No one would suspect them until it's too late. And that could end in disaster—a shopping mall attack like what had happened in Nairobi, or bombings and a shoot out, like in Mumbai...*

"That's why it's so important what we are doing—tracking them now and figuring out who is joining this mindset," Ken continued as he rubbed his forehead in concern. "But if you ask me, with so many already over there, it's just a matter of time before some are going to be sent back here to attack. *And* they'll also have an international network to rely upon. And who knows, aside from the Americans, how many others—also trained and ready to activate—will also manage to slip into our country with their visa waivers from Europe and Canada? For all we know, maybe we've got ISIS sleepers here already. Those guys are going to be *dangerous*," Ken frowned while leaning his lanky body on the counter behind him. He enjoyed talking to Cathy as it provided a respite from all the horror he took in watching gruesome ISIS and al Qaeda videos. At least with her he felt like there was a normal world somewhere, versus this sick terrorist world he immersed himself in daily.

"We'll I'm ready," Cathy said patting her hip as though she had her pistol there. "But maybe your computer is going to be more important than my gun in finding those types. Although, it's like finding a needle in a haystack isn't it?" she asked.

"Let's just hope they can't keep it to themselves and start to brag here and there on social media about wanting to join ISIS," Ken answered. "It seems for many of them it's all about building a new identity and in that case they just can't keep their mouths shut—they tweet about it and endorse ISIS sites and then at least we get some idea about what they're thinking and reading for that matter. I've got nearly fifty of those mouthrunners right now that I'm following on Twitter and Facebook.[4] Those that re-tweet the ISIS garbage—that's always a worrying sign. We've got signals on some of them—but not all—that's for sure. It's going to be a year of tracking and thwarting homegrown attacks—I'm certain of it," Ken warned.

"It's a crazy way of catching criminals," Cathy remarked. "I wasn't expecting to have to chase them on the Internet. I like stake outs much better than this kind of work," Cathy's mind wandered to her own young daughter growing up in today's world. Daniela loved to watch SpongeBob SquarePants while lounging around in her pink pajamas. The image made Cathy smile imperceptibly. *At least Daniela won't be trying to find her way as a young girl figuring out what it means be a Muslim,* Cathy thought.

"Yeah, but this is only the first step, watching what they post on social media…it goes step by step. And now with this Caliphate declared even more are going to take on this End Times mentality and want to go over. And for those who can't or don't leave here, they also have their stay at home attacks," Ken said as he picked up his empty coffee mug. Cathy remembered learning about the End Times prophecies of the Bible—that the world would suddenly go to hell in a hand basket, crazy weather events were prophesied and the antichrist would rise up in the Middle East—at least that's what she remembered. *Do people really believe that stuff?* Cathy wondered. *And if so, I guess global warming and all the earthquakes and tsunamis of late give some credence to their beliefs?*

"In regard to attacks, ISIS is different," Ken continued. "Al Qaeda favored command and control attacks—and liked spectacular, simultaneous and multiple assaults—the type that take a lot of planning. Like when they plotted to take a series of commercial planes down for Operation Bojinka, or using our planes to attack multiple sites for 9-11.

"Yeah, those kind played well on television for them. Got them a lot of media coverage," Cathy agreed remembering the nearly nonstop footage of the planes crashing into the Twin Towers in New York City. It seemed to her that nearly anytime terrorists were referenced those old photos would resurface as well.

"Until very recently al Qaeda didn't encourage simple, homegrown attacks," Ken explained as he gestured with his free hand, holding his coffee mug with the other, anxious for the coffee to be ready. "But ISIS is fine with the small time, self-organized, homegrown attacks and they are happy to use emotionally damaged and mentally ill people to carry them out. Right now, these smaller but still lethal, homegrown attacks are what we need to be concerned about."[5]

Cathy's mind wandered to imagining rounding up a small cell of terrorists. *How would they even find them?* From what Ken had been telling her there were literally thousands of youth endorsing ISIS but only a few of them took the next steps into violent extremism. *How to sort through and find that needle in the haystack?*

"The Muslims following ISIS believe this is all leading to the final cosmic battle and that Allah is calling them to the Great Jihad," Ken continued, as Cathy reached for the now ready coffee pot to fill their cups.[6] "There have been Caliphates declared before in recent years, but not one in the Middle East, and not one that looked like it might just make it. And perhaps most dangerous of all is the fact that people who believe in apocalyptic visions are often willing to sacrifice themselves and everyone else for their idea of the future. They won't stop at anything to bring in their vision of the new order and all bets are off on rationality. Remember Jim Jones and his purple Kool-Aid?"

Cathy nodded, smiling grimly as she filled her mug and poured Ken's too, handing his back—black and hot. Their hands brushed against each other briefly as she deposited his mug and she felt a tingle of enjoyment feeling his touch.

"Finally, I thought that coffee was never going to brew," he said smiling broadly. "I need my fix!"

Cathy laughed as she stirred half and half into her coffee.

"Thanks," Ken said as he took the carton of half and half from her offered hand. Cathy enjoyed listening to Ken and learned quickly from him but sometimes the subject area was so grim. The thought of all those suicides with Jim Jones made her stomach flop a bit. *How had he managed to convince otherwise rational people to fly to Jonestown in Guyana with him and set up a supposedly socialist paradise and then poison themselves and their children in order to commit "revolutionary suicide"?* Cathy wondered as she waited for her coffee to cool a bit. *There had been more than nine hundred people there and three hundred children killed—mostly by willingly drinking and giving their own children cyanide mixed into their purple Kool-Aid! Visions of little Daniela filled Cathy's mind as she recoiled at the idea of any parent asking their child to drink poison.*

Although she also remembered her own desperation when she found out Matt was cheating. Daniela had been only a baby. She'd had a lot of crazy thoughts during that time period—grief, shame, anger and thoughts of how to exit life without anyone realizing it was suicide—although she also had been firm at the time in the belief that she couldn't abandon Daniela while she was also completely baffled that Matt could. She'd been so hurt and angry—and still was—over how he could go on partying while she was left with all the responsibilities of parenthood. It had soured her on trusting men—until only recently. A little crack in that armor was opening as she hung around Ken. Yet for the most part she remained guarded and cynical about men.

"And look how ISIS is kicking everyone's butts in Syria and Iraq," Ken continued, his eyes burning with excitement as he paused for a minute to savor his coffee. "They can now appeal to anyone who is feeling down trodden, whose manhood is not on track, anyone who wants an adventure. Throw in kids who never fit in for one reason or another; they are the ones ripe for ISIS propaganda. Trust me—the hundreds that have gone over from the United States as foreign fighters for ISIS so far—that number is going to triple and from there it will rise exponentially. This ISIS Caliphate is bad news for everyone."

"Did you say Caliphate?" Russell, a junior team member and a regular smart-ass asked in an exaggerated Arab accent as he sashayed into the break room. "You make the coffee yet, new girl?" he asked as he turned to Cathy.

"Yes, I did," she answered laughing at his goofy, playful tone. Russell had been calling her the "new girl" ever since she arrived. She wasn't even sure he knew her real name. And while she didn't like being gender stereotyped into the role of female coffee maker, Russell could get away with teasing her that way. He was the resident cut-up and everyone knew to take him with a huge grain of salt. Russell was tall and dark with curly, short locks and a razor sharp mind. Cathy liked him, except when he took his attention getting gimmicks too far and was downright irritating. For the most part he was simply eccentric, sporting strange bow ties, muscle shirts, and regularly making everyone laugh with his wise cracks. Ken didn't look so amused with Russell's arrival, however. His brow was furrowed as Cathy glanced over at him.

"Where are they from—the kids that go over?" Cathy asked, turning her attention back to Ken as Russell filled his coffee mug and departed. "Ta, ta!" Russell called out as he left the room.

"Everywhere—some are from the Somali community in Minneapolis, others from New York, but that's the rub, there is not just one place," Ken answered. "It's a totally new game with ISIS. With al Qaeda, if you wanted to join, you had to get to know somebody—at the mosque or meet online—and they'd vet you for a pretty long time. That gave us time to track them and meant there were recruiting hubs and nodes of activity where we could place undercovers. With al Qaeda if you managed to meet someone and convince them you were serious, you *might* get invited to Pakistan where you'd get vetted some more and eventually, maybe just maybe, you'd make it into the training camps. So there was a lot of waiting around and risk of being picked up by security services in trying to get into al Qaeda."

He eats and breathes this stuff! Cathy marveled, reflecting on her own life that had far more of a work-life balance. Her commitments as a mother to Daniela always pulled her back out of the realm of FBI concerns after a long days work to the more mundane aspects of what's for dinner, what's for tomorrow's lunch and snack, and why didn't she remember to recharge the I-pad for Daniela to distract her with learning games?

"But it's not so with ISIS," Ken continued his blue eyes sparkling as they usually did when he got wound up talking about terrorists. "They don't work that way. They are taking everyone. If you are a Muslim, you are welcome. In fact they're telling *all* Muslims that they belong. They even have a slogan that they put out to Muslims around the world, *We are all ISIS!* And at the same time, they are building on the old al Qaeda narrative that Muslims, Islam and Islamic lands are under attack by the West and every Muslim has the duty to jihad. And ISIS is calling for mass hijra—that's Islamic speak for come and join us in the jihad *here*. Once they get indoctrinated online young men and women just pick up and leave for Syria."

Cathy smiled remembering all the times she'd seen Ken hunched over his computer—following all the wannabe jihadis he had on his radar. *Is he going to catch them before we do?* she asked herself realizing that in today's terrorist game the analysts were every bit as important in catching terrorists as the agents with the guns. *But it takes us both working together,* Cathy reflected. Ken could ID the terrorists online; finding them on his screen but without the agents like her to go and round them up it didn't amount to anything. But the converse was also true—without guys like Ken, agents like Cathy were lost.

"And for those who can't for whatever reason, make it over to the land of Sham and Iraq to join the Caliphate," Ken continued. "ISIS is telling them to *stay and act in place.* Those are the deadly ones that we're going to have to catch *before* they activate here," Ken said as he ran his hand through his wavy hair.

"But why are they attracted to ISIS? Is it parents not giving their kids a healthy sense of identity or purpose?" Cathy asked as her thoughts wandered anxiously to Daniela, reflecting on how little time she actually spent with her daughter. Daniela already knew how to type in her favorite shows on the iPad and could navigate her way around the Internet like a little pro. *What was she going to be exposed to growing up in the Internet age?*

"It's never just one thing," Ken answered. "For some it's a way to channel their anger, others want adventure, some want to prove themselves.

There are even those who are unemployed and think an ISIS fighter's salary sounds promising. Forget that it's hell over there. They drink the Kool-Aid and believe it's going to be paradise on earth—building this new caliphate. It can even be the weather for some of them—like the guys in Calgary, Canada that went over. For awhile the jihadis were putting up videos advertising five-star jihad—showing tough guys with Kalashnikov rifles eating pizza as they sat around the sunny pool of a Syrian house they'd overtaken. Imagine how that felt for the unemployed, bored guys sitting in the overcast, freezing, Canadian winter viewing those videos? They probably thought it looked like fun," Ken said laughing and meeting Cathy's eyes.

Cathy burst into laughter as well. "Five-star jihad! I'll book it for my next vacation," she quipped.

"We can go together," Ken said laughing back, and then continued with his 'lesson,' "It's different motivations for different people. Many are angered over geopolitics and believe the West is attacking Islamic people and Islamic lands. Our invasions of Iraq and Afghanistan didn't help with that. Recently our drone kills that are supposed to be precision attacks on terrorist leaders are problematic. Since most terrorist leaders don't live in barracks but live with their extended families, we rarely kill only the terrorists. And a few videos of burned up kids—our collateral damage—can go a very long way in motivating future jihadis, just like the pictures from Abu Ghraib were great recruiting fodder for al Qaeda in the past."

Cathy nodded, her brows furrowed in thought imagining how she'd feel if her child was killed as collateral damage. It wouldn't sit well that's for sure.

"Imagine being a Muslim mother trying to safeguard her teenager from such propaganda?" Cathy exclaimed as all these images went through her mind. *Burned up children in drone kills—that was a sick thought!* It was painful to think of Daniela growing up in such a world—she felt fortunate that they were not Muslims.

Ken nodded, "It's got to be rough territory for moderate Muslim parents to navigate, a lot harder than the sex talk, these days," he added chuckling briefly. "A lot of the parents and imams have no idea what's out there on the Internet trying to lure in the vulnerable ones—but their kids know."

At that moment, Cathy's FBI boss, Jason walked into the coffee room. Jason was a tall, well-built forty-three-year-old who wore his dark hair cut short and sported a short hipster beard that served him well with the "wannabe" jihadis whenever he went undercover, although most of the time he sent the younger agents to do that work.

"Getting up to speed on Islamic issues?" he asked Cathy as he made his way for the coffee maker. Ken pulled a mug down for him and Cathy filled his cup as Jason smiled at their efficient delivery of his much craved for morning jolt. "Thanks guys," he said, turning back to his office. "Cathy stop by and see me later this afternoon," he added, as he got to the doorway. "We need to discuss that drug stakeout I've got you on."

"Sure boss," Cathy called back. Jason inspired trust throughout the office. He was smart, fair and always one step ahead of his agents, and they respected him for that. They all knew Jason had their six. The analysts like him too—he could give any of them a run for their money on most of their topics.

"Sure that makes sense for the attraction," Cathy said continuing their conversation on motivations for joining. "But why would these young people go the whole way and throw away their lives and futures to go to ISIS when there's so many other things they can do to address these problems?"

"They've made it exciting," Ken answered. "ISIS has created an Internet contagion on social media and they know how to appeal to the young men at least. Some of their Internet outreach is using graphics from *Grand Theft Auto* and *Call of Duty*. You know how popular those games are with the guys."

"Not just the men," Cathy countered, as Ken smiled back at her remembering that she was as tough as the lot of them—tougher than him by far.

"But what about the women—why do they go?" Cathy asked arching her eyebrows. "Do they really just want to be ISIS brides? I read that the women that go over to marry the mujahideen buy into the utopian state, the whole purity thing of living by Islamic ideals and they want a part in building it. And ISIS fighters need women, I get that, but isn't it all a big lie?" Cathy asked wrinkling up her nose as she pulled her fingers back through her dark red, wavy hair. "Won't reality show them that many of the jihadis think nothing of beating their wives and totally subjugating them, as well as raping other women and that life in a war zone is not as much fun as they expected?" Cathy asked as she poured herself another coffee and held the pot out to him. "See, I've been studying up," she added as she winked at Ken and smiled.

"I can see that," Ken beamed back as he held out his mug and took a refill.

"Thing is, you can't convince young people of the dangers of joining these freaks. The militants in chat rooms on Facebook and Tumbler have Internet seduction down to an art. Find a lonely young Muslim woman who is looking for adventure, angered about geopolitics and already endorsing ISIS and then show her a manly fighter who starts telling her she's beautiful and how much her special talents are needed in the terrorist cause and BANG! She's up on Skype with a militant, being promised an exalted status, a good life, complete with devoted husband, beautiful house—stolen from others of course—and a big family of loving children, the works. Next thing you know she's falling in love and, soon after, on the next plane to Istanbul," Ken said as he shook his head. "It's not rational—a lot of it's emotions. The women that have gone over there are recruiting their sisters big-time as well."

Cathy nodded, watching as he lifted his coffee mug to his lips to take a sip. *Ken is so hot when he gets worked up,* Cathy thought. *His excitement is contagious. I wonder if he just reads counter-terrorism books every night,* she pondered as she thought about her own evenings reading *Goodnight Moon* and *The Chick and the Duckling* well before she could even think about cracking a counter-terrorism article. *Well at least Daniela is learning to read,* she consoled herself.

"Stop by my computer later and I'll show you some of their latest videos. They've got one where they've picked up the feed from Grand Theft Auto and they show a killing spree with a guy shooting up and driving his car over bystanders waiting for pickup at the airport. Everyone thinks it's the plane that's going to be attacked, but now they're encouraging homegrowns to take a car or buy a gun to mow people down outside the terminals. These are the type of small scale, but lethal, attacks that ISIS likes to promote."

Cathy squinted imagining such an attack at the Denver airport. Nodding she shook off the image. There was so much evil they witnessed everyday in their jobs from the work of punks to hardcore criminals, and now these homegrown terrorists hell-bent on killing innocents. She'd learned at Quantico that analysts who watched violent videos all day long— beheadings, murders and monitoring the terrorists' propaganda—were known to burn out and need the services of the company shrink from time to time.[7] Ken protected himself with black humor and chats like this.

"We sure have an awful lot of crazies to sift through to find the real threats," Cathy commented as they started walking back to her office. This was all new to her—tracking individuals espousing extremism through undercovers and informants in their mosques, social groups, and communities was the work she was used to doing in other venues—but tracking them over the Internet and trying to figure out who was making the step into committing violent extremism was new and strange to her.

"Yeah, that's for sure. Along with catching foreign fighters who've gone over there in the hundreds from Canada, Western Europe and now from the United States who decide to come back here to attack," Ken replied, his face looking serious and his eyes intent as he followed his partner down the hall.

Cathy nodded. It was fascinating—all he knew about Islamic issues. Cathy was presently preoccupied with other FBI work at the Fusion Center. She had a stakeout on some drug traffickers planned for later tonight—but jihadis were just starting to make it on her operational radar and she was trying to spend as much time with the analysts as possible to learn what this new threat looming over the horizon was all about. Ken's mentoring her all these months was helping a lot, getting her ready to chase terrorists as well. And after spending so much time with Ken, she was finding it was a pleasure in more ways than one.

Denial

Sophie jolted awake on the sleeper sofa the next morning. She gazed around the room, her eyes darting quickly from the window to the door. Something terrible had happened. What was it?

Sophie's hand darted down her leg as she remembered. Shots of pain stabbed her vaginal area. Crusty patches of dried blood covered her inner thighs. *Colin—if that was even his real name?*

Heart racing, Sophie hurriedly looked around to get her bearings as she sat up. She was dressed in the clothes she'd worn last night and Cara was still sleeping. Judging from the light in the room, the sun was only just now rising.

Sophie slipped on her sandals and bolted for the sliding glass door, wincing in pain as she went. Searching around on the patio she found her purse and phone laying discarded on the ground—she hadn't noticed losing them in the struggle last night. Scooping them up and breaking into a half run from Cara's backyard, Sophie spilled out into the street. It was May in Denver and not yet hot in the mornings. And just as she'd thought, the sun was only now rising on the horizon. Sophie sprinted two blocks from Cara's house to the bus stop and waited there, checking all the time over her shoulder for Colin, as her heart thumped haphazardly in her chest. She knew he was long gone, but somehow she felt he could suddenly materialize again out of nowhere.

Shit! Did all that really happen? Sophie asked herself as her sore and bleeding bottom screamed that it had. *No, that did not happen,* Sophie argued. *I'm still a virgin. He didn't take anything from me.* But even as she tried to reassure herself she knew it wasn't true. She heard her father's voice echoing in her head, *"You can't trust men, and if you don't protect yourself, they'll make you into something you don't want to become."*

What had Colin made her into?

Sophie's heart knocked hard in her chest as she remembered Colin pushing her down hard on the chaise lounge, forcing her legs open, hurting her. Sophie's stomach knotted up remembering.

You can't ever tell, Sophie realized. Her father would just think she'd voluntarily become a slut. She knew her Dad loved her, but he was old fashioned to the core when it came to women.

It's my own fault sneaking out to a bar late at night and doing shots, Sophie reminded herself. Her father had drummed that in from early on—to take responsibility for her own actions, particularly those that turned out bad. Her mind flashed back to Colin's remarks as well, about dressing and acting all grown-up, but being unwilling to act the part.

Fuck! Sophie thought as disgust rose in her throat, laced with the leftover nausea of a giant hangover. *I'm so stupid!*

Hot tears rolled down her cheeks as Sophie waited for the bus to arrive. No matter how she tried to deny it, flashbacks of the sexual assault intruded, unbidden into her mind—raping her over and over again with his despicable smell, words, groping hands and rough protrusions pushing their way into her mind and body. Reliving the horror, it seemed like full sensory movies going off in her head—more real than any IMAX movie could ever hope to be.[8]

It was a bad dream, that's all, Sophie repeated to herself once seated on the bus, but try as she might to deny reality, the reminders of the painful penetrations wouldn't stop. They kept forcing themselves into her consciousness— and a devil on her shoulder seemingly giddy with accusations, *You didn't listen, Soph! You went ahead and went partying at the clubs and now you're ruined.* A war of words erupted in her brain, with opposing sides of fault, blame, and culpability lined up at the doorstep of her mind. She, and she alone, was forced to answer for her own misdeeds.

Sophie had wanted to give her virginity to the guy she loved—not have it taken from her as it had been last night. She'd figured it would happen in college when she finally got out from under her old fashioned father—but not now, not this early. Her father was so strict—he never let her date. After the school play cast party last year a senior had driven her home and paused to kiss her before her father had abruptly opened the door interrupting their sweet moment. Sophie had wanted to date him but her father had adamantly refused.

"He's too old for you Sophie, and he drives. The last thing you need is a guy with a car trying to get into your pants," he'd said shaking his head and clenching his jaw. It was clear there was no reasoning with him. So that had been the end of that. All her friends dated, but Sophie hadn't even been kissed, except for that one interrupted time on her doorstep.

Sophie sniffled as she sat forlornly looking out the bus window without seeing anything but the revolting movies as they replayed in her mind. It went on and on, fear and shame flooding her mind so powerfully that no matter how she tried to escape her thoughts kept returning to the horror of it all. Colin had reduced her to a powerless pawn that he had used to pleasure himself while humiliating and annihilating her hopes and dreams, along with putting so much terror into her body that it seemed her life could never again be sane. There was no way to tell her parents about it. How could she ever explain? Maybe her father would blame her and think she was a whore? And Colin had threatened he would come for her again if she told. Sophie's heart raced in terror as she remembered.

The endless replay loop only came to an end as it had ended the night before when—overwhelmed with pain, terror and a feeling of complete inescapability and total responsibility—Sophie's mind spun off into a dizzying dissociative swirl, leaving her empty and emotionless, only half present in her body.

As she entered this barren space where she became emotionally numb, resolutely banishing memory from consciousness—*that did not happen to me*—Sophie felt a new cold-edged steeliness arise inside her, in which she was once again back in charge, at least in her mind. She finished her way home in this determined mindset, amidst a cold inner haze.

***

"You're home early," Sophie's Mom, Sarah noted without looking up from her laptop as Sophie entered the kitchen her head bent to the ground. Sarah was a lawyer with her own private practice and worked long hours at the office, followed by even longer hours at home. Struggling to make her practice viable, she always had reams of attorney paperwork piled up like small barricades around her.

"Yeah," Sophie said as she avoided eye contact, which was never difficult with her mother who was always distracted, and made her way through the kitchen down to her basement bedroom. There she stripped off her soiled clothing.

Her underpants were soaked in blood. Sophie recoiled at the blood and wondered if she was injured internally while she collected all her soiled clothes. Picking them up, she shoved them into a plastic bag. She tied and retied the bag into tight knots—trying to choke the life out of the memory that wouldn't be killed. Wrapping a towel around her body, Sophie walked down the hallway to the garage where she threw the bag into the outdoor trash bin.

Naked but still holding inside her body nauseating traces of the night before, Sophie stepped into the hot shower and began fiercely scrubbing herself under the scalding water. As she passed the loofah sponge roughly over her skin, she kept trying to force the memories away.

Despite the hot water, Sophie's body shivered as she showered. She shook harder as she stepped out of the shower and toweled off. Donning a new, clean, flannel nightie she climbed into bed. Grabbing her teddy bear, she rolled up into the fetal position and pulled her covers around her. She clenched her childhood bear tightly against her chest. Then, Sophie sank into a deep oblivion where thirty-year-old rapists could not follow.

The Lion of Islam

"Want to go over to the Sand Dollar for drinks and dinner, hang out, after work? I've got some cases I'd like to show you," Ken said as he poked his head into Cathy's office.

"Sure," Cathy answered after hesitating for a brief moment. *Is this a work invitation or a date?* she mused as she grabbed her purse.

"You asked about the female terrorists yesterday. I've got some that I've been following that I'd like to tell you about. They are foreigners—unclassified, so I can tell you about them at the bar," Ken offered, his blue eyes flashing.

Cathy glanced for a second at the photo of six-year-old Daniela on her desk as they departed, remembering that she was hardly carefree at night like in the old dating days. She needed to remember to text home to her mother telling her she needed to work later than usual.

"Your car or separate cars?" Cathy asked as they walked toward the elevator, thinking, *This is a bit like a date. I wonder if he's into me or just wants someone to talk with about terrorism?*

"Mine," Ken answered as they waited for the elevator.

The Sand Dollar was decorated in a Caribbean theme with colorful fishnets, painted, carved wooden mermaids and fish hanging from the walls—a bit out of place for being located in Denver but the seafood was excellent. Pink flamingos were perched beside the bar where Cathy and Ken sat waiting for a table.

"Howdy," the waitress said as she handed over menus. "What can I get you to drink?"

Cathy looked over her menu as her mind raced between what drink to choose and what to eat—mojito or white wine, fish or a burger, and then jumped to, *Is this a date or a work outing?* She couldn't stop her mind from going there. Her long legs swung from the bar chair as she noticed Ken catching a look at them in his peripheral vision. Smiling she ordered, "A mojito please." Ken ordered a beer.

"So, I've been collecting tweets from ISIS women and it's really alarming the things they say," Ken started up. Pulling out his phone he began showing them to Cathy. Look, here's one," Ken said leaning toward her so she could see his screen as he scrolled through his tweets.

"We loved death as you love life. That's Umm Khattab—that means mother of Khattab. She's a mother and widow at age eighteen and happy her husband was killed in Kobani. Lovely no?" he asked, as he looked up into Cathy's brown eyes while she sipped her mojito.[9]

"Who could possibly love death more than life?" Cathy asked, horrified by the prospect. Her life seemed so full of possibilities, especially right now, here with him.

The waitress appeared and showed them to their table where Cathy ordered grilled scallops and Ken ordered a burger. While they waited for their food Ken sat near Cathy in order to let her see his phone better. Feeling his shoulder leaning into hers, Cathy felt a shiver of desire run down her body.

"Look at this one, Muhajirah fi Sham—that means Immigrant in Syria, or Sham, as they call it," Ken said showing Cathy the screen. "She tweets: I wna b da 1st UK woman 2 kill a UK or US terrorist![10] She's believed to be a UK national, from Lewisham. She changed her name to Khadijah Dare, after converting during her teens in the UK. She is thought to be twenty-two now, and married to an ISIS fighter and they have a toddler son. Look here's a picture of her son that she tweeted," Ken said showing Cathy a picture of a little boy holding an AK47."

"The women you follow!" Cathy gasped. "Who would tweet a photograph their child holding an assault rifle?"

"Yeah, she's a real piece of work," Ken said his forehead wrinkling in concern as he read out another of her tweets. "Listen to this one: All da people back in dar ul kufr [land of disbelievers] what are you waiting for ... hurry up and join da caravan to where the laws of Allah is implemented. No one from Lewisham has come here apart from an 18-year-old sister shame on all those people who afford fancy meals and clothes and do not make hijra. Shame on you.[11]"

"Dar ul kufr is the land of disbelievers, by the way. These women call themselves warriors for Allah, but truth is they are not allowed into combat—at least not yet. But they are so proud of their men—their husbands and their sons, and most are eager to become widows. They see it as an honor," Ken explained.

Cathy shook her head in disbelief.

"You know if you ever have to go undercover to try to catch someone like this it may turn out to be a real advantage being a female agent," Ken commented. "A lot of these ISIS women, when they get all conservative, they won't spend time with the men anymore. They'll only hang with other women. That's why it's important that you're ready when the time comes. We could just as soon have a female homegrown appear on our analytic radar as a male. It may take a female to take her out."

"That's cool," Cathy remarked suddenly feeling pleased that her gender might afford her a rare advantage in the world of FBI agents.

"You know Princess Aisha of Jordan trained women to be in the Special Forces for exactly that reason," Ken continued. "Sometimes only women can go where the others go, and then it becomes imperative that the security services have thought ahead to making sure they're equipped to take out the bad guys, or women in this case.[12] Soon you're going to have it all—the physical and mental training," Ken said looking admiringly at Cathy. He was proud of all she'd learned under his tutelage. She however got suddenly shy under his prideful scrutiny, so he turned back to the matters at hand.

"Here's Bird of Jannah giving some marriage advice," Ken said, reading her posting from his phone: "Marry the person you know can uplift you morally and who will always remind you that Allah is sufficient in times of trials.[13] She's a doctor, from Malaysia. She married another ISIS fighter and didn't even speak the same language as him at the time of their marriage! They used phone translation apps to communicate."

"Wow, that's weird, but it sounds like fairly good marriage advice" Cathy commented with a laugh.

Suddenly the waitress appeared with their food, placing Cathy's grilled scallops down in front of her. Ken got up and sat on his side of the table, where the waitress placed his burger. Cathy felt sudden regret at his body no longer leaning into and touching hers.

"Any more drinks?" the waitress asked. Both ordered another.

"They all see their man as a lion," Ken explained, smiling as he looked up shyly.

"Right," Cathy smiled back as he quickly turned his eyes back to his phone and scrolled further through his tweets. Cathy dug into her scallops waiting for his next "find." The scallops were buttery and melted in her mouth, as tasty as she remembered from other times stopping at the Sand Dollar after work with colleagues. But never had the conversation been this interesting

"These marriages—their goal is not to be together long in this life," Ken continued. "Their aim is 'martyrdom' and to be reunited in jannah—or paradise. Bird of Jannah's husband told her, 'Jihad is my first wife, and you're my second.' Here's one of her Tumblr photos," Ken said handing Cathy his phone to show her a photo of an Islamic couple standing near the flag of ISIS, the man with a long, dark beard covering his face and the woman standing beside him covered from head to toe, only her eyes gazing out of a narrow slit of fabric covering her face. The caption read: Marriage: In the land of Jihad "Till Martyrdom Do Us Part"[14]

"Geez, I can't imagine getting married and bringing children into a family under those conditions," Cathy commented. "Or wanting to be a widow with children in a war zone!" Her mind involuntarily drifted to little Daniela who was surely in bed sleeping by now. It was hard enough on Daniela that her parents were divorced, but a wife celebrating her husband going to his death while leaving children behind? *What were these women thinking?*

"Here's another, Umm Anwar. She talks about seeing a Yazidi slave," Ken said, his face lighting up with excitement as he read out her words: "Walked into a room, gave salam to everyone in the room to find out there was a yazidi slave girl there as well... she replied to my salam."[15]

"You know the ISIS guys take the Yazidi's, especially the women—rape them and force them to be their sex slaves. Sick, no?" Ken asked, his face suddenly serious.

"That is *so sick*, how can their Muslim wives respect that?" Cathy asked her face cringing in horror at the thought.

"They sickly justifiy it as the bounties of war," Ken answered, his voice grim as he continued to search his phone.

Cathy took the opportunity to take in his shoulders and muscular build. It had been a long time since she'd been with a man. There were plenty interested in her during her twenty-one weeks of training in Quantico, but Cathy had shied away, fearful of a long distance romance conflicting with single motherhood. And she was gun shy after having been burned by Matt, her first husband—a guy that liked to drink and fool around. The partying had been fun early on but after Daniela was born it wore thin, along with the cheating.

The waitress appeared to check on their food as Ken continued his face lighting up in excitement as he located another one. "The ones that tweet from inside ISIS sound like they actually like it. Except they say it's hard for them to leave their families," Ken said. "Like this one, Umm Ubaydah, she writes, I yearn to hug my mother again, kiss her cheek or to even hear her voice, May Allah accept my sacrifice & allow me 2 intercede for her."

Cathy could relate to that one. She was close with her own mother and she hoped Daniela would grow up to feel the same way. She had really missed them both when she'd been in the FBI training. She even missed them now—despite the fun night out.

"Some of these are so chilling," Ken said. "Listen to this one, Drove past the body of the man who was crucified in manbij for raping a 70 year old. Perks of living under the shade of Shariah," Ken read.[16] "Okay, rape is bad, but crucifixion? And I'm sure he didn't get a trial."

Ken leaned across the table, staring into Cathy's eyes adding, "These ISIS women *want to be widowed and they want to die!* They are proud and actually celebrate when their husbands are 'martyred' and they long for 'martyrdom' themselves! Right now, most of what they are doing is domestic support for the mujahideen—along with providing marital sex for their jihadi partners—but things can change. *What if* one of them gets sent back here to carry out a suicide attack? What then?"

"That would be a problem," Cathy answered pushing away her finished plate and throwing her long, red hair back over her shoulders. "But why would their hubbies let them go on a suicide mission if they're keeping them all warmed up each night?" she asked arching her eyebrows.

"Good point," Ken conceded laughing as he dug into his burger. Inside however, Cathy was remembering her own desperate feelings and anger when things had been falling apart with Matt. Suicide had crossed her mind more than once.

Ken had been talking so much he still had his food to finish. As he ate, Cathy's eyes wandered over to a painted Mermaid hanging on the wall and it made her think again of Daniela snug at home in bed.

"But we do have widows," Ken added as soon as he washed a bit of burger back with his beer. "The Chechen Black Widows that took over the theater in Moscow—many of them were actual widows hell bent on revenge."[17]

"What motivates these women really?" Cathy asked remembering how she had wanted to lash out at others when she found proof that Matt was cheating. She remembered feeling enraged at the world and feeling the injustice of being left to raise their daughter on her own while Matt carried on partying, but she would have never gone out and taken her own life to hurt others.

"I'm not sure exactly," Ken answered. "Men and women both think they are fighting for social justice, but it's definitely different for the women. On the individual psychological level men often go to fight and prove their manhood and for the adventure of it all, but for these women it's a lot about being pure—living the uncontaminated Islamic life.[18] They really believe they are going to build an Islamic state—a utopian world where they will live purely and be respected in their entire communities, but sadly the reality is so unlike that," Ken explained as he reached for his fries and offered them to Cathy as well. She shook her head, pushing the fries back over to his side of the table.

It's so strange to talk about these dark things, and even darker relationships filled with death and dreams of glory, she thought as she looked into his eyes. *And all the same I feel like I want to be with you while we talk about the horrors of life,* Cathy thought. *Can he tell how I feel?* she wondered, suddenly worried.

"Listen to this one, Umm Ubaydah, We are trying to build an Islamic state that lives and abides by the law of Allah.[19] This purity thing is big for Islamic women," Ken continued.

"Yeah, luckily we don't have to worry about that over here," Cathy joked, taking a long sip of her Mojito as she flashed her brown eyes at Ken.

Ken caught her gaze and stared back into her eyes while he quipped, "What? You don't need to stay virginally pure?"

"Ha! You forget I've been married before so that's not on my list of regulations. And I have a six-year-old daughter," Cathy answered, thinking,

There now I've said it. I'm a divorcee with a child.

"I'm a free woman," she added, feeling sudden panic rise up inside her. Funny—she could face any criminal and had been in many an urban gunfight but thinking about dating again gave her the nervous jitters. Blushing she also realized what she had said sounded like a bold proposition—not merely an openness to going out again.

"Well then, maybe you could help me tame my wild side." Ken joked, confirming that she had been a bit far out there. They both got out their credit cards to split the bill.

Outside in the parking lot Ken walked with Cathy to her side of his car where he opened the door for her. *This is like a real date,* she thought wishing it wasn't ending. As he drove back to work to drop her at her car, Cathy glanced at his hands, admiring their strength.

Pulling up alongside her car, Ken turned to Cathy and smiled saying, "This was a great evening. We should do it again."

Cathy smiled back at him sensing that if she lingered in the car he might just lean over and kiss her. Panic rose up in her chest as she reached for the door handle and bolted out into the parking garage. "Yeah, it was great," she called over her shoulder. "See you tomorrow!"

Just as she said it, Russell emerged from the Fusion Center elevator, "Oh yessss...see you tomorrow!" he mimicked in a high voice, calling after her as he walked to his car. Cathy laughed although she was mortified at the thought that only moments earlier he might have walked out and seen Ken kissing her in his car. *Better that never happened,* she reassured herself. Although deep inside, she wished it had.

The Memory Vault

"**G**o ROTC?" Sophie's Dad, Jake asked when she emerged from her leaden sleep into the kitchen. She was ready for a run, wearing her navy blue running shorts and a matching zip-up hoodie, her blonde hair tied back with an elastic band. Jake was dressed in navy khakis and a yellow button-down short sleeve shirt—the same clothes he wore to his weekday job as a computer programmer—although today was Saturday.

"Sure Dad," Sophie answered, avoiding eye contact.

Can he see it? She wondered as she reached into the fridge to grab a yogurt. Peeling the plastic film off the yogurt container's top, Sophie dipped into it with a spoon. *Does he know that a stranger has just destroyed the person I was?*

"I need to run—clear my mind," she said as she escaped his gaze, tossing the spoon into the sink and the empty yogurt container in the trash and making for the door.

"It's a good way to pay for college! You'd make a good officer," Jake added before she exited.

"Yeah," Sophie answered listlessly as she slipped out the doorway. "See you in a bit," she called over her shoulder, thinking, *The ROTC and all his plans for me to join the military are so over. There is no way now, that I'd join an all man's club—not now—not after last night.*

Just like that, her father's well-laid plans to pay for college had been ruined, devoured in the roaring fire that had also taken the innocent and hopeful girl she'd been a day earlier. Sophie's bright future had vanished like smoke swirling into the sky, leaving only a dying ember in its place—an ember that had no idea how to rekindle itself into life again.

So much for all his rules and trying to protect me, Sophie reflected guiltily as she headed for the running path not far from the house and began to pump her legs hard as she ran along the soft surface. Jake was an IT geek and liked rules and order. He'd been overprotective since she'd been born and always so afraid of what men might do to his sweet, innocent daughter. Now it had happened.

Sophie felt sick with remorse as she ran. The trees and brick, two-story neighborhood houses disappeared into a dizzying blur as she broke into a sprint, her feet falling fast and lifting again, while the swirls of green trees, sun streaked blue sky and white clouds mixed with images of the rape that kept intruding into her mind. *Why didn't I just listen to him?* an inner voice condemned her. How many times had he told her, "I know best Sophie, you don't know men. You need to trust me on this."

Sophie pushed herself faster, as she tried to drive the memories of last night deep below the surface of her mind drowning the recollections into silence as she shoved them back down into a hidden vault in her mind. There she tried to lock them into oblivion so as not to disrupt her thoughts anymore. Trees blended with grass and sky as Sophie ran, letting the fresh, cold air cleanse her lungs as she breathed deeply and spit out her throat the unspoken horrors of the night before.

That did not happen to me, she kept repeating over and over again as she ran. But try as she might to deny the truth, it didn't work. It did happen and all there was to do about it was to try to cope with the reality of it all.

Doubling back at the mile mark, Sophie ran at full-blown speed back to the house. As she ran, Sophie mentally tried to ditch the memories—tossing them along the way into the neighbors' trash bins awaiting the garbage trucks and into the gully where the creek ran, letting them dissolve into the soil.

That didn't happen, she repeated. Having exhausted herself for now, Sophie could only concentrate on her labored breathing and her aching knees—a temporary distraction at best.

When she got home, Jake was still in the kitchen but didn't let her pass by so easily as before. "How are Cara's parents?" he asked.

Does he know something? Sophie wondered as she stared at the geometric patterns in the ceramic kitchen floor tiles, her heart racing. "They're fine," Sophie answered daring to look up briefly. "We ordered pizza in the basement so we didn't see much of them," she lied.

"You seem different," Jake commented as he stood looking intensely at her. "Anything wrong, baby?"

"No, nothing," Sophie lied as her heart pounded hard inside her rib cage. *He knows! He can see it!*

But Jake was silent as he let her pass. Sophie took another shower scrubbing her body vigorously again and using the hottest water she could stand, trying to remove the stain left inside.

A stream of texts from Cara filled her phone when she got around to checking. Everything okay? U left my house without waking me, r u mad at me for leaving u last night? I'm sorry I thought u must have left without me, the first text read. I was too drunk to drive, bed spins. U mad at me? the second one read. It went on: Everything okay? What's up? Sophie didn't bother to read them all.

Not mad just tired, She replied genuinely.

How could she blame Cara? It wasn't her fault that Sophie had been so stupid to trust Colin. Sophie clicked her phone into silent mode and tossed it into her purse. Cara was the last person she wanted to think about right now. She just wanted to forget—everything.

That night Sophie tossed and turned in her bed before finally falling asleep. Sometime later she awoke with a start. Intense fear clutched at her heart, weaving a web of dread through her arms down into her stomach like a colony of spiders searching for a place to nest. *No! Don't hurt me,* Sophie cried out as she sat up in her bed realizing that she was in the middle of a nightmare.

Sophie rolled off the bed and crept upstairs. Tiptoeing in the darkness, she made her way to her parent's liquor cabinet. She took out a bottle of vodka knowing that she needed something really strong to deaden the emotional pain, stop the screams she hadn't been able to force out the night before, those that were now rising up in her throat, threatening to bellow out into the darkness. She needed something—anything—to banish the pain and to calm her mind and body that kept reliving the penetrations that had been forced upon her.

They'll never notice, Sophie thought as she crept back downstairs with the bottle in her hands. Sophie's father rarely drank, but always had hard alcohol on hand for guests. Her mother favored wine. Taking the bottle, Sophie sat on the edge of her periwinkle blue comforter and poured one shot after another into the little shot glass she'd picked up in the Grand Canyon on a family visit there.

Warmth crept from her throat to her stomach bringing instant relaxation, easing her tormented mind, and bringing her a sense of floating and a grateful-to-God peace. She sighed and slumped down onto the bed. Sophie felt close to slipping into another kind of oblivion—one where she was safely locked into the vault and the memories were free to fly out wherever they wished, as long as they left her lying there undisturbed.

In a blurred haze she rose and tucked the bottle into the back of her underwear drawer, hiding it in a place neither of her parents would ever think to look. Then she lifted the comforter, grabbed her teddy bear and hiding herself under the covers, fell into the deep sleep of drunken unconsciousness.

In her dreams, the cottony clouds painted on her ceiling years ago moved lazily along the summer sky and Sophie revisited happier memories of being young and innocent with her mother pushing her on the swing out back. She was dressed in a little white eyelet dress, her skinny little legs pumping hard with each swing up to the sky. She kept trying to reach the blue beyond but found she was always tethered back to this earth returning in a long arc into the safety of her mother's arms. Sarah pushed and laughed with her as Sophie called out for more, "Higher, Mommy! Push me higher!"

The Instigator

"**A**nwar al-Awlaki—this guy is showing up in nearly every terrorist plot we've seen over the last years," Ken said as he met Cathy at the coffee machine on Monday morning. "Look, here's a picture of him," Ken said pulling a glossy photo out of the manila file folder he was carrying. "Last night I was checking him out on the Internet and I ended up spending the entire evening listening to his lectures. He's evil, but he's really quite mesmerizing."

"Oh so you like a Yemeni, American imam, better than me," Cathy joked. "I see how it is—you go both ways." Inside she was feeling a low level panic. *Stop flirting with him. What am I doing? Workplace romances are always a mistake!* Cathy's inner critic reminded her as her heart flip-flopped at the pleasure of seeing him today. Avoiding Ken's eyes she looked at the photo he was holding and reflected, "He's got soft eyes."

"Oh yeah—me and the Arab boys—we get on well," Ken answered laughing as he caught and gazed into her eyes. "Hey, I had to do something to distract me—it was a damn boring weekend."

"Oh yeah?" Cathy answered laughing and nervously wondering, *Is he into me or just another player? I don't need any players in my life right now—I've got my hands full with work and Daniela.* Tonight in fact, the two had plans to build together the log cabin Daniela needed for her class project on pioneers. *It's always so hard to figure his motivation for talking to me,* Cathy thought eyeing the folder in Ken's hands. *He's probably just talking to me as my mentor right now,* she realized, hoping it wasn't the case.

"A lion can't appear needy," Ken answered reaching for the coffee cups. "But if you are not busy this Friday night and Saturday and Sunday," he joked placing the cups down for Cathy to pour. His blue eyes were searching and her brown ones met them with a smile. *He is interested in me!*

"Let me check my schedule. Hmm, looks like I'm free until 2025,"

Cathy answered blushing slightly while her inner critic warned, *And how long before he moves on to the next woman?*

Is he asking me out? She wondered and then warned herself once more, *You're going to get hurt and you can't afford to get a broken heart again.*

"Okay back to my 'date' last night," Ken said, his face flushing with pleasure. "This Anwar al-Awlaki guy is actually dead. But he lives on via the Internet, inspiring from beyond the grave."

"What?" Cathy asked not wanting him to stop the banter just yet. "Dead, but still inspiring?"

"You can find immortality on the Internet," Ken quipped. "Make a few hundred videos and you can live forever!"

Cathy laughed as Ken continued—pleased that he stayed for more conversation, "Cathy, you need to be up to speed on this dude because chances are that any terrorists you get to chase have been downloading and studying his teachings. He's implicated in nearly every homegrown, Islamic-related terror plot we've seen here in the U.S., in Canada and in Europe over the past five years. Look at this list of plots," Ken said taking a paper from his folder.

"Looks like a regular bevy of spies meeting over a manila folder," Russell remarked as he roared into the break room. "What is this? M briefing 007?" he asked as he took a mug and held it out for Cathy to fill. "Coffee please, new girl," he demanded.

"Oh please!" Ken complained.

Reaching for the pot, Cathy good-naturedly filled his mug. Russell left the room as quickly as he had entered calling, "See you later, agitators!" over his shoulder.

Still smiling, Cathy took the paper from Ken's outstretched hand and began reading aloud from the list, "The 7-7-2005 London metro bombings. Who carried them out?" she asked. Her job didn't require her to know much about foreign plots but some of the British one's involved trying to take down U.S. bound jets.

"There were four of them—all homegrown—three British-born sons of Pakistani immigrants," Ken answered. They exploded three London underground trains and a double decker bus in Tavistock Square, nearly simultaneously; all involving suicide attacks that killed fifty-two and injured over seven hundred. That's what I'm worried can happen here,"[20]

"I hope not," Cathy responded as she reflected, *Daniela is never going to ride the subway in Denver.*

Ken began taking pictures from the folder to show her. "This is Hasib Hussain," Ken said showing her a grainy CCTV photo of one of the bombers wearing a blue button down polo shirt with a zip-up sports jacket over it. The only clue that he might be a bomber was the large backpack on his back. He looked relaxed as could be walking through Boots, a London drug store. *How would I know to take him down?* Cathy marveled examining his jaunty demeanor and innocent looking face.

"Here's Germaine Lindsay," Ken said pulling out a glossy print out of a tall, lightly bearded black man. He was a convert born in Jamaica. Ken pulled out pictures of Shehzad Tanweer and Mohammad Sidique Khan next, while Cathy silently asked, *What in God's name turned such men into killers? They lived in England for God's sake! Wasn't that a good enough place to live?*

Full coffee cup in hand, she motioned to Ken to follow as she walked slowly toward her office down the hall. It was the first time she'd suggested they meet in her office rather than hang out in the break room or in his tiny cubicle. She was breaking a new boundary—inviting him into her space.

"The London bombers were also *not all* young men, like we commonly think of terror suspects," Ken explained. "One of them was thirty-years-old and two were married with children, so you need to keep that in mind as well. There is no clear profile of the modern day militant jihadi. The Jamaican, Germaine Lindsay—the black man I showed you, he left behind a young son and his pregnant wife," Ken added.[21] Right after the attack, she pleaded shock and innocence but then disappeared and resurfaced in Kenya as a terrorist in her own right. "She's Caucasian, and now known as the 'White Widow.' See why I was worried about Tamerlan Tsarnaev's wife—Katherine Russell?"[22]

"Yeah, I remember that Tsarnaev's widow said she knew nothing after the Boston bombings," Cathy answered opening her office door and holding it for Ken. "No one believed her because they were making their pressure cooker bombs right in the kitchen, but I always thought it could be true, because she had a young child and a fulltime job being a caretaker for elderly folks at night. She may have been exhausted and completely clueless," Cathy remarked, thinking back to when Daniela was a baby. Remembering that sleepless time period and all the stress with Matt and how she hadn't known what he was up to, it seemed plausible that Katherine Russell was also clueless.

"You have to remember, it's impossible to profile these people anymore," Ken said as he flopped into the overstuffed chair by Cathy's desk. He looked around curiously, noticing that she had laid a deep blue carpet with a splash of primary colors woven into the design—probably from Ikea—on the floor to cover the government-issued beige carpet. The walls were decorated with three framed art posters—one a copy of a blue Matisse cut out and two Van Gogh's—*Starry Night over the Rhone* and *The Evening Cafe* mixed alongside her daughter's artwork scotch taped to the drab white walls near her computer monitor.

Not your usual government office, Ken reflected as he made himself comfortable. Small attentions to details in Cathy's office caught his eye as they continued to talk, details in which the tactile and colorful were emphasized. A small bronze sculpture of a wolf on her desk, its nose pointed to the sky as it howled, caught his eye. It was finely sculpted and looked vaguely restless seated on its haunches on her desk—*a lot like her, always wanting to get out into the field, get her hands dirty with the real work*, he thought as he looked around. Her bookshelf, although packed full of criminal justice and counter-terrorism texts, also showcased a small pink conch shell, surrounded by some star fish and a few smaller seashells interspersed with small, rock formations spread out on each of the shelves. The rocks were a mixture of crystals and cut semi precious stones—small pieces of purple amethyst, pink quartz, blue lapis and a halved malachite stone, each scattered haphazardly in front of the books, their colors echoing the bright hues in the carpet. The bottom bookshelf had what appeared to be a basket of small toys, although he couldn't make out what exactly was inside the basket.

She's got another side to her, Ken thought, taking in the artful way she'd managed to breathe elegance into her government issued furniture and office. Sensing it better to stay with business, he refrained from commenting on it. "Terrorists used to be mainly young men, but nowadays the homegrown can be just about anyone—male, female, married, unmarried, parent or childless," he said, carrying on their conversation. "Although, most are young men and the most lethal ones right now are connected with a hijacked form of Islam. We can credit al-Awlaki for spreading that into the Western world."

"So who is this al-Awlaki guy? What makes him so convincing?" Cathy asked looking again at the photo Ken had handed her earlier. She seemed unaware of the effect her office had on him. She was simply glad to have Ken in her space at the office.

"Well, for starters, he was born here, in New Mexico to Yemeni parents," Ken answered, leaning forward and taking a swallow of his coffee "He lived here until he was seven-years-old," he said handing her another picture of a younger al-Awlaki, brown, curly hair tucked neatly under his white haji cap. "Then he returned again for his higher education and he lived here for twelve years as an adult. He preached at a mosque just outside of Washington, D.C. before 9-11 and he interacted with at least two of the 9-11 bombers. There are still unanswered questions about his involvement in that plot. He also lived in the U.K. So he spoke perfect English and he knew how to appeal to Westerners."

"You see that white haji cap he's wearing?" Ken asked.

Cathy nodded. "That means he's been to Mecca for the Hajj, an obligation for all Muslims to carry out once in their lives."[23]

"It says in the Qur'an that the End Times are going to begin in the Middle East and that an army of ten thousand will rise up in Yemen and march to Syria and Iraq to fight in the Great Jihad. Al-Awlaki started to believe it was the End Times, before we droned him in 2011 and that's why he was calling for the endless jihad—thinking maybe he was going to lead the army of Yemeni jihadis," Ken explained.

"But what's his message?" Cathy asked as she leaned back in her desk chair. Her office was small but she'd made it comfortable and she felt good here behind her desk. She was proud that Jason had given her an office.

"He's got this lecture—Constants on the Path of Jihad—that has been downloaded all over the world. It's actually the teaching of Yusaf al Uyayri who founded al Qaeda in Saudi Arabia," Ken explained as he pulled the big chair he was seated in toward her desk. As he did so he noticed the photos of Daniela on Cathy's desk. "She's cute," he commented catching Cathy's eye.

"That's my daughter, Daniela," Cathy said blushing slightly. *Divorcee, single mother, undateable, boring,* she thought as she tried not to feel suddenly unattractive in his eyes.

Taking her cue, Ken reverted from the personal back to their conversation, "Al-Awlaki translated Uyayri's lecture into English and added real-life examples and religious stories from the Qur'an and hadiths to interpret it. It seems to be very compelling to some young and impressionable Muslims," Ken explained.

"Here let me show you one of his videos,"[24] Ken said pulling his chair around the corner of Cathy's desk. "Can I open a website for you?" he asked as she pulled her chair to the side to make room for him to pull up beside her. He reached for her mouse.

"He preaches in his Internet sermons that the faithful need to return to the great, eternal and unchanging principles of Islam," Ken explained searching for some of the al-Awlaki lectures. "He claims that it's an 'innovation'—what they call bid'ah, a sin—that jihad be temporarily suspended or cease entirely. And he puts forward something he calls the 'Constants of Jihad,' which are basically that believers need to fight jihad until the end times and that nothing should hold them back—not family, not those who might argue against, or anyone or anything because those who oppose are clearly from Satan. According to al-Awlaki, true believers must fight jihad endlessly until the final Day of Judgment. And he's got a hell of a lot of followers." Ken explained.

"And more joining the cause everyday it sounds like."

"The London bombers studied his lectures. As did the Toronto 18," Ken continued.

"Who are they?" Cathy asked leaning closer to Ken as he scrolled through YouTube. She liked the way he felt, so near.

"Here's one," Ken said clicking on it but the message that appeared showed that it had been deleted from the web. "YouTube keeps deleting his videos but they pop back up on other sites," Ken explained as he kept searching.

"The Toronto 18 were an international terrorist group in Canada that almost got to the point of detonating three Oklahoma City type truck bombs placed strategically around Toronto," Ken answered her earlier question. "They were also feeding out of al-Awlaki's hand. They planned to storm their Parliament *and* behead their Prime Minister. They had two American members who were aiming for targets in Washington, D.C. Those two carried out reconnaissance of the U.S. Capitol and other sites and even sent their surveillance video over to Pakistan for al Qaeda to consider funding. The so called 'Atlanta cell's' plan was to attack here and then slip over the Canadian border to hide out in a safe house set up by the Toronto cell,"[25] Ken explained.

"Oh geez," Cathy said raising her eyebrows as she listened. She imagined the FBI response to that kind of event.

"Remember the five New Jersey guys who tried to mount an attack on Fort Dix?" Ken asked sipping his coffee that he then placed on her desk as they sat near one another talking. "They also were sucking up al-Awlaki's poison. He inspired a shooting attack at the Little Rock military recruiting office. And do you remember Nidal Hasan—the military psychiatrist who carried out an active shooter attack on his coworkers at Fort Hood?"

Cathy nodded and Ken continued, "Hasan was an al-Awlaki follower—he was actually in e-mail contact with al-Awlaki and got his blessings for that type of attack. Hasan was disturbed about all the Muslims being killed in Iraq and Afghanistan and felt our military was doing the wrong thing. And now, even though he is a psychiatrist, he is such a nutter that he wrote a letter from his prison cell to ISIS requesting to be made a citizen of the Islamic State!"[26]

"Wow!" Cathy replied. This was all fascinating, but at the same time creating anxiety inside of her. She wanted to do something about it and wasn't content like Ken to observe and dissect terrorists virtually, from a safe distance. She needed to feel like she was doing something and she wasn't content to sit idly by and watch terrorists reap havoc in other's lives. She was eager to translate Intel into action—to get out in the field to do the work she loved best—capture and arrest. That's where the thrill was for her. Ken however, was clearly worked up just reading about terrorists.

"And Faisal Shazaid, the Times Square bomber—he was studying al-Awlaki's lectures," Ken said, while pulling up Faisal's Internet profile to show Cathy.[27] "It just goes on and on, all the people poisoned by al-Awlaki. The Christmas underwear bomber—he tried to detonate his bomb in an airliner over Detroit," Ken continued. "Al-Awlaki is thought to have directed his plot and Rajib Karim was trying to bring down British Airways planes while corresponding with al-Awlaki.[28]

So in 2011 we had enough and we droned the guy. You think that would shut him down, no?" Ken said slapping his hand down on her desk.

Cathy shrugged as she listened.

"But no, Anwar al-Awlaki lives on. He's alive and well on the Internet and has tons of followers. Imagine this—Roshonara Choudhry a King's college honor student, top in her class, starts watching his sermons online, gets hooked and watches *all* of his videos over a matter of months. She suddenly drops out of college and ends up bringing a kitchen knife to visit her parliamentarian—who voted to go into Iraq. She comes up to him nice, as can be, and stabs him right in the stomach—trying to kill him. She didn't care if she was killed—she wanted to be a 'martyr.'[29] Honor student to 'martyr' in a matter of months—no handler, no trainer, and no group—just our man, Anwar al-Awlaki doing his thing in his recorded Internet sermons. And even though we droned him, he lives on in cyberspace and is recruiting even more jihadis after his death."

"So what's his magic?" Cathy asked.

"After I spent the night listening to his lectures, I can see how he works," Ken answered clicking on another of al-Awlaki's videos to see if it would play. "Here just listen to this small clip," Ken said clicking play. The two watched as al-Awlaki, an imam, with a kindly forty-year-old bearded face wearing wire rim round glasses, a white haji hat, white thobe and combat vest, posed in front of what looked like a peaceful garden wall and began animatedly lecturing on jihad.

His voice was a strange combination of soothing authority mixed with fiery anger as he raised his index finger to make his points. His face and his eyes peering through the screen were intense and penetrating. Cathy could feel how mesmerizing a speaker he was in only the few minutes they watched before Ken hit stop and commented, "First of all he's charismatic. Second, he's got this authority to him—that probably comes from being from an important Yemeni family and tribe—but his authority is combined with a warmth and kindness. And he's also humble, while fiery."

"Muslims with an axe to grind could be directed into jihad simply by listening to him long enough. He's good—he catches all the psychological and emotional hooks. He uses real examples of where we've screwed up, been too harsh or made mistakes—like Abu Ghraib or those rapes by the Marines, and he points his angry finger at the West while making his case."

"So what does it mean for us?" Cathy asked glancing at the clock. "I need to get to a meeting soon," she said, immediately regretting having said it. She was enjoying his company immensely.

Maybe he's for real? She wondered. *He doesn't seem like a player.* But then remembering back to how she'd trusted Matt too, she pulled herself back—*Why risk it? You'll just get hurt,* an inner voice warned. Trusting again was not in her near future.

"Staff meeting in five," Russell suddenly announced, poking his head in her door. His bowtie was bright, lime green today and he looked ridiculous in it.

"I don't know what it means for us," Ken answered as soon as Russell departed. His eyes looked irritated as he gathered his papers back into his folder. Russell always had that effect on Ken, Cathy noticed. *Is he jealous?* she asked, smiling inwardly, but then quickly dismissed the thought. *Probably neither of them would be seriously interested in a single mother divorcee,* she reminded herself.

"I'm just worried that we're going to miss the one that slips through our fingers—perhaps someone like that white, Belgian, convert girl—Muriel Degauque. She totally blindsided the Belgians when she became a suicide bomber.[30] It's the perfect storm and we won't see it coming, until it hits."

"But then it will be too late, Ken," Cathy said as she stood up, her eyes serious, her brow furrowed with concern.

Purging

Trying to pretend she hadn't been raped was exhausting. Try as she might to avoid reminders that triggered recall, or using alcohol at night to numb herself out—no matter how hard she tried—Sophie kept ending up back on that chaise lounge pinned beneath the rapist, feeling him once again forcing himself into her body. And then her heart would start to race uncontrollably. Breaking into a cold sweat with the room spinning and fragmenting out of control happened nearly every time she got swept up in the flashbacks, just as it had in the actual event. Sometimes Sophie wasn't even sure she was still in her body. She felt like a point of consciousness without any body, no mooring connecting her to the earth.

At school her mind wandered far from the classroom, going back over Cara's idea to make fake IDs and go dancing. It had seemed like such a fun idea. She had been so tired of her father keeping her in a cage. He was so afraid someone would hurt his baby—she had needed to escape. But then when she did, it all went bad. And now it all went round and round in her head.

She could hardly talk to Cara. What's wrong, Sophie? her friend had texted her at least a hundred times but Sophie couldn't bring herself to tell Cara what had happened. It was too horrible and if she put it into words then it would be real for sure. Better to leave it buried where it at least had the chance of becoming undone. *She could wish for that couldn't she?* Luckily Cara didn't attend the same school so she didn't risk running into her.

Are you avoiding me? Cara texted, asking her what was wrong most weekends, and why they weren't getting together as usual. Don't you want to go back to the Solar again?

No, not avoiding. Studying for finals. Sophie texted back, although the truth was she didn't want to see anyone, including Cara. You know how my Dad is. She added, using her father as her excuse.

In truth, Sophie was finding it impossible to study. When she sat down to do her homework her mind wouldn't focus. The words swam on the page so much that she could hardly read anymore. Her head ached as she tried to keep the memories out and focus on the text in front of her, but the words just hopped around on the page, seeming to mock her. Sophie feared she was going to flunk her finals.

At dinnertime she felt terrified her father would ask her questions again, discover her secret shame. With each bite of food she felt panic rising in her throat and she found she could hardly enjoy her meals anymore.

The unbidden flashbacks came over her at any moment, startling her with their lifelike intensity. When she was doing the dishes after dinner Sophie suddenly felt Colin's hands holding her down, his legs forcing hers open, his fumbling between her legs and then hurting her. Reliving it, Sophie dropped the crystal glass she'd been washing and jumped back as if she'd been holding a poisonous serpent, watching in horror as the crystal smashed into pieces in the kitchen sink.

"Sophie!" her mother cried. "The crystal glasses I hand carried from Poland! You broke another one? That's the second one in a week!"

Tears slipped down her cheeks as she murmured, "Sorry Mom, I'll be more careful next time. I didn't mean to break it."

"Honey, you've got to pay attention!" Sarah chided, adding more pain to her already overwhelming burden of guilt and shame.

That's when she found the great comfort food could be—ice cream, chips, candy, anything sweet—and the more the better. She'd shovel in a quart of Ben and Jerry's chocolate chip cookie ice cream — with a chaser of potato chips and a Coke. Buzzed from all the sugar she'd feel better, until the pounds started to pile on. Two, four, and then ten pounds showed up on the bathroom scale as Sophie perched in anxiety, pulling in a bloated belly that blocked her sight from the dial. The Great Comforter—food and drink— had become her best friends and confidants, but they were also making her overweight. Nothing like legal substances to dull the mind and drown the senses.

Her morning runs had fallen by the wayside. She was too hung-over in the mornings from the vodka shots she downed to sleep through the night to have enough energy to run in the morning.

"Wake up!" Sophie's mother had come down to her room to shake her awake just this morning. In the dull haze of a hangover, Sophie quickly glanced around the room to be sure last night's vodka bottle was safely back in the drawer and her binge foods tucked under the bed.

Thankfully, Sarah saw nothing awry as she chided her daughter, "You are oversleeping so often these days! You think it's a growth spurt? You sleeping okay?"

Sophie nodded. "I'm fine Mom, just tired. They're cramming us for finals."

Sophie found that she was pouring the shots earlier and earlier these days, disappearing each evening to her room to binge on chocolate, ice cream and candy—to be followed by vodka. Her parents had no idea—believing her when she told them, "I've got a big test tomorrow, better go study."

In fact, Sophie was failing most of her classes. Her high school grades had tanked and along with them any hopes of ever getting into a good college—along with her plans of paying for it via ROTC, which she was absolutely not going to do. Sophie thought about dropping out. She'd already checked out getting a GED instead.

Panicked over the weight gain, Sophie learned how to end her binge sessions by pushing her fingers way back into her throat causing her to gag and vomit up the sugary, comfort food. It didn't stop the weight gain, although it did deliver a strange, calm feeling of empowerment. To battle the extra pounds, Sophie began running again, substituting afternoons instead of early mornings—pumping her legs hard—trying to burn off the excess weight. But once home, back in the cocoon of the basement, she found herself going back to the sugar and junk foods.

Tonight it was Ben & Jerry's chocolate, cookie dough ice cream. Sophie had bought two pints of it on the way home from her run and was now frantically opening the first pint. Digging in her spoon she shoveled the ice cream in and let the cool, sweet cream fill her senses. The sugar buzz went immediately to her brain as she kept devouring the first pint and then turned to the next. The pleasure was so filling, her mind totally focused on the sugar, cream and chocolate. Tastes from childhood delivered now, when she needed it—a fix from the pain.

Just as soon as she finished the second pint, Sophie ran to the toilet. She'd read on the Internet about how to purge and she knew that some of the calories—even when vomited back, absorbed into her system. She needed to act fast to keep her weight under control. Ramming her index far enough down her throat to push hard on her uvula, Sophie gagged and her stomach violently flip-flopped and sent the ice cream back up her throat ejecting it into the toilet as she pushed her long locks out of the way.

Sophie's head spun as she stared at the mess, undigested chocolate chips mixed with stomach acid and melted ice cream. *At least I control this,* Sophie thought with a grim mix of satisfaction and disgust as she felt stomach acid burning the back of her throat and gums and smelled the foul aroma of vomit surrounding her. Her heart raced in her chest as she felt her blood whooshing through her body. Flushing the toilet Sophie tried to calm her body and shut down the overwhelming feelings of shame as she went back to her bedroom and tried to study. Of course it was impossible, which led her to break out the vodka shots.

In panic over the weight gain she couldn't restrain, and terrified of losing control, Sophie started purging *all* of her meals. Unknowingly, by inducing vomiting four or five times a day, Sophie had stumbled upon a heroin-like drug. Her natural endorphins kicked in as she vomited up her meals giving her a peaceful high that—along with the bingeing—helped her keep the memories at bay. Sophie had found her path out of the rapist's brutal grip—but she was free falling into bulimia and alcohol abuse and all the shame that went with both.

The tell tale signs were starting to show as well. With all the vomiting, Sophie's throat and face started bloating up strangely—making her look pale and ill. That added to the vodka hangovers and fitful sleep, Sophie was starting to see in the mirror a face she hardly recognized—one that was puffed up, pale, and worry-worn.

Sophie's parents noticed the changes as well, but were clueless as to the cause, chalking it up to normal, teenage stressors. Jake especially was delighted with Sophie's sudden hermit-like seclusion in the basement, no longer arguing and begging to go out nights and weekends with her friends. He believed her stories, thinking that his daughter was busy studying in the basement, eager to learn.

"You know, we're really lucky, Sarah," Jake remarked at night to his wife. "While other kids are doing God knows what, our Sophie's downstairs hitting the books." When Sarah failed to answer—her mind so deep in her legal briefs—he asked, "But did you notice her face looks puffy recently and it seems like she's gaining weight. What's that about?"

"It's probably just baby fat," Sarah answered without looking up from her reading. "She's going through puberty, remember?"

A sucker for fitness, Jake wasn't so sure. He stopped Sophie the next day in the kitchen, on her way home from her run. She'd picked up the usual two pints of ice cream and tried to hide it from him, holding the bag partially hidden under her running jacket.

"What's in the bag?" Jake asked.

"Aw just some ice cream," Sophie answered already filled with shame at his even asking. "I got hungry running today."

"You don't think you are overeating a bit?" Jake asked. "You used to be in such great shape, but lately it seems you're slipping in the self-discipline department."

"Sure, Dad," Sophie said staring at the kitchen tiles. *Even he can see I'm turning into an elephant!* Sophie groaned inside. *But I need this*, she remembered, knowing the sugary ice cream could at least momentarily fill the hole inside that constantly needed to be fed.

"Well take it easy on the sweets," Jake said. "You've got a good figure and should keep it that way," he added as he turned and went back to his office.

Filled with shame Sophie went to the basement and opened the first Ben & Jerry's pint. Today it was mint chocolate chip. As she shoveled it into her mouth, it didn't deliver the same pleasure. Instead she ate numbly as tears rolled down her face. The shame of her father seeing her falling apart filled her with self-loathing. Yet she couldn't stop. She ate the entire first pint, finished off the second as well, and then went through her usual barfing routine. Although today it brought her no sense of control or pleasure whatsoever.

Premonitions

"**S**omething is going to happen," Ken said as he caught up to Cathy in the morning for their coffee meet-up. Today was Monday and Ken was eager to talk with her after the weekend.

"Did you hear the news out of Canada?" Ken asked as he reached for the coffee cups. "Martin Rouleau Couture, an angry Muslim—and a recent convert—took his car and ran down two Canadian soldiers, killing one of them, injuring the other.[31] And guess what? He's been listening to Anwar al-Awlaki and following ISIS. He'd been stopped from going to Turkey the year before—probably to slip into Syria, but when that got foiled…"

"A *stay and act in place* attack?" Cathy mused remembering how Ken had explained that if the ISIS adherents couldn't travel to the battlefield they should bring the battlefield to them.

"Yep, just what I've been telling you is going to happen here," Ken said. He sipped his coffee as he looked over the rim appreciatively at Cathy. Glad to have something to keep her attention, he went on, "I don't know why, but I feel something brewing here—something big. I don't know where it's going to come from, but there's going to be *a stay and act in place* attack here, I just know it."

"Oh, so you are a fortune-teller now," Cathy quipped, smiling over her coffee cup although she also felt that this homegrown terrorism thing was looming just over the horizon, threatening to take them all by surprise.

"No, just reading the signs," Ken answered. "And the writing on the wall seems all too clear to me. We simply need to figure out *who* it is and *what he—or she*—has got planned for us. I hope I'm wrong, I really do."

"I don't think you're wrong, Ken," Cathy said while turning up the volume on the TV in the employee lounge. It was time for Michael Steinbach, Assistant Director of the Counterterrorism Division of the FBI to give his Investigation Statement before the House Committee on Homeland Security in Washington, D.C. The other FBI team members entered the lounge also wanting to watch the newscast. Everyone turned his or her attention to the special reporting on CNN as the Assistant Director began his statement. [32]

"Good morning Chairman McCaul, Ranking Member Thompson, and members of the committee. Thank you for the opportunity to appear before you today to discuss the dynamic threat of foreign fighters traveling in support of the Islamic State of Iraq and the Levant (ISIL) and the rising threat to the United States from homegrown violent extremism. This threat remains one of the biggest priorities not only for the FBI but for the Intelligence Community (IC) as a whole and our foreign partners."

"Conflicts in Syria and Iraq are currently the most attractive overseas theater for Western-based extremists who want to engage in violence. We estimate upwards of one hundred and fifty Americans have traveled or attempted to travel to Syria to join extremist groups. However, once in Syria, it is very difficult to discern what happens there. This lack of clarity remains troubling to the Intelligence Community."[33]

"No shit, Sherlock," Russell remarked. Russell had complained in their last staff meeting about not being given enough leeway by the upper management to take down suspects. "It wouldn't be so 'troubling' if we were allowed to knock down doors and ask questions later."

"Russell, shut up. You might learn something," warned Jason, the team supervisor for the FBI Agents assigned to the Fusion Center.

"...ISIS has proven to be relentless and continues to terrorize individuals in Syria and Iraq, including Westerners. We are concerned about the possibility of homegrown extremists becoming radicalized by information available on the Internet," Assistant Director Steinbach continued.

"The *possibility* of homegrown extremists? Oh my God...what the hell does he think we've been doing here?" Russell broke in.

"Russell, he's talking to the Senate, not us. Chill out," Ken spoke up.

"There is little doubt that ISIL views the United States and the West as a strategic enemy. A year ago, the leader of ISIL warned the United States will soon be in direct conflict with the group. ISIL recently released a video via social media networking sites reiterating the group's encouragement of lone offender attacks in Western countries; specifically advocating for attacks against soldiers, patrons, law enforcement and intelligence members. Several incidents have occurred in the United States and Europe over the last few months that indicate this 'call to arms' has resonated among ISIL supporters and sympathizers." [34] Assistant Director Steinbach went on, not saying anything they didn't all already know.

"Okay," Jason said as he turned off the TV. "Nothing new here. He's just catching up our beloved Congress on what's going on," Jason said with a note of sarcasm. "Since we are all here, let's take a look at where we're at. Ken, have you got anything new from the social media tracking?"

"There's a lot of bragging going on but nothing serious yet," Ken responded. "But in the chat rooms I'm hearing some chatter between kids endorsing ISIS, that getting into the drug trade might be a good way to raise funds. Hard to say, as these guys are all big talkers, but something is buzzing on that," Ken replied.

"Keep on it and keep me in the loop," Jason said. "Cathy that sounds like you should get back out with the drug lords and see if you can learn anything. You ready to go undercover again for a few nights?"

"Sure," Cathy answered with a big smile crossing her face. She felt proud to be singled out. Over the past three months Cathy had developed an undercover persona who hung out with the drug lords and she was starting to gain their confidence. It was work that built on her previous career as a Denver cop who had a good grasp on the local crime scene.

"Sir, we also got a tip from one of the local librarians about a young Muslim using the computer library," she added. "Nothing definite but she said he seemed suspicious. I know we shouldn't be profiling Muslims but..."

"I can fill you in on that, Jason," Russell said as he jumped into Cathy's spotlight.

"Of course," Cathy said with a smirk. Russell could be so irritating when it came to hogging the boss's attention. Russell had lately abandoned his bow ties and today was wearing a tight, black Armani lounge top that showed his chiseled chest, just one of his many attempts to get noticed—and he rarely failed.

"Why thank you," Russell came forward, puffing out his chest as he stood next to Jason and took a bow. The room laughed. Cathy didn't.

He's so muscle bound he probably couldn't climb over a fence, yet he thinks he knows it all, Cathy thought as Russell began speaking. She could usually take his quips and laughed when he called her the "new girl" and demanded coffee, but this time he was pushing her out of the boss's radar, and that stung.

"I had that computer snatched and brought to me. Seems that young towelhead—er, I mean Mohammed Said, is a minor. He's only sixteen but he has been using the library computer to communicate with some ISIS fighters over in Syria. He has been asking how to travel through Turkey and what to bring. He's even gone so far as to cover his tracks by using a 'dead drop' system for his e-mails. It's not really that sophisticated, just of a method of trying to be incognito, by setting up a false account to be shared with other nefarious creatures, and leaving messages for them to read in the "drafts" folder to avoid sending any that could be intercepted..."

"Russell, cut the crap—we all know what a dead drop system is. Just get on with it," Jason commented in an irritated tone. He tolerated Russell and his excessive ego because Russell was the best forensic technician they had, but they also didn't need a lecture on the basics of Internet detection methods right now.

"Right. The short of it is that I was able to hack into their so-called 'dead drop' e-mail account only to find that our towelhead applied for, but hasn't gotten his passport to travel to Syria. He has been talking about leaving via Denver International Airport to Ankara, Turkey—via Toronto and Istanbul. However, he hasn't raised the money to buy his ticket yet. That's as far as I've gotten." Loath to give up the spotlight Russell slowly returned to his chair.

"Thanks Russell, good job. Keep on that and report to me with anything new. This young man sounds serious," Jason said. "Cathy I think we need to get eyes on him and maybe send someone out to talk to him and his parents. And Russell, you should get him on the no-fly list."

"Yes sir, I already did," Russell stood again and answered before Cathy could reply. She noticed Ken looked annoyed as well.

"Anyone else got anything?" Jason asked glancing around the room. When no one answered, he added, "ISIS delving into the drug trade is a chilling thought. That could be a whole new situation. Let's hope that's just chatter. Let's get to work," Jason said as he exited the staff lounge for his office.

Drop Out

"Sophie, can you come up here?" Jake called down the stairs leading to Sophie's basement room. His voice was laced with concern.

When she appeared in the kitchen, Jake was standing with a letter from her school gripped tightly in his hand, his brow was knit, and he had a deep frown on his face.

"What's this about you dropping out of high school?" Jake asked incredulously as he waved the letter about. "This letter says you dropped out last week. What the hell?" It was late June and Sophie had failed most of her final exams. Figuring there was no use in trying anymore, she'd let her school know she wasn't coming back in the fall.

"Yeah, Dad, I was going to tell you," Sophie answered, pushing her hands down into her jean pockets while an overwhelming sense of shame kept her eyes glued to the ceramic kitchen floor tiles. Her hair fell across her face as she explained, "I'm going to take the GED."

"The GED! Only losers take their GEDs," Jake stormed, tossing the letter down on the table and crossing the room to stand over Sophie. "What about ROTC and college?"

"I don't think I'm cut out for college anymore, Dad," Sophie said tracing the geometric patterns in the ceramic floor tiles with her downcast eyes. "I'm going to be a CNA instead."

"CNA! What the hell is that?" Jake ranted.

"Certified Nurse's Assistant," Sophie explained. "I've already signed up for online courses."

"Not cut out for college?" Jake fumed. "What are you talking about? You were getting straight A's last semester."

"Not anymore," Sophie said, a tear trickling down her cheek as she gazed briefly up at her father's face. It was filled with disappointment and concern. "I failed both my Algebra II and Biology tests last week."

"But every night you said you had to go and study. What the hell was that all about?" Jake fumed.

"I think my brain has shut down lately," Sophie answered, stifling a sob.

"You want me to hire a tutor?" Jake asked, fury still filling his voice.

"No Dad," Sophie answered, her tears falling freely now as she wiped them away with her hands. "I've got this. I'm going to become a CNA. It's not a bad life. I always thought I'd do something in the medical field. Maybe I'll go to college later," she said, wiping her face with her sleeve.

"Emptying bedpans?" Jake fumed as he furiously ripped a paper towel from the hanging dispenser and handed it to her. "You can still turn this around. You're strong."

"No Dad, not everyone is a computer geek like you. I just can't study right now," Sophie answered taking the paper towel to dry her tears. It felt rough against her eyes.

"Come on, Sophie," Jake ranted. "You only have one year left to go. It's totally stupid to throw it all away when you are so close to graduating," Jake said. "You've always been a good student. You can get back on your horse. You just need to get serious, no more fooling around, lazing around and eating Ben & Jerry's in the basement."

"No, Dad, I can't right now," Sophie answered, stifling a sob. *There's nothing I can do right to please him, not anymore,* Sophie thought in desperation.

"What do you mean you can't? You've gone slack lately—gained a lot of weight, failing out in your classes. It's not like you!" Jake raged.

But Sophie just shook her head as her face contorted into another grimace. "No, Dad, everything's cool. I've got a plan." Sophie answered.

"A plan? You mean dumping college so you can empty bedpans? Doesn't sound like much of a plan to me. A person doesn't just suddenly drop out of school for no good reason, Soph!" Jake seethed as he held his hands on his hips. A better part of him yearned to wrap his arms around his little girl. He never could stand it when she cried. But the bigger part was damn furious. *How could she throw away the future he'd worked so hard to make for her?* He'd watched her grades all these years, helped her with her homework, and made sure she did all her assignments. *And now this?*

"Yeah, Dad. I'm sure about this," Sophie answered, wishing she could just disappear, vaporize into thin air. "This is the right thing for me right now," she said, a sob catching in her throat as she turned to descend back down the basement stairs.

"God almighty, I'll never understand girls!" Jake said as he scratched his head and went to the living room looking around for something to distract him. Picking up the remote he flipped on the television to a college football game. But unable to contain his agitation he turned instead to punch the wall, creating a small hole where his fist went right through the plasterboard. "Damn it all to hell!" he shouted, as the pain in his fist equaled the pain in his heart.

Downstairs Sophie heard his anger, punching the wall, and his cursing. Terrified she wondered, *What should I do now?*

Truth was Sophie had no plan—other than to take the online CNA course and somehow find a way to get out from beneath those cruel hands that kept holding her down, pinned to the lounge chair.

Lunch

"**Y**ou want to catch lunch over at the Olive Garden?" Ken asked poking his head in Cathy's office door.

"Yeah, I'm starved," Cathy answered, smiling up at him. "I'll drive today," she offered remembering last time they'd sat together in his car. A warm ripple of pleasure accompanied the memory along with a touch of anxiety. She wanted to be in charge this time.

At the Olive Garden they got a table pretty quickly and both ordered pasta, tortellini and lasagna, with iced teas for both.

"You ever get discouraged by working in counter-terrorism?" Cathy asked as she picked a breadstick from the basket. Lately the culmination of all the evil she'd been taking in over the years—the bad things she'd seen on the streets as a cop—and now this talk of the world becoming unhinged with terrorism was getting on her nerves. "I'm doubting the inner goodness of mankind," she explained smiling sadly. "Does it ever seem like too much to you?"

"Yeah, sure, all the time in fact," Ken answered with good humor filling his voice. "You don't spend your days on the computer like I do watching those hideous jihadi films. I've seen so many beheadings I think I'm desensitized to it. AllahuAkbar! The whole damn thing! I dream about those videos sometimes."

"Nightmares?" Cathy probed as the waitress set down their food. Ken waited for the waitress to finish and leave before answering.

"Yeah, sometimes I relive them in my dreams," he answered as he picked at his lasagna. "We live in a really lame world, you know?"

"I've felt that so often," Cathy admitted. "Sometimes I don't know why I became a cop. What was I thinking? And now trying to get up to speed on this whole militant jihadi thing—it's overwhelming. I don't like to admit the kind of world we live in and I get afraid—not for myself, but for my daughter. Into what kind of world is she growing up?"

Ken gazed into Cathy's eyes before answering, "You can't let it get you down, kiddo."

"Yeah, I remember it took awhile to get used to the drug dealers and mafia types. I was afraid and disgusted by them too, but now they seem run of the mill to me. That's kind of sick, isn't it? The way we get desensitized to violence?"

"Yeah, of course it is. But the important thing is not to lose your heart. You learn to take distance, but you keep your heart open, don't forget that," Ken answered, his eyes soft as he gazed into hers.

"Okay," Cathy answered, thinking, *He's really cool, the real deal maybe?*

"Sometimes I wonder if stressing myself out, watching all this disgusting jihadi stuff, if I could develop Tourette's and one day I'll start shouting jihadi slogans by accident," Ken suddenly joked with a big smile on his face. "Can you imagine it? Me shouting 'AllahuAkbar!' by accident in the airport security line?" he asked, chuckling as he began to eat in earnest. That was typical Ken—find the joke in the middle of the horror.

"I wonder how long you'd last before four or five TSA guys would have you on the floor, if not dead?" Cathy answered giggling at the thought. "Geez that would be a terrible form of Tourette's!"

"Yeah, I better keep a lid on the inner Tourette's thing," Ken answered, smiling.

"Yeah, you better keep that corked up inside," Cathy agreed laughing freely now.

"Or how about this?" Ken asked. "I once interviewed this Palestinian woman who was visiting Paris with her best friend who was also a Muslim and his name was Jihad. For real—his mother had named him Jihad. So they get separated around the Eiffel Tower and she doesn't give it a thought. She starts calling out his name, screaming at the top of her lungs, "Jihad! Jihad!"

Of course the Paris police surrounded her before her friend came running and explained their way out of the situation. I think he had to show his ID to prove it was his name. They were lucky they weren't both thrown in the slammer!"

Cathy laughed at his story thinking about how Ken had such a good way with black humor—lightening the pain when it got too heavy.

They ate in silence for a few minutes until Ken's face suddenly became perturbed, "Ever see a lady with both her legs blown off?" he asked. "I had dinner with one of the victims of the London subway bombings—it was heart rending," he went on.

His eyes clouded over, remembering seeing the woman hobble about on her artificial legs as they had all been seated for dinner. "She'd been visiting in London and just happened to take the tube that day. Her legs got totally blown away in the explosion. She was lucky—she lived, but it was really horrible being there with her as she balanced on those artificial limbs going all the way up to her hips."

Why am I telling her this? Ken suddenly thought. Yet he felt compelled to tell her more.

"And she was so naïve about terrorists. She told us all at the dinner that she planned to enter a parade on the anniversary of the 7-7 bombings and walk the memorial route with her fake legs and canes. She thought that would make future homegrowns think twice about the violence they cause to innocent victims."

"I felt so bad telling her the truth. I told her these people are so filled with hate for us, and sympathy for the victims they think that *we cause*, that they won't see you as a victim or feel any sympathy," Ken said grimacing at the memory. "I felt so terrible telling her that."

"Oh geez," Cathy responded, sadness filling her eyes.

The two sat in silence for a few moments, a comfortable silence—one that said all the comforting things that were impossible to put into words.

A Live Lead

"**I** saw your write up on Abdur Rahman, aka Sammy Stillman," Russell said as he stopped by Ken's cubicle, their boss Jason appearing alongside him. "It looks to me as though you may have a live one. I've asked Jason if we can move in on him," Russell announced. Russell had blue suspenders on today over a tightly stretched, knit T-shirt. He snapped his thumbs in his suspenders as he spoke. Ken wanted to roll his eyes at Russell's outfit and make some remark, but he saw that Jason appeared in a hurry.

"Let's take a look," Jason said signaling to Ken to pull up the case, as they gathered around Ken's computer. Jason saw Cathy leaving her office and motioned for her to join them.

"What's up?" Cathy asked, sticking her head over the cubicle wall.

"Meet Abdur Rahman," Ken said clicking on his computer to show a picture of his lead. "Also known as Sammy Stillman."[35] The screen showed an ordinary looking eighteen-year-old slim, medium height, Caucasian, young man with a bit of a scrawny beard appearing on his chin. His curly, dark brown hair reached almost to his shoulders.

"He converted two years ago and has been becoming more and more radical ever since. Here's his Facebook feed. He's all over ISIS," Russell said taking over the briefing to their boss—as usual. "And he's managed to get himself into some of the serious chat rooms where he's saying he's interested in taking out the infidel government here at home."

Russell handed Jason, Ken and Cathy printouts of what Ken had documented earlier, the content of chat room discussions. Jason began avidly reading. After some time, he looked up at the assembled group, his face solemn and said, "This one looks serious."

"I'm thinking it's the right time to make an undercover visit to him—tell him I'm with ISIS and I can help get him equipped for a mission," Russell remarked, trying to gauge Jason's reaction.

"You don't want to lead him further than he's already gone," Ken jumped in, caution filling his voice.

"And we also don't want to miss finding out how he equips himself," Russell answered, his voice cynical and his eyes steely with determination as he stared Ken down.

"I guess you have a point there," Ken answered, his face wearing a look of concern. "I just don't like the idea of entrapping a young man who hasn't yet gone into terrorism—no matter what he's spouting in the chat rooms. Young men tend to be braggarts you know."

"There will be no entrapment," Russell answered his voice growing cold as he looked to Jason for approval. "He's already determined to pull the trigger or I wouldn't be standing here telling you why we need to go meet with him. While you're worried about entrapment, Ken, Americans may end up murdered by someone like him."

Jason remained silent, listening as his two experts argued it out.

"You know Russell, there's one counter terrorism expert that says there are four ingredients that make up the lethal cocktail of terrorism" Ken said listing them off as he held up his fingers. "One, a group that's decided to use terrorism to advance its political goal; two, an ideology that somehow wrongly justifies attacking innocent civilians in pursuit of the group's goal; three, the social support the group and its ideology enjoy; and four, the vulnerabilities and motivations of an individual interacting with the group and its ideology.[36] We need to think hard about if we are providing one of those ingredients. It seems to me that coming alongside a vulnerable kid like this and saying we're ISIS and can help him, is providing that crucial element of social support," Ken said pulling on his third finger. "Without that he might never pull the trigger and just remain an Internet braggart," Ken added as he faced Russell down.

"Don't lecture me, Ken. I did two tours in Iraq and I know what these types can do," Russell answered his voice becoming sharp. "I saw three little kids playing ball in the street one day. Happy as you please in the sunshine of life one minute and the next minute there were body parts splattered all over the place. The bomb not only killed them, but an old man minding his own business watching, and some innocent bystanders walking to the market," Russell said as he stared at Ken with cold, hard eyes. "Screw entrapment."

"Russell," Ken started quietly as he glanced at their boss who still said nothing. "Of course they harm innocents once they are activated, but I'm talking about *if* this guy would ever become activated without us coming alongside of him, offering him support." He looked over to Cathy to see if she had a reaction. Cathy just stared back without comment. Jason seemed to be weighing it all in his mind, deciding whether or not to give Russell the green light on moving in on Abdur Rahman.

"Look, these bastards don't play touchy feely with their gear, their weapons and their cold-hearted plans to kill us," Russell answered. "By the time we get around to deciding if they're not playing around after checking under every single rock, they've already done their blowing up. I don't know about you all, but I'm not willing to fool around and take any more chances with simply watching and waiting. Not after 9-11."

"I get it Russell. I just don't want a lack of due diligence to bite us in the ass in case we're moving in too fast," Ken said backing down. He had to remember he was the analyst. They were the agents.

"Forget it, Ken," Russell answered still looking annoyed. Turning his full attention to their boss, Russell continued, "Jason, I'd like to start chatting with this fellow on the Internet and I think he warrants an undercover visit."

Russell then paused and mused in his usual staged way as he turned to Ken, adding, "You know, I could really use an Islamic issues specialist on this mission. How would you like to *really serve your country* Ken, and join me when I pay this kook a visit?" Russell asked, cocking his head as he left his offer hanging in the air.

Cathy looked over at Ken for a reaction. She wished Russell had asked her but didn't say a word while Russell waited for Ken's reply. *He's trying to make Ken out as a wimp in front of our boss,* Cathy realized. She knew how Ken felt about entrapment and the legal hassles it could cause, but on these issues she sided with Russell one hundred percent. *These guys are lethal and need to be stopped and if it takes a sting operation that's what it takes,* she thought while she watched Ken's face.

"Yeah, I'm in." Ken answered after a few moments of silence. He shot a look at Cathy that told her he hoped everything about this Abdur Rahman had been vetted properly. If not, the powers that be could make life miserable for all of them.

"It sounds justified to me," Jason said giving the final approval. "You two work together on this."

"Let's get these bastards before they get one of our own," Russell said smiling approvingly. "You might even enjoy this," he added as he reached over to pat Ken on the back. Ken winced at Russell's condescending touch but didn't pull away—he'd said enough already.

Party Time

There's a party tomorrow night at Stuart's!! Everyone's asking where you've been? Cara texted. It was late July and Sophie had been avoiding everyone, especially since dropping out of high school. After running into a few of her friends Sophie had decided that she couldn't face the questions and the shock of her friends' speechless stares when they found out. It was like seeing her father's judgment mirrored again in their faces. It stabbed at her heart, painfully, bringing back his wrath when he found out.

Just hangin, Sophie texted back.

Why didn't you tell me you dropped out? What's going on? Cara asked.

It was only a few weeks ago, Sophie answered, unsure of how to explain. How could she explain without telling the truth, when the truth was something she could never admit? There was no explanation. Her own father couldn't even get it.

Everyone is asking if you're preggers??? Cara texted.

No! Not preggers, Sophie answered, feeling a sinking shame pervade her body. *The kids at school think I'm pregnant? Oh fuck!* Sophie moaned. It was so humiliating.

Of course I knew you couldn't be preggers. How could you be with your old man keeping you locked up in a virtual chastity belt? You were always the innocent one! LOL, Cara texted back.

Definitely not preggers, Sophie answered, horrified reading Cara's assessment of her as the "innocent one." *I'm hardly that anymore,* Sophie thought as a deep sadness lodged in her heart.

So why are you avoiding everyone? Cara demanded.

I was studying. I took my GED, Sophie answered still avoiding the question. I'm studying to be a certified nurse's assistant now.

Bedpans, LOL!!! I'll pick you up 8:30 tomorrow night – no excuses, Cara texted.

OK, Sophie answered cautiously. She knew Cara's personality—there was no telling her no, when it came to a party. Sophie had begged off of all Cara's invitations up to now, but she knew that eventually Cara was going to show up, and make her talk, if she didn't agree to come out. And then Cara was going to demand to know why Sophie was no longer interested and Sophie wasn't sure she could keep her secret hidden if Cara pushed hard enough.

That, and the stifling disapproval from her Dad ever since she'd dropped out, made her finally feel she needed to get out of the house. *Might as well be the failure he thinks I am,* Sophie rationalized.

Wear a short skirt, high heels and loads of makeup, Cara texted. Let's get this party on!!!

LOL, Then I'll need some heels from you, Sophie wrote back and switched her phone off. Tomorrow would arrive soon enough and she wasn't sure she could handle partying again with Cara, or any of them for that matter.

"I'm going to sleep over at Cara's tomorrow night," Sophie told her mother that afternoon.

"Did you discuss it with your father?" Sarah asked, knowing Jake was the one that liked to give Sophie permission for overnights.

"No, but I've stayed there before," Sophie said. "He'll be cool." In truth, Sophie wasn't sure if she could stand to go to Cara's house again. Would she be able to sleep there? *Unlikely,* Sophie realized. Maybe she'd need to find somewhere else to crash.

The idea of seeing Cara again was causing a constricting anxiety in her chest and throat as she imagined facing her questions in person. Although staying at home living under her father's seething disapproval was also getting her desperately down. Her comfort came with hiding from people she knew, keeping a low profile, avoiding questions and forced answers. It was the only safety she had anymore. That and the vodka shots that she poured for herself each night to induce sleep. Tonight she poured out a few extra.

***

Sophie took Cara's advice and picked out a red knit skirt, that wasn't a mini, that she could roll up at the waist to become one, coupled with a sleek sleeveless button-down shirt to wear to the party. Only problem was she didn't own any appropriate high heels for partying—how could she when Jake oversaw her wardrobe? So she texted Cara, Can I borrow your red platform heels?

Sure baby! Cara texted back.

Pick me up at the 7-11, ok? Sophie wrote.

"See you tomorrow, Dad," Sophie called out as she left, hoping he wouldn't think to check the overnight bag she was carrying that had all her party clothes and make up in it.

Arriving at the 7-11 Sophie headed for the ladies room and after locking the washroom door, slipped out of her jeans, discarded her bra, and stood briefly under the fluorescent lights in front of the washroom sink wearing nothing but her black lace panties. At least Jake didn't try to control her underwear purchases. They were from Victoria's Secret and very sexy. Staring at her nakedness, Sophie saw that her breasts were fuller and rounder than months before and she now had a little round pillow at the waist, but she was still hot. She just didn't feel hot. That was the trouble.

Sophie pulled on the red knit skirt, rolled it at the waist to be a mini and pulled the black button-down shirt over her head unbuttoning the buttons down below her bra line. Glancing sideways into the mirror she saw that her breasts showed. *Who the fuck cares?* Sophie thought. *It's not like I'm a virgin anymore.*

Then she got to work on her face. She was already made up—but only to her father's allowable standards. Now, staring at her reflection under the cold fluorescent lights she added a dark ring of black eyeliner around her eyes, mascaraed her lashes over again to highlight them and applied shiny lip-gloss to her lips, all to the effect of making her eyes and lips pop. Standing on her tiptoes in front of the mirror, Sophie checked out the full effect.

Her face still looked puffy and pale—even made up—but as Sophie loosed her hair from the elastic band she had tied it back in, she saw that she had achieved the desired look. Braless, her blonde hair falling over her shoulders, her long, naked legs poking out beneath the red knit mini and her lips pursed into a pout—she could definitely draw male attention.

So maybe I'm just a little slut after all? Sophie thought sadly as she stared at her reflected image staring back at her in the chrome framed mirror. She sure could sex it up, no question about that, even after what had happened to her—maybe even better now that she was "ruined", Sophie realized.

Nothing more to lose, she thought as she took in her sexy new image.

All grown-up, Sophie reminded herself with a sadness jabbing at her heart as she remembered the things Colin had said to her as he'd stripped away her clothes, and her virginity.

Cara texted that she'd arrived and Sophie quickly gathered her jeans, bra and t-shirt into her sleepover bag, threw on a pair of sunglasses—just in case her Dad happened by, and ran out of the washroom to Cara's car.

Can she tell? Sophie thought as she slipped into the passenger seat. *Does she know what happened to me that night?*

"Sophie! You look hot!" Cara screamed as her friend slammed the door shut and squealed out of the parking lot. "How did you get away from the Virginity Vault? The usual sleepover story?" Cara asked as they sped away from Sophie's residential neighborhood toward the highway.

Sophie nodded, wincing at the joke as she saw a bottle of vodka on the seat lying between them.

"How did you get your hands on that?" Sophie squealed in delight as she picked it up. It was just what she needed to get through tonight.

"I have friends," Cara answered, throwing her long, straight, brown hair back over her shoulders and letting out a sultry laugh.

Knowing it would stave off the anxiety that was rising up in her chest and constricting her throat, Sophie twisted open the cap. She'd never been a partier before. Cara liked to get drunk when they went to parties, but Sophie had always been too afraid to drink much until that first night they'd gone out to the bar with their fake ID's and the plan to sleepover at Cara's. Up to then she had always been goody-two-shoes that didn't want to get caught—too afraid her parents would find out and she'd be in a heap of trouble.

None of that mattered anymore. Getting caught for drinking was the least of her worries.

Sophie took the bottle and after opening it, took a long swig, and then another, and two more as they pulled up to Stuart's house.

"Whoa," Cara said as she parked the car. "Easy girl," she warned, "You'll be drunk on your ass before the dancing even starts."

"No, I'll be fine," Sophie answered. She'd built up a tolerance since they'd last met.

Cara stared in disbelief and then let out a snort of laughter. "Well don't be a hog, pass it over," she said as she too took a long swig from the bottle.

Maybe they know, somehow? Sophie thought as she walked beside her friend—both long legged and short skirted—into the party at Stuart's house. She made her way straight to the bar he'd set up on his parents' dining room table. "What do we start with first?" she asked out loud. "Let's begin with that yummy looking Tequila there," she said as she poured three shot glasses and lined them up in front of her.

"Here we go. One for me…"

Undercover

"Goodnight Daniela," Cathy said as she stood up from her daughter's bed and put Daniela's favorite book, *Goodnight Moon*, back on the shelf. Switching off the light she went to kiss Daniela's forehead. *If she had any idea what Mommy is up to next,* Cathy thought wondering what would happen to Daniela if anything happened to her. But she banished the thought as she walked out of the room. Risk-taking was a part of her job. And if homegrown terrorists were right around the corner she had to be ready to put it all on the line—to keep Daniela safe.

"Okay Mom, I should be back in about five hours," Cathy said to her mother, Gina, as she prepared to leave her apartment. Cathy was dressed in black leggings, a long sleeve, low-necked, thin black sweater and high-heeled boots over which she threw a well-worn, black, cropped leather jacket. Her red hair was piled atop her head and her makeup was heavier than usual.

"You look awful," Gina, said wrinkling up her nose as she looked over her daughter. "Don't you think you could give the undercover work to someone who isn't a single mother?" she complained. "You've always loved taking chances, ever since you were a child!"

"Oh mother, don't," Cathy said as she edged for the door. Picking up her purse from the hook inside her coat closet she let herself out. "Bye Mom, love you."

In this purse Cathy was identified as Angela Maden, complete with a Colorado driver's license with her "Angela" persona's heavily made-up picture on it. Her credit card and her phone provided by the FBI, and even her fake e-mails on the phone—corresponded with this name. It was all false information, but done well. No one who grabbed her purse and tried to take her down as an undercover agent would be able to discover who she really was. Same with the Ford Taurus she would soon pick up from the Fusion Center. The license plates put on it tonight traced back to Angela Maden and the fake address associated with her persona.

That didn't mean she couldn't be followed, forced into a car, stabbed, shot, raped, taken hostage, or encounter the myriad of other risks of going undercover among criminals. Anything could happen while working undercover. Cathy was well aware of the dangers as she drove to Sancho's Lounge, the bar where the drug dealers liked to hang. Angela Maden, unlike Cathy, liked the money that came with drugs so she hung there too—at least whenever the FBI wanted to figure out more of what was going on in the underworld. Tonight was one of those nights and Angela has already won the trust and attention of some of the biggest dealers in town.

Driving along route 25, Cathy saw the bright pink, neon light for Sancho's Lounge. Swinging her car into the parking lot she wondered, *Who will be there tonight? I wonder if my man, Larry will show?* Larry seemed to be a big-time dealer and Cathy would love to bring him in, but the time wasn't right yet. It was hard to wait, but she knew the best operations take time. Reapplying her shiny pink lip-gloss, Cathy checked herself out in the rearview mirror and then made her way to the bar.

Strutting into Sancho's, Cathy noticed more than a couple of heads turn her way. The upscale, dark bar was full of drug dealers and the kind of women who liked their money.

"Angela!" one of the better-dressed dealers called out and recognizing Miltie, Angela waved and made her way to the bar stool nearby. "What are you drinking, babe?" Miltie asked as she sat down and smiled sideways at him. He looked her up and down appreciatively.

"Scotch on the rocks," Cathy answered in a coquettish voice. When her drink arrived, placed on the gleaming black marble bar, she made small talk with Miltie as she listened to the buzz around her.

"We're getting Internet traffic that somebody from ISIS is trying to break in on the Denver drug trafficking," Ken had coached her that day, helping her identify what to be listening for before she came here. He'd looked intense while he was briefing her. He had looked anxious in fact—she'd seen the look of tender concern in his face and eyes as he told her what to be asking about.

He's worried about me! Cathy had realized, and now she was suddenly in the thick of it with Miltie obviously happy to see her and waiting to see if she'd get drunk enough to go home with him or at least let him try to make out with her in the parking lot like he had once before, luckily allowing her to slip away before he got too far.

"How've you been, Miltie?" Cathy asked, as she used her finger to draw circles in the water from her drink condensing on the bar. She thought about reaching out to touch his hand but thought the better of encouraging him too much.

"Not bad, even better since you showed up," Miltie answered with a big smile taking in her long legs, high heels and the cleavage that her black, tight, low necked sweater revealed. "It's been a long time since I seen you. We had a good time last time, remember babe?" he said hinting at their last parting in the parking lot. "But then you ran off. Why'd you go and do that baby? We would of had a good time together!"

Cathy just laughed and played with her drink as he recalled how he'd tried to kiss her last time, even tried to stick his tongue in her mouth. *Yuck!* she thought remembering. One attempted French kiss from Miltie was enough for a lifetime. But she had gotten him to talk…

Maybe he'll talk this time too, Cathy thought hoping she could get what she wanted without enduring another near make-out session with a would-be felon. Having sexual encounters in her undercover role wasn't part of her job description, although she was well aware that being a good-looking woman was part of this undercover gig. Dressed like this and playing the part of a dumb redhead, no one would suspect her of being FBI. But it did have its dangers—of getting the men she was trying to open up so excited that they lost control. And they were brutes, after all, used to taking and discarding women at their pleasure.

A few drinks later Cathy was starting to feel the alcohol and wondering if she needed to get out before Miltie made his moves. She remembered how strong his arms had been when she'd tried to get away last time, how he'd held her firmly as he tried to French kiss her. She'd almost broken cover and kneed him in the groin when his tongue had reached into her mouth, a move that she would have finished off with a few chops to bring him to the ground. Luckily she had shaken free in the usual female manner and ran to her car leaving him puzzled over why she'd teased him all night and then ran away.

It's time to get out of here, Cathy thought, as it got late. Looking up the sleek granite bar, she searched for a way to keep Miltie from following her out to the parking lot. There were a lot of men here, Cathy noticed, and too many platinum blondes hanging around—women intent on going home with a guy and his money. Suddenly Cathy's ears pricked up as she overhead talk that made the whole trip worthwhile.

"They want in on our operation," a man down the bar named Andy complained in a low voice. He was wearing an expensive looking suit. "I don't know about doing no business with a Muslim, but then again if they have cash they need laundered, why the hell not?" The others snorted in laughter as Cathy's attention turned to him.

"What's he talking about Miltie?" Cathy asked leaning provocatively closer. She'd worked Miltie before and knew he'd talk to her. Although she wasn't planning on letting him touch her tonight. Not after last time.

"Doing business with Muslims? I didn't think they did drugs?" she asked as she spun her toothpick-spitted olive on her shiny glossed lips, working her dumb redhead look to the hilt.

"They don't as far as I know," Miltie answered, "But there are more and more of them showing up wanting to do business. I don't know where they're from—Syria or the Gulf. How the hell would I know? I'm Italian."

Cathy smiled and nodded her head. "Miltie why would they deal in drugs if they don't take them?" she asked as she rubbed her high heeled black boot over his shin. "You think there's some new Muslim drug lord on the scene?"

"No kid, there's no Muslim drug lord breaking into our business," Miltie said as he reached his hand to put on Cathy's hip. Despite hating the feel of his hand on her body she let him touch her.

"So who is this Muslim, Andy is talking about?" Cathy asked finishing her drink. "I'll take another one of these," she said standing up to signal the bartender and to avoid Miltie's groping hands. It didn't help though. His hands just followed her backside to the bar as he started rubbing one of them up and down the backside of her thigh. *Thank God I'm wearing leggings and not a skirt tonight,* Cathy thought.

If it wasn't Miltie doing it I might have found it pleasurable, Cathy noted as her next drink arrived and her mind drifted briefly to Ken. *Yeah, that would feel great if it was his hand.*

"I don't know baby," Miltie said, his face looking exasperated with her questions. He was clearly ready to leave the bar—with her. "There's some kid—Abdur Ramen noodles, or something, that has been hanging around asking if he can get in on the business, but he don't do no drugs either. It's weird."

Abdur Rahman? The same guy Russell is following? Cathy wondered to herself as she listened hoping to learn more. *Is ISIS trying to break into the drug world?*

Cathy reached into her purse and tapped her phone to make it ring. On cue it rang and she took it from her bag, pretending to answer. "Oh, no! Yeah of course I'll come right home," she said to her pretend caller.

"What's wrong baby?" Miltie said as he moved in closer, his hand moving closer up along her backside now, getting way too familiar.

"It's my son," Cathy answered lying as she pulled herself away. "He's sick and I have to go right home. He's only four and got a fever. The babysitter is scared. I've got to go. Damn it all to hell, Miltie!" she said looking into his eyes, her own eyes wide and sincere and her mouth making a pout at him. "I was looking forward to seeing you tonight. I hoped you'd be here again," Cathy said softly extricating her bottom half from his groping hands as she leaned in and gave him a soft peck on the cheek. "You forgive me?" she asked in a crooning voice. "I'll be back soon," she promised as she ran her finger down his hand.

Miltie's face was priceless—the look of disappointment on it staggering. *He was so counting on this,* Cathy thought as she turned and quickly made her way for the door without looking back until she was ready to exit. Then her training turned on and she quickly took a three hundred and sixty of the bar, checking to see if anything unusual had happened, if anyone was following her. No one was. Everyone important was right where they'd been when she stood up. She was clean as she walked out the door.

Hangover

"Come on, let's dance on the tables!" Sophie shouted to Cara above the loud music now blaring throughout Stuart's house. The party was in full swing and Sophie was getting it on. The last weeks had been too hard and pushed her to her final limits. Four or five shots of vodka and Tequila had worked their magic and she suddenly felt released from all the pent up tension.

If Dad thinks I'm a loser, then maybe I am? Sophie thought as she drunkenly pulled out one of Stuart's dining room chairs and climbed onto it and then up onto the dining room table. Luckily it was a sturdy table that held her weight. Sophie stood tall on one side of it and raised her arms above her head as her little red skirt gyrated over her long bare legs as she strutted back and forth on one side of the chandelier and spun her hips in time fo the music. Cara's red platform heels made a good clatter on the wood when Sophie decided to beat out the rhythms onto the table below.

"Go girl!" Cara yelled in amazement. She'd never seen Sophie this drunk, or this much fun either, for that matter. Sophie was usually the quiet one that lurked in the corners and laughed it up with the others later, but was rarely out in front leading the partying.

"Come dance with me!" Sophie screamed. Unable to resist, Cara followed her lead and jumped up on the table as well, after stopping briefly to turn the chandelier on to its dimmed setting. It made a beautiful dance floor to showcase the two young girls as they swirled and gyrated across the tabletop, rocking out on either side of the chandelier. Both girls somehow managed to keep their balance perched on their high heels as they swayed and spun their bodies to the blaring music.

It wasn't long before they drew a crowd and someone brought one of the bottles over to the table and began handing out shots as they clapped and cheered the two girls on. "Nice panties," one of Stuart's male friends yelled out as Sophie danced on. "Here have another shot," he said handing her a small vodka-filled glass. Taking it Sophie didn't miss a beat as she whirled and rocked and tossed the shot back, returning the glass to her new admirer. Across the room, a few couples were making out on the living room sofas in the dark shadows of the dimly lit room but Sophie didn't notice. She was too busy enjoying her power to enthrall.

Later, getting down from the table Sophie spotted a tall, dark guy with big brown eyes. "What's your name?" Sophie asked as she drunkenly reached out to pull him forward to dance with her.

"Kareem," he answered smiling back at her. Kareem followed her lead and started gyrating along with her. He was hot, and a good dancer, Sophie noticed.

After a bit of dancing, Stuart passed by with another tray of shots. Sophie reached out for one but Kareem refused. "What? Not into the partying?" Sophie asked her eyebrows arching in genuine surprise.

"I don't drink," Kareem answered, gazing into her eyes unabashedly. "I'm Muslim."

Sophie walked over to the patio door with her shot glass in hand, walking outside to cool off. Kareem followed her out and they stood under the stars together listening to the music while Sophie downed her drink. "The stars are beautiful," she remarked.

"You can see so many," Kareem answered. "There's no moon tonight, that's why."

They stood together gazing upward until Sophie reached out to pull Kareem toward her. He resisted.

"You're really beautiful," he softly said, holding her out at arm's length and smiling warmly. He seemed to mean it which confused Sophie.

"If I'm beautiful, why are you staying so far away?" she asked in slurred words as she stood, frustrated in front of him.

"I guess I just don't understand why you non-Muslim women don't respect yourselves more," Kareem answered. "You're beauty is obvious but it makes me sorry to see you put it on display for everyone."

Sophie snorted and walked back inside, going to join some other dancers across the room. His words lingered in her mind, and stung.

***

"Oh shit," Sophie mumbled as she woke up on someone's bed at Stuart's. Rubbing her eyes, she blurrily looked around the room. A couple of her high school friends were passed out nearby, one was drooling and snoring lightly on the carpet. Sophie stood up and made her way over the bodies and litter of beer, vodka and wine bottles to the kitchen. Cara was talking with Stuart and some of the others. Judging from the sunlight peeking in the windows, it looked like early morning.

"Let's go home," Sophie said.

"Oh you came to," Cara answered smiling sarcastically at Sophie. "I've been waiting for you to come around. I didn't think I could haul your carcass to the car and I didn't want to deliver you back to your folks passed out anyway. I didn't think they'd like that very much."

"Yeah, you were right about that," Sophie answered, rubbing her eyes. Her mouth felt fuzzy and her head ached.

Sitting at the table with Cara was Kareem, the guy she'd tried to make out with the night before.

What's his name? Sophie searched her mind remembering some haze of conversation from the night before. *Kareem—the Muslim guy! Oh yeah, the guy who doesn't drink and wouldn't kiss me.* Kareem was eating a bowl of Cheerios looking up at her smiling.

Beautiful, really? Sophie thought remembering how he'd said it and suddenly smiled shyly back at him. *But don't respect myself enough—well if you only knew the half of it. It didn't start out that way!* Sophie thought taking in his big brown eyes that seemed to genuinely appreciate her—just as they had the night before.

"Let's get going," Cara said standing.

"I need my shoes, I mean your shoes! And I have to pee," Sophie said as she turned to look around for Cara's red high heels. She had no memory of kicking them off before passing out on Stuart's bed, but it didn't take long to find them under the couch.

It was in the bathroom staring at her owl-ringed eyes in the mirror that she realized her panties were missing.

Shit! What happened to me? Sophie wondered as panic started her heart fluttering in her chest. Nothing hurt down there—nothing like last time.

What the hell? I guess it doesn't matter anymore. I'm one of the sluts now, Sophie thought as tears slid down her cheek. *Yep that's what I'm here for,* she thought looking at her messed up make up in the mirror, her beauty from the night before now spent. *Use me up and spit me out,* Sophie thought bitterly as she splashed cold water over her face and tried to get the smudged eyeliner off her cheeks. *Kareem was right,* she thought. *I am beautiful, but so fucked up!*

Remembering why she'd come to the toilet, Sophie peed quickly and then stood to flush the toilet, disconcerted that there were no panties to pull back up afterward. Instead, Sophie yanked at her red knit mini skirt rolling it back down from her waist as far as she could to cover her bare bottom.

"Let's get out of here," she said looking around in disgust as she rejoined her friend, unable to meet Kareem's eyes again.

What the hell did I do last night? Sophie asked herself as they made their way to the car.

***

At home Sophie hurriedly passed her mother in the kitchen. Sophie had changed back into her jeans and t-shirt and had rubbed all the extra make up off with a make-up wipe in Cara's car so there was little to tell of what had gone on the night before. It was Saturday, but Sarah was working—

sitting at the table, coffee mug in hand—making her way through a stack of legal documents.

"Hi, Mom," Sophie mumbled her head hanging down, her feet making a beeline for the basement steps.

"Sophie," Sarah called, but her daughter didn't answer or slow down. "Sophie!" Sarah called out again.

"Yeah, Mom," Sophie answered, turning to face her Mom at the door to the basement steps.

"Did you have a good time at Cara's?" Sarah asked looking genuinely interested, unlike her father who would have been wondering what she'd been up to, if she'd been behaving, and that whole routine.

"Yeah, it was fun," Sophie said as she gazed past her Mom's open laptop screen out the window to the backyard where the wooden playground Jake had built for Sophie years ago still stood. It was surrounded by the pink and red impatiens her mother planted every year. Memories suddenly flowed through her mind: mornings at the park with her Mom, going to the zoo together, baking cookies and how her father had built this playground for her.

Her mother had always been a good sport, making popcorn for their family movie nights, setting out tea parties when Sophie wanted to play dolls, and singing songs together that she learned in preschool. Years ago Sophie had helped plant all the flowers, her mother letting her carry the watering can and be the one to place each annual in the holes they'd dug together.

Sophie knew her mother had cut her legal career short and opted to start her own practice so she could work more at home than if she had stayed with the big firm. Her mother had succeeded in going solo, but had underestimated how much work it would take. Now her mom seemed to always be buried beneath piles of legal briefs. Home—but not really present.

She was present now though, as Sophie looked into her mom's sad and searching eyes. She seemed worried but Sophie couldn't find any suitable answer to the concern she saw in her mother's eyes.

What can I tell her? Sophie thought as her heart ached to pour it all out to her Mom. *There's no way anything I tell her won't go right back to Dad,* Sophie realized pushing the truth back down into the dark hole reserved for *what had never happened.*

"We watched movies and popped popcorn, like we used to do on our movie nights," Sophie lied. Then throwing her Mom a bone, she added, "It was fun, but not like it used to be with us." Then she turned and disappeared into the basement, happy to be alone with her shameful secrets.

In her bedroom, Sophie flipped on her computer and tried to study for her CNA exam, but as usual her mind flitted from one painful subject to another and she couldn't concentrate. There was no sugar left in her cache and she didn't want to go back upstairs so Sophie tried to distract herself by surfing the Internet.

Mindlessly, Sophie Googled the name Kareem and learned it was an Arabic name, meaning generous or giving. That led to other sites, most of them related to Islam. On one of these sites, Sophie read the words, Islam-the Path to Purity, written across the website banner in big blaring letters.

Restoring purity—is it possible? Sophie wondered with a furrowed brow. *Probably just a big lie,* she thought, sighing sadly as she read the links under the website heading. For a second, she considered clicking on one of them.

Kareem was Muslim. *But what the hell does he know?* Sophie asked dismissing it all as she shut down her computer and stared blankly out the window. A brief mountain thunderstorm was gathering in the sky and Sophie could see it was about to rain. The threatening sky matched her mood.

***

"Hi honey," Jake said as he came in the kitchen door and threw his tennis racquet on the counter.

"Oh hi. How was your game?"

"Brutal! Where's Sophie?" Jack asked while getting a beer out of the fridge.

"She's in the basement as usual," Sarah answered. "Jake, I've been wondering. She doesn't give us the time of day anymore. I'm wondering why?" Sarah asked while turning back to her computer and the legal brief waiting to be finished.

"I dunno. It's a phase," Jake replied while moving into the living room to turn on the television. He was disgusted with his daughter and her decision to drop out of high school and didn't want to think about it anymore. *Let her find her own way out of this mess she's made of her life!* Jake thought as he flipped through the channels.

Abdur Rahman

In the next week Russell started chatting with Ken's live lead, Abdur Rahman and eventually suggested they chat privately. Brother, I've been following your dedication to the cause and I can help you achieve your goals against the infidels, Insha'Allah Russell texted. But I want to meet in person.

Where? Abdur Rahman asked. And when?

Wednesday night at 8 pm. Come to 8306 East Colfax Avenue. The brothers have a safe house in one of the apartments there. Take the elevator to the 10th floor and wait for me there. I will be with another brother. Meet us there, Russell wrote back, referring to Ken.

Two days later, on Wednesday evening, Ken and Russell were getting ready to go. Russell, Italian by bloodline, was olive skinned and had just grown a short, well trimmed, dark beard that could make him look Muslim—especially when he wore a Palestinian, black and white cotton keffiyeh wound around his black turtleneck sweater, tucking it inside his black leather jacket. It was so Russell to have grown his beard for this part.

"Nice getup," Ken remarked as they prepared to leave.

Russell smiled in return, clearly satisfied that his "look" was garnering the appropriate approval from their resident Islamic expert. He was wearing jeans and sneakers and looked street smart tough. Adding to it, he took his pistol out of its FBI issued holster and slid it down the back of his pants.

Cathy stood nearby, wishing this was an operation she could play an active role in. She knew the "brothers" didn't usually mix with the women so she'd have to wait this one out, but it pained her to see Russell leaving with Ken, instead of her.

"Hmm, obviously I can pass as an Arab, but you'll need to be a convert," Russell remarked in a snarky tone as he glanced over at Ken who looked like an ordinary dude with his sandy brown, wavy hair, navy checkered, long-sleeve shirt and faded jeans. "At least you don't look like an

FBI flat-footer," Russell commented looking Ken up and down.

"Don't you have anything you can put on to Muslim him up a bit, new girl?" Russell said turning to Cathy, clearly happy to have her attention. "My Muslim name is Abdullah by the way," he said sidling up to Cathy wanting as much of her approval as he could win in this moment.

"How's this?" Ken answered, smiling widely as he unbuttoned his shirt revealing a black T-shirt below with Arabic writing across the chest. "It's the ISIS flag," Ken explained, seeing Russell staring at it uncomprehendingly.

"Oh yeah, I thought it looked familiar," Russell answered as Ken ditched his button down shirt on the chair nearby and threw a jean jacket over his ISIS emblazoned chest. Glancing at Cathy he raised his eyebrows to mock Russell's lack of Islamic knowledge. He knew Cathy recognized the flag right off.

"Okay, so if I'm a convert, I'm going to call myself Samir and don't worry I've got the Muslim talk down pat," Ken said beaming. He was starting to get into this undercover gig. Although he too wished it was Cathy accompanying him instead of Russell. Russell was fit, but he seemed like a loose cannon—unpredictable. Ken wanted to know what to expect, when, how and where. With Russell he felt he was joining a one-man show, only problem was there were two of them, and Abdur Rahman might use deadly force if Russell blew their cover.

As they readied to leave, Cathy pulled Ken back to his cubicle. "I'm worried about you," she said as she leaned against the wall near his desk, her brow furrowed into a frown.

"Yeah, like I was crazy over you going out to Sancho's to meet that Miltie creep?" Ken shot back. "I didn't get to sleep at all that night."

"Aw, Miltie? I can take him down with one hand tied behind my back," Cathy laughed, although she was heart warmed that he'd been worried about her. "Didn't sleep that night? Worried about me?" she teased.

"Yeah, I was worried about you," Ken said gazing up into her eyes.

"A redhead out with the mafia drug lords of Denver, yep I was worried sick," he confessed.

"Well I guess it's my turn to worry now," Cathy replied. "What if it is a trap? What if he's a nut case with a gun, or a bomb or something else and he figures out you guys are coming from the Fusion Center? He might kill you both, and you've got no training, Ken. You don't even know how to shoot a gun, do you?" she asked.

"I can smite him with scriptures from the Qur'an," Ken joked.

"Oh God!" Cathy said as she burst into laughter and rolled her eyes. "Then I hope Allah is real and protects you," she added with a softness filling her voice.

"Don't worry Cath," Ken said coming to stand beside her. At that moment Russell appeared.

"Ready for the rodeo!" he shouted out, pretending to wave a lasso over his head. "Gonna ride me a buckin' bronco till I tames him right down. Oh yessiree!"

"Geez, Russell," Ken answered, irritated to have his private moment with Cathy cut short.

"It's time to go," Russell said glancing at Cathy. "Speak into the microphone little lassie," he joked as he suddenly lifted up his black turtleneck sweater to show off his well sculpted, tanned chest and to show her he was wearing a wire, taped to it—hidden well beneath his sweater.

"Cool it, Russell," Ken said as Cathy put her hand over her mouth and tried to stop giggling at his hijinks.

"You are *crazy* Russell," she said as she walked along with them to the elevator, taking it down to where they walked together to Russell's FBI issued car.

Ken was still not sure how good he felt about the wire, if what they were about to embark upon wasn't some sort of entrapment.

Cathy accompanied them as far as the car and called out, "Good luck guys. Ken, call me later and tell me how it goes," she added, worry filling her voice.

"Call me later," Russell mocked in a falsetto voice making a phone with his hand held up to his ear as he got into the car. "Ta! Ta!"

"Seriously, dude" he continued once they were inside the car and driving away, "What's with the workplace romance? You don't think that's a bit unprofessional?" Russell teased with raised eyebrows.

"What?" Ken answered, feeling his face flush and his heart skip a few beats. "There's nothing going on between us."

"Oh, so the new office hottie is up for the taking?" Russell jabbed, using his usual irritating tone of voice. "Then I'll just be snapping up that piece of fruit soon as possible. The ladies are often into guys like me—you know the agent danger business and all that."

"No, I think you better leave her alone," Ken warned, his voice becoming icy. The thought of Russell trying to seduce Cathy made him suddenly physically nauseous.

Russell took out a pretentious looking jazz album from his briefcase and popped it into the drive player of the car and the two drove on toward their target, the music filling in the cold silence that had descended upon them.

***

He's probably just a braggart, Ken thought as they approached the tenth floor. Reflecting on all the Facebook accounts he'd been monitoring of young kids who were into "jihadi cool," thinking endorsing terrorism was a way to look tough, Abdur Rahman's was pretty much run of the mill—except that he'd said he was looking to make an attack. His latest Facebook entries had been to like an ISIS T-shirt that read "Fight for Freedom, Until the Last Drop of Blood"—not exactly a criminal offense, but worrisome all the same.

I guess we'll find out how serious he is, Ken thought as they arrived to the tenth floor and saw a scared looking nineteen-year-old waiting for them

"As salamu alaikum wa rahmatullah wa barakatuhu," Ken said holding out his hand to Abdur Rahman. *May the mercy, peace and blessings of Allah be upon you.* "My name is Samir and this is Abdullah," he said indicating Russell.

Russell probably has no clue what I just said to Abdur Rahman, Ken thought as Abdur Rahman answered slowly, still clearly struggling with his Arabic.

"Wa alaikum salam wa rahmatullah wa barakatuhu" Abdur Rahman said, as he offered up the blessings of Allah in return to Ken's greeting.

Ken smiled ruefully, looking at Abdur Rahman's scrawny beard, slight body, and coke bottle glasses. *This kid is a real loser—probably looking for something to make him feel good about himself. But then most of them are.*

Checking out his clothing, he noted that Abdur Rahman had the requisite Islamic pants that ended above the ankle, and a medium length Arabic shirt worn over that, as the jihadis like to wear. He also wore a small skullcap over his dark, curly hair—although it was not the white crocheted haji cap that those who had visited Mecca wear to show their status.

He's got the full get-up, Ken thought, as he noted that Abdur Rahman still looked a little uncomfortable and out of place in his foreign, Salafi style costume.

The threesome walked down the hall together, pausing as Russell unlocked the door to the safe house. Russell flipped on the hallway lights as the three entered. The apartment was vintage seventies, sparsely furnished and small. Russell led them through the kitchen, past the mustard yellow, old fashioned appliances, to the seating area between the kitchen and living room. He flipped on the hanging overhead light there, as they seated themselves at the brown, wood-grained Formica dining table.

Russell took some Cokes from the refrigerator and handed them around saying, "My brother, it appears Allah has brought you to us at the right time. The Caliphate has been declared and fighters are needed to bring its expansion to all parts of the world."

"Insha'Allah, it will come to pass," Abdur Rahman answered as he accepted a Coke from Russell's hand.

"We live in the land of infidels, but it's all changing fast," Russell answered. "We are lucky to be able to change the course of history with our brave actions and our deeds," he added as he popped open his Coke and put a bag of chips on the Formica tabletop.

"Insha'Allah, we can make a difference," Abdur Rahman said as he looked to the two older men. *He's just a kid,* Ken thought noticing how impressed Abdur Rahman seemed to be to be in what he believed to be a real "safe house" with the "brothers." *This is so sick, we should have never brought this kid here, seduced him out from behind his computer screen. He's just an Internet troll endorsing stupid stuff.*

"Of course we can make a difference!" Russell bragged, his normal bravado shining through in this role as well. "We are Allah's holy warriors! We've nothing to fear but the Final Day of Judgment. Then our sins will be called out," Russell said.

Ken stared at him thinking, *You dork, you have no idea what you are talking about, and if anyone's going to be reading out sins on the Day of Judgment, yours will be top on the list as big fat dickhead who was always too full of himself.*

"Yes we are Allah's holy warriors," Abdur Rahman echoed and sat taller as he caught a bit of Russell's showy bravado. "We are the mujahideen in America!"

"Fucking embedded, sleeper cells we are!" Russell added, ripping open the bag of chips.

God almighty, he's encouraging this loser, Ken reflected as he wondered if he could steer the conversation a bit away from leading their contact into greater commitment to ISIS.

"Have you been in contact with our brothers?" Ken asked zeroing in a bit; wanting to know whose network Abdur Rahman might belong to, if any.

"Just on the Internet," Abdur Rahman admitted. "You are the first mujahideen I've met in person. It's an honor for me," he said as his hand went up to cover his heart as he bowed forward. The same hand then went to uncertainly rub his scruffy beard. Abdur Rahman looked over to Russell with beaming eyes, clearly in full admiration of his Islamic big brother.

That's when Russell went for the kill. "If you are really serious about carrying out an attack we may be able to help you," he offered. Ken winced, thinking, *this punk, he's going to go for it. He's so needy for validation. He'd probably blow something up just to have Russell smile his way. I wonder if he even has a father at home?*

"I am ready to die in the path of Allah," Abdur Rahman said, his eyes shining brightly, "but I want it to be something big."

"Big? What did you have in mind, my friend?" Russell asked exuberantly as he took a long swig from his Coke.

Abdur Rahman looked from Russell to Ken. "Well, I want to hit the Capitol building in Washington, D.C. and kill those who voted for airstrikes in Iraq. Can you imagine this?"

"You're serious?" Russell asked—even *he* was surprised. Russell's eyes met briefly with Ken's.

"Oh yes, it will be magnificent. You will see," Abdur Rahman said. "Those Senators deserve to die. They voted for the first invasion and now this. So many innocents have died because of them. I've seen the videos of the women and children killed by their airstrikes, the burned up bodies."

As he spoke Ken and Russell watched this shy, lost kid transform in front of them. His voice filled with authority and his face flexed in anger as he parroted a tirade he had obviously ingested from the Internet, "Why does the Great Satan bomb our Iraqi brothers—to save the Satan worshipper

Yazidis and the Christian minorities, or to steal our oil? Why didn't they help our brothers in Syria and Gaza when they were being slaughtered in the thousands? It's always a crusade against Islam and now the Great Satan needs to be punished and cut down. And I am willing to give my life to achieve that."

Ken and Russell hid their horror at what this young kid could so quickly morph into with just a bit of encouragement. His hatred for American and his wish to die as a "martyr" transformed him completely. It was like his scrawny self suddenly altered into a wiry, angry animal ready to fearlessly lash out at any target within range.

Russell listened nodding all through it, clearly encouraging Abdur Rahman's tirade until he finally had enough and stood saying, "Brother, we have to go now, but we'll meet again and talk details. We'll message you."

Ken and Russell left Abdur Rahman at the bus stop in front of the safe house as they walked back to their undercover FBI car.

"God almighty, Russell. He's serious," Ken admitted as he opened the car door and got in, although he still wondered if a young man like Abdur Rahman would ever figure out how to activate without the help of outsiders.

"Yeah. Ready, willing and able—a real live one," Russell answered. "We'll have fun with him."

"This isn't supposed to be fun, Russell," Ken reminded him, feeling horrified that Abdur Rahman was going to be taken down hard before he had any real chance in his life.

A Path to Purity

It was an October evening and Sophie was in the basement bingeing again on Ben & Jerry's. This time is was The Tonight Dough flavor—a recipe filled with extra-chunky chocolate and caramel ice cream with chocolate chip cookie dough and crunchy, chocolate cookies swirled inside. It was inspired for Jimmy Fallon and the carton had a big picture of him on the outside that made Sophie smile as she shoveled it into her mouth. She liked Jimmy Fallon but she liked the ice cream even better. The sugar went straight to her brain giving her the most delicious sugar buzz. As usual Sophie binged on two cartons and then ran to the bathroom to shove her fingers back into her throat to make her vomit it as quickly as possible into the toilet.

This time however, when she finished ejecting the contents of her stomach and chunks of chocolate and vanilla foam floated in the toilet, Sophie suddenly felt intensely dizzy and off balance. Her heart started pounding wildly, then oscillated into slow and then wild heartbeats. Sophie collapsed to her knees in sudden weakness, feeling her vision tunneling into a concentrated point of light. She was passing out—but then regained her vision. Meanwhile her heart constricted painfully. It felt like someone was using a blunt instrument to pierce her heart again and again. The pain was excruciating. Sophie bent over the toilet, clinging to it. The acrid smell burned her nose as she tried to calm her body and set her heartbeat slowly back on course. Gradually her heart stopped beating out erratically wild rhythms and calmed. Satisfied that she was safe, Sophie crawled out of the bathroom to lie on the floor of her bedroom, gasping with fear.

When she felt the strength to rise, she went straight to her computer and Googled *bulimia*. There she read about electrolyte imbalances and cases of heart attacks caused by the fatal disruption of normal heart rhythms.

Oh my God, I'm killing myself doing this! Sophie thought as she stood and went back to the bathroom to brush her teeth, feeling revulsion for herself and this foul habit filling her soul.

She already knew her back molars were rotting out from all the stomach acid and she had a constant sore throat from the acid burning her soft tissues as well. Flushing the toilet, Sophie felt dizzy again and went back to her bed. *What am I going to do?* Sophie wondered as she lay curled in a ball of shame with fear gripping at the edges of her mind. *I can't stop!* There was a hole inside that begged to be filled, but she had no idea what could fill it beside sugary food and alcohol.

Just then Jake walked downstairs. He rarely came into her room but this time he was faster than Sophie could hide the evidence of what she'd just been doing. Seeing the two empty Ben & Jerry's cartons on the floor he immediately chided, "Sophie are you back at the ice cream? Honestly how could you eat two whole cartons?" he asked, disgust wrinkling up his nose.

Glancing over at her open laptop he saw the page she'd been reading. "Bulimia!" he gasped reading it. "You've got to fucking be kidding me? What else is it going to be with you?" he shouted as he clenched his mouth in anger. Sophie lay curled up on the bed, wincing in pain at the revulsion filling his voice. "I never thought you'd be one of those stupid girls bingeing and puking back your meals. Bulimia, seriously Soph?"

"No, Dad," Sophie tried to protest. "I was studying about it for my CNA work," she lied, lamely.

"Yeah, right," Jake sneered. "Geez, you just puked now, didn't you? I can smell it! What's happened to you? You used to be such a successful girl, but now?" His body shook as he continued, "God, Sophie! I really give up! I just throw in the towel where you are concerned," he said as abhorrence dripped from every syllable he uttered. Shaking his head he walked back upstairs, Sophie remained curled up in the fetal position and sobbed while clutching her pillow to her chest.

I'm so fucked up! I'm never gonna get right, never! She sobbed until there were no more tears. Then she slowly stood up to have her shots. It had gotten to the point that she couldn't sleep without them—otherwise her hands would shake, and once asleep, the rape would slip out of the memory vault and return in full Technicolor and sensory images to taunt her. *Whore! Slut! All grown-up, disposable girl!* Only the vodka could keep the memories and horrible new identities at bay.

Fuck it! Fuck everything! Sophie thought as she downed the vodka through a haze of tears and overwhelming shame and self-hatred.

* * *

The next afternoon, Sophie was riding the city bus, making her way home from her nursing assistant classes, when she noticed a pamphlet left behind that changed everything.

Islam-the Path to Purity it read, same as the website she'd seen earlier while surfing the Internet. As Sophie's eyes took it in, something in her heart leapt. She'd been drinking heavily since the fateful sleepover five months before, and she was no fool. Sophie was well aware that she was already on a slippery descent into the black hole of alcoholism. She'd learned that much in her D.A.R.E. drug and alcohol prevention classes in high school.

But she also recognized that there was no way she could sleep without it. And she was frightened by the recognition that she was drinking earlier and earlier these days—not waiting for bedtime to slip into her nightly, alcohol infused oblivion. Her hands shaking with anticipation, she was cracking the bottle right after supper most nights, and sometimes taking her meal with her into the basement to hit the sauce even earlier in the evening.

Why wait? Sophie's mind argued nightly as she shamelessly slunk to her dresser drawer to pull out the hidden vodka bottle and pour out her first shot—one that she now expertly threw back, to be followed by five or six more before the evening waned. She even had a supplier now—the older brother of a guy she knew from high school that charged her twice the cost, but kept her in vodka—no ID needed.

Same thing with the bulimia—it was consuming her. While it gave her a brief feeling of being in control, her binge-purge cycles were making her feel weak. And now that she realized it could give her a fatal heart attack, she understood that she was on the road to doom.

And her father knew she was doing it. *How am I going to hide from him now?* Sophie thought as shame washed over her again, remembering his look of disgust. *It is so sick, but I can't stop!* Sophie knew she needed a way out. All these addictions but no way to stop?

Sophie stared at the pamphlet wondering if it was a message meant for her. Why had she seen this same message twice? As she stared at it, she remembered Kareem. He was a Muslim. There was something very pure about him—the way he refused to drink or make out. The way he had spoken to her, respectfully, not shaming her—but telling her she was truly beautiful and should respect herself. Maybe that was the purity it was referencing?

Restoring purity—is it possible? Sophie wondered as she wearily took out her iPhone and typed in the website. A little flicker of hope danced in her heart while her mind doubted.

Highly unlikely, she thought as she glanced blankly out the window waiting for the website to load. The leaves were already falling from the trees and many lay lifeless in the gutters. The sky was grey and overcast—matching her mood.

How can a leaf that's fallen from the tree ever get back up from the gutter it's fallen into? Sophie thought as she looked down at the dead and dying leaves rattling about in the gutter as the bus sped by.

The website opened and Sophie began studying it.

Allah loves those who repent and purify themselves (2:222) Sophie read.[37] A small spark leapt again in her heart as she reread the words, letting them reach deep inside, imposing a small thaw on the freeze she had cast over her feelings in the past months—vowing to feel nothing—rather than remember what she kept telling herself had *not* happened.

Islam, the mercy of Allah, is for all of mankind and makes no preference to sex. Men and women have an equal calling and a place in nature. Neither has a greater value, nor is one of greater importance, Sophie smiled and nodded as she read on. The words were comforting and beautiful in their simplicity. They didn't sound so different than the Christianity she had been exposed to in her childhood.

Islam protects a Muslim woman's morals and decency, guards her reputation and dignity, and defends her chastity against evil thoughts and tongues, and tries to foil tempting hands that seek to harm her, Sophie read. *Foiling tempting hands that seek to harm—oh how I needed that.*

As she read on her mind skipped again back to Kareem telling her she was beautiful and refusing to make out with her. He was Muslim. He'd told her she should respect herself. And he hadn't said it in a judgmental manner—so different than how her father always lectured.

Maybe the Muslims are on to something? Sophie wondered, her heart missing a beat as she remembered dancing with Kareem. He was hot. His dark brown eyes, ringed by his long lashes, had looked so appreciatively at her. And he seemed to be having fun—even without drinking or trying to get in her panties.

Tell the believing women to lower their gaze (from looking at forbidden things), and protect their private parts (from illegal sexual acts etc.)[Surah 24:31], Sophie read, seeing from the notation that it was a quote from the Qur'an.

Rape is an illegal sexual act, Sophie thought, letting a rare glimpse of the truth of what had happened to her become a full admission.

Is there really a way of becoming restored? she wondered. *Would someone like Kareem ever be able to love someone like me?*

Preserve a decent, unrevealing manner of dress and ornamentation without being oppressive towards her. At the time of the Prophet (blessings and peace be upon him), Sophie read, now completely fascinated by the text, it was customary for some women to cover their faces. The flexibility of Islam allows the woman the option of covering her face, or not.

Sophie had seen Muslim women—their head and necks wrapped up in headscarves, some of them wearing long, floor-length robes. She'd always thought they were strange, but covering herself now sounded safe and good. Sophie sensed the promise of security as she contemplated hiding herself in billows of fabric, winding her blonde, flowing hair up into a bun and disappearing its silken allure beneath a black hijab.

Take on a new identity? Become someone completely new? It suddenly sounded wonderful to Sophie. *Leave the past totally behind. Yes! I want that!*

Muslim women hide themselves from the gaze of men and thereby protect themselves. Sophie read.

Cover the other attractions that do not show, such as the hair, neck and throat, arms and legs, from all people except her husband, and her consanguineous, non-marriageable relations whom she finds it hard to hide these from, Sophie studied the text, imagining covering her body completely—head to toe— in impenetrable fabric—a barrier to prying male eyes, male hands or other despicable male body parts. *That would feel so good,* Sophie thought almost feeling the silky fabric hiding her body, wrapping her up in soft protective layers that no one would dare try to strip off her.

"...and [Muslim women are] not to reveal her adornment except to their husbands, fathers, their husband's fathers, their sons, their husband's sons, their brothers or their brother's sons, or their sister's sons or their (Muslim) women (i.e. their sisters in Islam), or the (female) slaves whom their right hands possess, or old male servants who lack vigor, or small children who have no sense of the shame of sex". [Surah 24:31] Sophie read.

The shame of sex, Sophie reflected, feeling the words burning deep into her heart. That's how sex felt to her—shameful. That's how her whole body felt. It made her want a drink even now, as the memories threatened to resurface.

Sophie's mind wandered back to Colin—her rapist. He'd burnt up all her dreams of excitement and romance. He'd ruined her. She was no longer a desirable girl. Because of him, she'd become a jumpy, frightened drinker that puked up most of her meals.

But here was a system of purity and redemption—safety from prying hands, from unwanted male attention. She'd seen how respectful Kareem had been at the party.

Sophie imagined being pure and virginal again, sharing herself only with a guy like Kareem. It had a good feeling to it. *But would a guy like him accept a girl like me—with my past?*

Remembering how she'd woke up without her panties after the party Sophie felt a flush of shame overtake her. *Probably not,* she concluded.

Be above all acts [that are] meant to excite and tempt men. Avoid being in seclusion with a man who is neither a husband nor a non-marriageable relation, so as to keep a barrier between herself or the other man and all thoughts of sin, and between her good name and false rumors, Sophie read.

She remembered Kareem holding her out at arms length, refusing to let her be the slut she felt she had become. *Even if he may never want a girl like me, maybe Muslims know how to respect their women?* Sophie wondered.

Can it apply to me? Sophie asked as she continued to read, her hands shaking as they did each evening. She needed to drink soon.

The Prophet (blessings and peace be upon him) says, "No man should be in seclusion with a woman and no woman should travel except with a non-marriageable relation," or her husband, of course. Avoid male gatherings except on the grounds of necessity or an appreciable interest and only to the necessity or limit.

Never be alone with a man, Sophie thought deeply comforted by these rules. *Live covered and safe...* It all sounded so good as she read on.

With these directions and regulations, Islam provides safety for the woman and her femininity from impious tongues; it preserves her decency and chastity by distancing her from all factors of deviation. Islam guards her honor against the slurs of slanderers and spreaders of calumny. Above all, it protects her soul and calms her nerves against the tension, instability and trepidation that spring from wild imaginations or between the factors of agitation and excitement.

Sensing her bus stop approaching, Sophie looked up, switched off her phone and disembarked with a small flame growing in her heart.

I need to study this religion, Sophie decided as she walked the few blocks to her home. *Maybe this is the way to become pure again,* she wondered. *And then no one will take that from me ever again.*

Conversion

For the next month Sophie scoured the Internet to learn more about Islam. She found a website that read: Upon converting to Islam, all of one's previous sins are forgiven, and one starts a new life of piety and righteousness. And as a Muslim, when one makes a mistake thereafter, he/she can always repent to God who forgives the sins of those who repent to Him sincerely.[38]

All my sins forgiven, Sophie thought. Becoming fully cleansed, taking on a new persona—it sounded so good—leave her old self behind and become someone totally new.

I wonder what he'd say if he knew I want to convert? Sophie wondered, remembering Kareem. Remembering how handsome he'd been, she felt a thrill of excitement run through her. Too bad she never crossed paths with him anymore. *But there are plenty more Kareems out there,* she reassured herself as she screwed up her courage to take the plunge and make herself into a new woman.

Searching the Internet, she found a website to take her there.

La ilaha il-Allah, Muhammad-ur-Rasulullah—There is no God except Allah; Muhammad is the Messenger of Allah was all she had to say, and believe, to become a Muslim—it instructed. Simple steps to become new and clean, leaving her soiled past behind.

After committing the Arabic to memory, Sophie even found an online chat room where she could recite these important words, via Skype, to an imam who then pronounced her a member of her new religious tribe.

"Congratulations, you are a Muslim now. Peace be upon you," he said blessing her with his kind eyes. "All your sins are forgiven."

Sophie immediately joined the Muslim chat rooms where she found lively debates going on about everything from world politics to the length a proper Muslim man's beard should be. She read that Muslims don't drink which created a dilemma as she was still drinking nightly to banish the nightmares.

However, as she found more comfort in her newfound faith and the belief that she could be totally cleansed and made anew, Sophie began to cut down on the vodka—slowly giving it up. The bingeing and purging also decreased as she stepped into her new persona. She even took a new name—Halima. In some ways her new obsession filled the void she was creating by giving up her other addictions—at least attempting to give them up.

As Sophie immersed herself in chat rooms and Skype with her new Muslim brothers and sisters, she suddenly felt herself surrounded by love and acceptance.

Don't worry sister, if you can't do it all at once. Conversion is a process, but you must eventually become pure to stand in front of Allah, Raheema, one of her new "sisters" wrote to her. I'm a convert too, she wrote. It doesn't happen overnight, it's a gradual process coming into your Muslim deen.

Indeed Sophie was beginning to feel she was leaving all the past behind her, making a complete and total cut-off from the girl she had once been. It felt so good that Sophie studied long hours in front of her computer trying to find out what being a Muslim really meant. In some ways one addiction was replacing the others.

On the one hand it meant covering her body and Sophie was all for that. To complete her transformation Sophie found and ordered a black cotton abaya for seventy-eight dollars on Amazon. And for an additional twelve dollars and ninety-four cents she found and ordered a three layers long Saudi niqab to fit over face, head and shoulders, falling in neat triangles over her to completely block out any view of herself as a woman.

When her purchases arrived, a few days later, Sophie was surprised at how her hands shook as she ripped open the boxes, and the plastic bags inside them, surrounding her new accessories. Donning her new black abaya and niqab, Sophie stood in front of her floor length bedroom mirror—the same childhood mirror that had reflected back to her signs of her budding adolescence. Gazing at herself covered from head to toe with the black niqab draped over her head, neck and chest— Sophie felt suddenly safe and at peace. Only her eyes peered back at her through the thin oval slit allowing her to see out. Buried beneath black, she once again found the safety she had felt so long ago, as an innocent young girl.

***

"I've become a Muslim," Sophie told her parents one night at dinner. She was dressed again in her ordinary clothes. She wasn't ready to try out wearing her abaya and niqab in front of them—not yet at least—and it wasn't necessary to cover at home anyway. "I'm going to start dressing like a Muslim, so don't get all freaked out."

"You mean you're going to stop wearing short skirts?" Jake asked as he shoveled another forkful of spaghetti Bolognese into his mouth.

"Yes, I'll be wearing a long black robe and a face covering now when I go out," Sophie answered. "It's called a niqab."

"That sounds crazy," Jake answered sarcastically. "Although it's also a father's dream come true," he remarked as he stood up from the table, his hands still on it as he leaned toward Sophie to add sarcastically, "To tell the truth Sophie, nothing you've been doing lately makes a bit of sense to me, but I've given up! It's your life and you can make whatever mess you want of it," he said as he shook his head in disgust and walked away from the table.

Sophie's eyes filled with tears and a lump formed in her throat as she sat silently watching him depart.

Sophie's mom, Sarah said nothing and just stared off into space as she absent-mindedly picked at her food. She was preoccupied by a legal argument that had been put forward on a case she was working on that day.

Sophie cleared her throat. "Mom?"

"What? Why would you want to be a Muslim? We're Christians," her mother commented distractedly.

"It just feels real for me," Sophie said trying to catch her mom's attention.

"To wear a burqa?" Sophie's mom asked, raising her eyebrows as she turned momentarily to face Sophie. "We feminists fought hard for our rights—seems to be going backwards to me," her mother commented as she looked away again, her mind elsewhere.

Sarah hadn't told the family, but her practice was on the edge of failing and she needed to get more clients to keep ahead of expenses. Looking at Sophie in exhaustion, Sarah thought, *I think I'm ready to resign my subscription to motherhood.* Work was so demanding and it took too much out of her to keep up with Sophie's latest ups and downs.

And now this niq-bob nonsense. Or whatever it's called. What will it be next? Sarah thought before turning her thoughts back to her legal case.

Choosing a Target

"**I** want to hit the Capitol building in Washington, D.C., as I told you before," Abdur Rahman announced in their next meeting, where they were again seated at the dining room table of the Denver FBI safe house. "Those are the people who voted for invasion of Iraq and for the airstrikes on ISIS. They are the ones who should pay with their lives," Abdur Rahman added, his voice low but intense. His eyes glowed with conviction and determination.

Russell and Ken exchanged glances as they listened to Abdur Rahman. *He's serious about offing himself and he believes this shit about going straight to Paradise when he "martyrs" himself,* Ken thought trying to hide his revulsion.

But he's also just a kid, Ken reflected. *He can vote, but he's not old enough to drink yet—not that he would, being a devoted Muslim.* Russell had brought a bag of Lay's potato chips along this time, and Ken dipped his hand into the yellow plastic bag as he mulled over what they were doing with this kid.

"If you could carry out such an operation it would be a great victory for the brothers. But such an operation requires serious planning. Are you ready to conduct surveillance on the target?" Russell asked.

"You mean figure out where the security is and how to get through?" Abdur Rahman asked.

"Yes," Russell answered, rubbing his dark beard as he spoke. Ken reached for some more chips, noticing that he was the only one munching on the junk food.

"I can do that," Abdur Rahman eagerly answered, leaning forward in his chair. "But how do I get to Washington, D.C.?" Abdur Rahman asked. "I don't have any money. I've been trying to figure out how to raise the funds for this whole operation."

"We've got funds," Russell interrupted brusquely.

"Okay, I could probably make surveillance videos on my phone," Abdur Rahman suggested, starting to show some hesitation in his voice as he pulled at his scrawny beard.

"No, your phone won't hold enough data," Russell answered. "We have a video camera you can use for surveillance and the brothers will give you cash for the trip, but you must be very serious about this."

"I am totally devoted," Abdur Rahman said as he breathed deeply, regaining his confidence.

"Subhan'Allah, I can see that," Ken jumped in. "But are you really ready to give your life for it? And kill others at the same time? You can't have any doubts about this mission," Ken asked, concern knitting his brow and filling his voice.

"I am ready to die in the path of Allah," Abdur Rahman repeated his voice steady as he spoke. "And no one deserves to die more than those infidel Senators in Washington."

"We can send you to D.C. to make a reconnaissance trip, but you have to do a good job—find the chinks in the security," Russell continued unrattled by this declaration of misguided faith and hatred. "Find a way to enter the Capitol building, or to get as close as possible to it when the Senators are leaving the building at the end of the day—so we can kill as many of those dogs of hell as possible. I can equip you with an automatic rifle and a suicide vest for this operation when you a ready, Insha'Allah."

"I can do it," Abdur Rahman answered, his eyes shining fiercely. "I am very honored you put your trust in me. Together we will punish the infidel dogs," he snarled as he clenched his fists.

Russell went to retrieve his backpack from where he had set it, near the safe house door. Coming back to the table, he pulled out a video camera, charger plug and a wad of fifty-dollar bills stacked up in a neat bundle. "Here my brother," he said sliding it across the table. "Go and find out what is possible. But you must be careful, pretend to be a tourist. And don't get caught," he warned.

Identifying with the Struggle

Sophie emptied her vodka bottles down the sink a few weeks after she converted. She no longer needed to binge, purge and drink to keep her memories at bay. She used the Internet now to keep her mind diverted—studying late into the night—searching all the websites she could find to learn how to become a new and pure woman in Islam.

Outside the home she hid herself inside her new black abaya and niqab. And just like the Internet sites proclaimed, she suddenly began to feel the hatred and fear that others held in their hearts against Muslims. It seemed no one liked her as a Muslim and often people made rude comments. She saw their stares and how so many people crossed the street to avoid her or gave her wide swathe to pass.

"There should be a law against wearing that crap," she had once overheard a husband tell his wife. "You could get away with murder and no one would know who you were. And you know they all want to kill us Christians," the husband had gone on, as he steered his family in another direction away from Sophie. Another time, while waiting to check out at the cash register she'd overheard two women looking at her and murmuring, "Islam is such a violent religion!"

Sometimes she enjoyed scaring people. It was fun to hold the power for once, the ability to fascinate and terrify, all while hiding safely inside her black robes. She began to mock them back from behind her veil. *Stupid kafirs!* she thought, mimicking some of the extremist chatter she read each night in the Internet chat rooms discussing the sinfulness of unbelieving Westerners.

Also on the positive side was the fact that although people often stared at her in horror, made remarks about her to others, or even occasionally directly insulted her, no one dared touch her. Most just gave her odd looks and avoided her. Sophie liked that—if her black niqab scared them away then it was working just as she wished.

Sophie was also beginning to feel "born again"—a virginal Muslim girl. Her black abaya and niqab gave a new sense of purity and safety.

As Sophie explored the Internet for tips on living a pure Muslim life and how to fully enter into the ummah—that is the worldwide family of believers—she was soon also introduced to the plights of her new family the world over and to her brothers and sisters in Islam.

The Islamic chat rooms were full of questions like: Do you see what's happening in Gaza? How can we fail to act? or This baby was killed and burned by a U.S. drone. Usually the comments had websites or pictures attached and Sophie surfed onward to view the pictures and videos and read more before returning again to chat—often angrily with her newfound Muslim family.

Infidel Jews did this, she read, beginning to believe Jews were an evil people. The Great Satan kills innocent children targeting them from the sky, Sophie read while she looked in horror at the photos of burned up corpses. Disgust wrinkling her forehead, she found it hard to disagree.

Sophie began to learn of the struggles of the Palestinians, who according to the websites she read, had been driven from their homes by harsh Israelis. Read this terrible report about the horrors in Gaza and act.

Call the media, the President, Congress, one woman wrote, while another vowed, I'll give my body, anything, to end this evil occupation.

Underfunded and ill equipped to fight back, Sophie studied how the Palestinians had taken to donning suicide bombs to deliver their messages into the civilian underbellies of their enemies. Sophie could identify with their anger and hate. She had her own reasons for hate, but she could understand people that would give their lives to strike back trying to win their freedom.

The websites she read from conveniently brushed over that the terrorists were striking at innocent civilians—blowing up pizza joints and nightclubs filled with women, children and young people rather than fighting against the soldiers they believed oppressed them.

Sophie also read about the Kashmiris whose country had been founded and then torn in two—caught now in a frozen conflict between Pakistan and India.

She learned about Khava Baraeva who was the first Chechen "martyr" who along with another Chechen woman drove an explosive laden truck through a Russian checkpoint. The rebels had written a song to glorify her after her brave act, Sophie read as she imagined the courage it took to give her life for the cause. What more did the disempowered have to fight with, but to give up their bodies by exploding themselves amidst their enemies? If it accomplished nothing else, it was a powerful expression of pain—and forced their enemies to feel it as well. Sophie could relate to that.

She read about the Chechen "black widows" who dressed in black abayas and suicide vests, had gone to protest the disappearance, torture and killings of their husbands, brothers and fathers by threatening to explode a theater of eight hundred Muscovites to smithereens. They had given their lives to demand that Russian forces withdraw from Chechen lands. Sophie also read about Wafa Idris the first suicide terrorist among the Palestinians. Sophie smiled as she read the songs written to Khava and the poetry and praises made for Wafa and all those women who bravely followed them.[39] They seemed like heroes to Sophie whose focus was on their bravery and standing up for what they believed was right, rather than the violence they chose to enact and who they hurt doing so.

As Sophie poured over websites detailing the Islamic struggle with Western powers that were attacking Muslim lands, Muslim peoples and Islam itself, she found herself being drawn into the struggle and romanticizing it. It was, after all, her struggle too now that she was a Muslim—and she understood from the extremist websites that it was a fight between a disempowered people and a much stronger enemy—an enemy that was fueled by the evil Western powers.

Unable to discern the various streams of Islam, Sophie also stumbled into a hijacked version—radical Islam—and without even realizing it, she fell headlong into extremist thinking. Despite hate filling her mind as she read from extremist sites, compassion filled her heart, as she imagined the desperation her Muslim sisters must feel in the midst of so much loss and anguish that they would use their bodies to deliver bombs.

Sophie felt their pain so much that tears filled her eyes and determination rose inside her heart to join this worthy cause. It gave her the sense that she was not alone in what she had suffered and it provided the sense of belonging and usefulness she had been searching for.

I now have a family who understands pain and humiliation, she thought. *And I will do everything I can to show my brothers and sisters my support and love.*

Washington, D.C.

It was late morning when Abdur Rahman landed at Ronald Reagan National Airport. It was his first trip in a plane and his legs had been jumpy the whole way. Now as they finished taxiing to the gate at Reagan National, Abdur Rahman looked down to see he was still anxiously gripping the armrests. He was glad to be safely on the ground.

Without luggage, Abdur Rahman bypassed the waiting crowd at the luggage carousel and went straight to the taxi stand. Hopping in a cab when his turn came, he told the driver, "The Capitol please."

The driver headed out on the George Washington Parkway north to the Memorial Bridge as Abdur Rahman gazed out the window. The sun was shining brightly and the grass was still green here, despite it being winter. Driving along the Potomac River, Abdur Rahman recognized the tall, white obelisk of the Washington Monument and crossing the Memorial Bridge, he recognized the Lincoln Memorial. *It's beautiful,* he thought looking out across the shimmering water and vast green expanses around the monuments, *but not for long.*

The driver wound near the tidal basin on the Washington, D.C. side of the Potomac River to get to the Capitol, where Abdur Rahman paid his fare in cash and got out of the taxi. Standing in front of the Capitol Building, he gazed downhill along the long green expanse of the mall. In the middle he saw again the Washington Monument. From this vantage point he could see it was encircled by fifty-six poles all flying American flags. Farther down the mall, the sun shone on a long reflecting pool, and beyond that he could see the Lincoln Memorial located alongside the Potomac River.

Abdur Rahman turned and faced his target—the U.S. Capitol. *So how is this place guarded?* he asked as he began walking uphill around its perimeter. After he had made one long circuit around the Capitol, Abdur Rahman got out his video camera and began filming. In short order a policeman arrived at his side.

"Sir, you can't film here," he said. "I'll have to ask you to put your camera away."

"Okay," Abdur Rahman answered, his eyes screwing up in annoyance as he complied with the policeman and put his video camera back in its carrying case and turned away. Then he walked back up the Hill to the visitor entrance of the U.S. Capitol located at First and East Capitol Street. As it was still early in the day and not tourist season yet, the lines were short. Abdur Rahman stood in line and waited for his turn to go through the security check.

Anticipation laced his nervousness. He was preparing to pull off the biggest terrorist plot Washington D.C. had ever seen.

Him! Abdur Rahman with a suicide vest wrapped around his body loaded with fatal bombs that would reach far and wide in death and destruction. *Wow!* He grinned as he imagined his future glory and then quickly wiped his mouth. *Be careful. Remain calm. It will happen soon enough,* he reminded himself.

Finding Him

It didn't take long to find *him* on the Internet. In fact, it seemed to Sophie that he found her—bringing with him a message of purpose and love, if she could call it that. Yes, love.

Anwar al-Awlaki, she learned was a Yemeni imam that had been born and raised in the United States. Although he was a Muslim scholar, he spoke in perfect English with an authority, clarity and sense of purpose like she'd never heard before. His voice was soft, but convincing, as he translated from his mother tongue the Arabic teachings of Sheik Yusuf al Uyayri and explained in his lecture *Constants on the Path of Jihad,* that militant jihad was a necessity and incumbent upon every devout Muslim.[40]

After listening to the first al-Awlaki lecture she stumbled across, Sophie went from one to the next. Many of his YouTube videos started with beautiful melodic singing of the Qur'an. She could recognize some of the Arabic words now—Bismallah, for instance, which was one of the names of Allah—labeling Allah as most Gracious, most Compassionate.

The loving words describing her new God were joy to her heart. The more she read, peace filled her soul like a cool drink of sparkling water after a long, parched thirst. Sophie no longer craved alcohol to calm herself. Now that she found al-Awlaki, he was enough to take her mind into other spaces where she forgot all that Colin had done to her. Al-Awlaki also helped her see that righting wrongs and correcting injustice was her mission as a new Muslim.

Hope danced around the edges of her mind. A new belief, new clothes, and a new name. With this new identity she could snuff out the guilt and shame that threatened to pull her apart by the seams every single day. For the first time in a long while, Sophie felt a bit of optimism that it might be possible, after all, to achieve a new life that would not include shadows of the rape teasing daily at her sanity.

Sheik al-Awlaki was not a big man but his message was huge. On his videos, he appeared in the pure, shining white, floor-length robes of an imam and sometimes wore a short combat fatigue jacket over them. His head was covered with a haji cap. He was bearded—like authentic Muslim men should be, and his jet black, curly hair fell down beneath his shoulders. Something about his hair and his eyes had a softness that attracted Sophie.

"We have chosen the path of war to defend ourselves from your aggression…" al-Awlaki announced as he lectured Muslims the world over about how President Obama could never defeat the Arab mujahideen while he was also dealing with a recession back home. Arguing that George Bush had failed, despite having the United States and its full economic might behind him, al-Awlaki predicted that Obama too, would fail in the fight. And he vowed that Muslims would never stop fighting.[41]

Sophie listened in rapt attention to al-Awlaki's lectures about jihad and the need to take up arms against the West to defend Islam, Islamic people and lands.

I could be with him, Sophie thought, wondering if al-Awlaki already had his regulation four wives. *I'd feel safe with a man like him,* she mused watching as his slender hands moved to make his points and his brown eyes penetrated across cyberspace, gazing softly at her through her laptop screen, entering into the private space of her bedroom. With him she didn't mind his peering gaze—in fact she welcomed it, as she devoured lecture after lecture of his authoritative teachings. She felt dizzy as she drank in his honeyed words of hatred for the West.

Sophie only later learned—after listening to over twenty of his lectures, and with each one falling deeper in love with his curly black locks, gentle hands and soft authority-filled voice preaching hatred of the West, and the need for constant jihad—that the West had dutifully hated him back. He'd been killed a full three years earlier—before she'd even converted to Islam—in an American drone strike on September 30th, 2011.[42]

Her beloved al-Awlaki had died on a road in Yemen after his traveling group stopped alongside the road to eat breakfast, Sophie learned as she angrily read accounts of his death. As Anwar and his companions dined outside, two Predator drones, launched from a CIA airstrip in Saudi Arabia, laser pinpointed his truck. Within minutes, hellfire missiles fired from remotely controlled Reapers exploded into his group of believers, enveloping them in a ball of fire.[43] The missiles were followed by helicopters filled with U.S. Navy SEALs who slid down long cables slung from their hovering craft to verify the kill.

Sophie mourned the man she thought was a hero. Going to her Facebook page she expressed her sorrow, May Allah accept his martyrdom. Then she moved to her Google Plus account and fired off an angry question: When there are so few mujahideen, is it not our duty to fight regardless of our country of birth and/or residence?[44]

Returning to surf the Internet a bit more she found an article reporting that al-Awlaki's teenage son, also an American, was soon after also struck down by an air-strike. He was killed as he ate lunch with friends at an outdoor terrace in Yemen, on October 14, 2011—only fourteen days after his father was assassinated.[45] Sophie stared at the picture of the sixteen-year-old boy, as his big brown eyes gazed back at her, his brown curly hair framing a child-like face. Grief, mixed with rage, filled her heart and mind as she read that this beautiful son wasn't even the real target that day. *I hope I have a son just like him someday, and that he will rise up to avenge these murders,* Sophie angrily thought.

Somehow with his gentle, but hate-filled words, al-Awlaki—speaking to her even from beyond his grave, via the Internet, had awakened in her a dormant sense of sexuality long deadened by what Colin had done to her. Somehow he had reminded her that even beneath her black abaya clad persona was a young, sensual woman that longed for love—the kind of love only a devoted Muslim man such as al-Awlaki could give. That, along with the soft tones of his firm words warning the West to stop the callous aggression toward his people, he spoke to Sophie as if his video was made just for her. His soft eyes in the pictures she had around her room also seemed to look out and really see her—the innocent girl she'd been and the pure woman she wanted to become.

Being a newcomer to Islam, Sophie completely missed the fact that al-Awlaki was twisting the sacred scriptures in ways most Muslim authorities would never condone. His words were dripping with hatred and were not even preaching Islam according to most, but Sophie had no idea. For her, now steeped in extremist thought, they were the words of a devoted Muslim imam who dearly loved and worried for his people.

Somehow he'd also reached down into the deep recesses of her soul touching the place where she had locked inside her memory vault, the unspoken, shame-filled and numbed memories of being assaulted. Collecting all of that anger she held hidden inside, he deftly redirected it into a fiery rage as powerful as a Hellfire missile, to be sent back to her country—fired back to its senders as revenge for his death. He'd taken all her pain and turned it into hate for her own country and made it ready to strike out for the Muslims that he directed her to help defend.

As she mourned the only man who seemed gentle enough to heal the scars of that fateful night, and rekindle the fires of a sexual self that had been burnt down to cold, dead embers of fear, Sophie felt a slow sense of fate building—a fate that would tie her forever to her beloved preacher. As he'd reawakened her sexuality, he'd also redirected her anger over what had been done to her toward a much wider sense of Muslim victimhood. The West, al-Awlaki had convinced her, was the biggest rapist of all, and it needed to be brought to its knees.

Learning to Hate

The hatred of kuffar [those who reject The Truth] is a central element of our military creed, Sophie read in al-Awlaki's *Forty-Four ways to Support the Jihad*.[46]

Hating, it turned out, wasn't all that hard for her. There was a furnace of burning anger always ready to leap to the surface and she was finding it harder and harder to control. The memories she could suppress, but it took a lot of energy and effort to keep the emotions that went with them locked up, buried beneath the surface while she pretended to be normal—pretended she was the same girl—the one she no longer was, the one who hadn't been seen again since Colin had taken her innocence.

Her memories, pushed down under the surface, became like a trafficked girl who gets lost in a maze of handlers—lost in the maze of avoidance and misinformation she fed herself daily. *It did not happen,* she told herself as she slipped deeper into extremism and distanced herself from inaction and pacifism—things that made her vulnerable to being used and thrown to the wolves.

Sophie had tried so many ways to make the memories go away. Like bitter pills she just had to push down, swallow hard, and make them disappear deep inside as she turned to distractions. As she fed from the extremist groups over the Internet, Sophie found her memories could go missing temporarily—just like the girl she'd been, drowned in the pool of innocence she'd lost. Self-respect and a sense of being able to master her own destiny were slowly replacing guilt for having ever invited Colin into her life. She was learning that Allah loved his daughters and hellfire waited for those who exploited their sacred potential.

But somehow the memories always found a way to keep resurfacing, like dead bodies floating back up to remind her of what had happened. And at the times when she could run no more and had to admit it, she clung to her conversion.

All my sins are forgiven. I'm living a pure life now, Sophie told herself. And above all, Allah loves and cherishes me, his daughter.

***

Sophie woke, startled with Colin holding her down, his legs savagely pushing hers open, his hand over her mouth. She couldn't scream. She struggled, but couldn't get out from under him as he plunged into her body painfully ripping at her insides.

"No!!!" she screamed, suddenly waking. Sweaty and her heart pounding in her chest, Sophie ran to the bathroom and bent over the toilet trying to retch. There was nothing to vomit—no sense of control in directing her own body—rather than have someone else overtake it.

Sophie thought about running upstairs to search the cupboards for something sugary to fill the hole inside, but then remembered her newfound faith.

She grabbed her laptop instead and flipped open the chat rooms. Immersing herself in the chatter about kafirs and infidels and hatred for the West, she felt her body calm itself. Hate had its own logic and it too could capture her mind and keep her thoughts away from the painful memories that kept intruding.

Strangely—even though she knew she hadn't done anything to cause it—Sophie felt guilty for having been raped, like it was her fault. *Slut! Whore!* Those words—they'd never actually been said to her, but they entered her mind all the time. She felt Colin had taken her innocence and turned her into someone bad, disposable, trashy and used up. And while converting had helped, she still didn't feel totally pure or completely safe yet. The rape kept repeating itself in her mind, penetrating even beneath her veil, reaching inside to assault her abaya clad body.

The anger it brought along with it was even harder to banish. It took too much energy to keep the memories *and* the anger buried. There were too many reminders. The television was constantly flashing up images of sexual violence. It seemed all the images she encountered—except on the Muslim sites showed scantily clad women and men abusing them.

Sophie had learned to walk out of the room, or if she was alone, switch off the television every time a violent sexual assault was depicted or talked about—which she was starting to learn could be any time on the television—unless she watched cartoons. She couldn't read normal things anymore; all the newspapers and news magazines were filled with stories of sexual violence, and most novels were too.

And so too were the friends she used to have. Everyone it seemed, had a rape story to share—although it was never their own—but the story of *some other girl*. And it was always the girl that was speculated upon, why she'd been raped, what she'd been wearing, where she'd been, what she'd been doing, drinking, thinking—*never why the rapist had assaulted her.*

It was never about *him*, always about the girl and figuring out some fault that had somehow made her the victim of her crime. For Sophie, these things made the anger roar up inside—made her want to strike out. The fight or flight defense mechanism welled up in her and panic forced her to flee somewhere, anywhere private, to be alone.

Sophie recognized that after the rape she'd become a much different girl—angry, afraid and lonely. And she was hiding inside an abaya, at least whenever she left the house. Even if Colin hadn't made her a whore or a slut, she felt he had, and he had for sure fundamentally changed her into someone pathetic and out of control—that much she knew for sure. The Sophie that now hid inside an abaya—at least whenever she left the house—was anxious, shamed and lonely until she got on the Internet to read and increasingly to chat with other extremist-leaning Muslims.

Her bedroom was no longer a place where she binged on Ben & Jerry's. Instead it had become a sanctuary that held pictures of al-Awlaki, her hero baptized with fire in his fight to right so many wrongs done to his people; the picture of the beautiful son so innocent, a tragedy of senseless death brought on by evil Americans who hated Islam. Sophie would take the laminated photo of him off her wall to sleep with it under her pillow as she prayed to Allah to help her somehow be able to help her new family—the Muslim ummah.

And she loved to stare into Anwar's deep brown eyes. In her favorite picture of him, he was sitting in a silky white robe that covered him from his neck to his feet, his white crocheted haji cap on his head, his right hand raised and pointing upward to Allah. She stopped and gazed into his soft brown eyes at least once a day, if not more. *Oh how she loved that man!*

***

At home her parents were just plain irritating. They were always asking stupid questions. "You sure you don't want to enlist?" her father still asked, even after she'd told him she wasn't going to finish high school, wasn't going to college, and for sure wasn't joining ROTC—being a nursing assistant was good enough for her.

Emptying the shit from the bedpans of invalids—that fit her just fine now. Endless shoveling of shit—it was the same on the inside as the outside. She was shoveling the shit in her mind all the time anyway—why not get paid for it?

Just this afternoon her father had asked her, "So you ever going to go to college? Or you just plan on carrying on with this burqa nonsense forever?"

Sophie shook her head in confusion. *What could she say in reply?*

The look of disgust coupled with disappointment on her father's face made her want to put her niqab back on and wear it at home to hide from him too. She wanted to hide her pain, bury it behind the black abaya and stifling hot niqab, not let him see her face, stare back out at him with angry eyes and not have to answer *why* anymore.

Why so angry? Why so different? Why she didn't want to join the Army anymore? Why she didn't want to go to school? Why she didn't call, or answer the calls, from any of her friends anymore? Why all the anti-American talk?

Don't you understand how evil our American military is? Sophie wanted to shout at him. *They are the evildoers. They killed Anwar! Sent him a missile from a Hellfire Predator that cut his body into pieces, same as the missile that cut my life into pieces,* Sophie thought. *And the Beautiful Son,* as she now called him, *murdered as he ate lunch with his friends! Cowards killed him—don't you see this?* All she felt was shame for the parents she wished would leave her alone.

Sophie comforted herself by listening to Anwar's lectures every night. Even though he was dead, she found his voice soothing and his call to jihad reassuring. He offered a way to work out all her anger at injustice. He gave her a focus and purpose and the promise that she could be renewed.

All Muslims must participate in *Jihad* in person, by funding it, or by writing, Anwar instructed and Sophie was convinced.[47] Her Anwar, his photos were plastered on all four walls of her bedroom, his beautiful son as well. He knew best. Whatever he said, she knew it was right. If he said jihad was her Islamic duty, then it was.

It was all she thought about now—how she would participate in jihad, how she would contribute.

All Muslims must remain physically fit, and train with firearms to be ready for the battlefield, he'd taught.[48]

Sophie was fit. Her father had drilled her throughout high school, readying her for ROTC. And he'd taught her how to shoot at the local firing range. Maybe that's how she should join—become a sniper for ISIS?

Scouring the Internet, Sophie found a webpage that encouraged the faithful that weren't ready to make hijra—that is come to the land of jihad—or to stay and fight in place. One of the ways to attack at home was to purchase a gun and mount a VIP attack.

Getting her hands on a gun and accurately taking out an enemy of

Islam couldn't be so hard—but who should be the target? Sophie wondered. She began studying Colorado's politicians. That's when she found her target.

Senator Mark Durham—he'd voted in support of the 2003 invasion of Iraq and now he was leading the charge for airstrikes against ISIS in Syria and Iraq. Mark Durham was an enemy of the Islamic State and the newly formed Caliphate. Sophie didn't have a rifle yet, but she had the target clearly located in the crosshairs of her mind.

Bread Crumbs

"**S**he's like a raven hanging around our church—all wrapped up in black," the woman caller complained. Ken glanced up at the round clock hanging on the wall across the Fusion Center. This sounded like a crank call to him. He could use a cigarette right about now.

"Well, wearing black and hanging around a church is not a crime," Ken answered back into the phone.

"She seems to be scoping us out," the woman continued. "Some of our parishioners asked her to go away and she told them that all Christians are going to hell and that Americans are going to pay for the war in Iraq," the woman explained.[49] Her voice sounded middle-aged. "She calls herself Halima, but her real name is Sophie Lindsay. She converted to Islam last year at age seventeen. Now she's always wearing that black burqa and black face covering thing."

Ken's ears perked up. *A recent convert wearing a burqa and niqab— telling Christians they were going to hell and saying Americans would pay for Iraq? Could be interesting,* Ken mused.

"Okay, I'll give it a look," Ken replied. "Thanks for calling."

Sophie Lindsay, Ken thought as he typed the name into his computer. *Facebook page with no profile picture, but there are pictures from a year ago,* Ken reflected as he poked around on Sophie's now mostly inactive Facebook page. One was of Sophie wearing denim cut-off jean shorts and a bright blue halter-top. Her blonde hair fell down over her bare shoulders and she was smiling at the camera. Another showed her lounging in a little, yellow bikini on a beach chair, iPhone in hand with her hair caught up in a clip atop her head. *Nice looking, nothing to hide there,* Ken thought noticing Sophie's lithe figure and silky blonde hair. *Shame to hide that hair under a headscarf and that body under a burqa!*

Checking her history of likes Ken's interest piqued even further.

There were thirty or more al-Awlaki and ISIS videos among her latest likes.

So she's met our friend, al-Awlaki and she thinks the war in Iraq was all wrong, and she's interested in Islamic State. This is getting interesting.

Hamid

Sophie found Hamid in the chat rooms. He was a Tunisian. Thirty-one years old and bearded—like al-Awlaki, but less gentle, and lacking his sense of authority. He made up for that by being a mujahid—a holy warrior—the kind that al-Awlaki had said needed to rise up to fight the West.

Hamid was true to that vision. My parents didn't want me to go, but I made hijra, Hamid wrote referring to his move from Tunisia to Syria where jihad was being fought. I was with al-Nusrah in Syria at first, but now I'm with ISIS, Hamid wrote.

You are a hero of Islam, Sophie wrote back as she admired his profile picture. He looked strong and capable.

They chatted a lot the first month—he telling her about the battles and the victories they'd won and what the Americans had done to the Iraqis in the latest airstrikes. Maliki is a despicable Shia. He's backed by the Iranians. And the Shia security forces pick up random Sunnis from the street and take them to prison where they are tortured and murdered. They even take women and rape them in prison, Hamid wrote. But we freed them.[50]

Sophie had learned about the horrible divide between Sunni and Shia Muslims—a sectarian schism that went way back to ancient times when the Prophet had died and there were rivalries over who would carry on in his stead. What she didn't understand was that the current struggle for leadership in Islam was fueled in part by a rivalry existing even today between Shia Iran and Sunni Saudi Arabia, and that there were dark elements on *both* sides that fueled killing and marauding to further their own interests.[51] For Sophie, steeped in extremist Sunni teachings, the Shia were heretics. And now with Hamid as her teacher she was learning to hate the Maliki government in Iraq and all the Shia death squads that hurt Iraqi people. She was oblivious to what ISIS itself was doing and simply enjoyed pouring all her hurt and wrath out over what had happened to her, on what seemed to her, to be a legitimate target.

We had to fight back, Hamid told her in one of his texts. She'd given him her phone number after getting to know him better. And now we have declared the Caliphate! Hamid announced, clearly euphoric over their claimed victory. It will extend to all the ends of the earth and we will reign victorious over all Allah's enemies, he typed as Sophie too became caught up in his rapturous joy and vision of a utopian Sunni state, freed of the Shia and Western infidels ruling them.

Now finally we can live free of the kafirs, throwing off their despicable ways. We can pursue pure and true Islam and live under Sharia law. You should come here and join us, Hamid texted. Sophie felt a thrill of excitement move down her body in response to his suggestion. *Is he interested in me?* she wondered.

Sophie didn't at first answer his call to jihad. Instead she asked about his family in Tunisia, his childhood, and life now in Iraq. As he spun tails of a warm and loving family life and a heroic battleground, she slowly began to open up to him as well.

I was raped, she told him after two months of intensive, daily chatting, a frown filling her face, her down cast eyes threatening to break into tears as she typed the horrible words. He was the first human being she had shared these horrific words with. Maybe it was easier since it was over chat and he was halfway around the world. I was sixteen. He stole my soul, she typed as hot tears coursed down her cheeks. I found Islam after and now I have become pure again, she shared.

Masha'Allah! The mercies of Allah are boundless, he wrote. I am sure you are innocent as a flower. I should kill this man if I could, he wrote adding, The West is an evil place that allows such things to happen. Sophie warmed to his strength and protective kindness.

After another month, he convinced her to exchange more pictures than the ones that showed up on their chat icons. He sent a picture of himself as a bearded man dressed in combat fatigues and she sent him a fully covered picture of herself in a blue abaya and matching headscarf. Staring at his picture, Sophie felt a tingle of pleasure running through her body. He looked so manly!

You are like a lily-white lotus floating in a pond of pure blue water, he wrote and she smiled, giddily reading it—drinking in his kindness and forgiveness of her past. Shivers ran through her body. No one had ever complimented her with such sweet, poetic words. And no one had offered to avenge her attacker before. Maybe she could escape her past?

Come now, send me a picture of yourself without the scarf, he begged. Don't you realize I'm in love with you?

Sophie smiled in delight at those words, too speechless to reply. *He accepts me as I am,* she marveled joyously.

Join me on Skype, he pleaded in the days that followed.

Studying his picture, particularly his brown eyes and genuine smile, with the creases wrinkling around his eyelids—Sophie decided to give in and agreed to a Skype chat—although with her headscarf firmly tied around her head and neck. He could see her face, but nothing more—at least not yet.

Hatching a Plan

"Here's the surveillance videos and pictures of the Capitol," Abdur Rahman said as he slid a memory stick across the table to Russell.

"You have the video camera and any cash left?" Russell asked, his face screwing up into a cynical expression. He was used to dealing with undercovers and informants that kept anything he didn't ask for.

"Yes it's all here," Abdur Rahman said indicating a bag at his feet.

"So what do you think?" Russell challenged, still not buying that Abdur Rahman had it in him.

"I now know how to do it," Abdur Rahman answered leaning across the table excitedly.

Russell nodded and Ken watched carefully as Abdur Rahman spoke, noting, *He seems to have grown in confidence since working with us.*

"I just need you to help me carry out the plan because I don't know how to make explosives," Abdur Rahman explained. "I hope you can teach me."

"So, what's your plan?" Russell asked.

"It's impossible to enter the Capitol with any kind of weapon," Abdur Rahman began, excitement filling his voice. "They have way too many security guards, metal detectors—the whole works. I went in and out of the Capitol five or six times and I couldn't find any way to breach their system."

Are we creating a monster? Ken wondered as he listened. *Am I right to trust Russell on this?* Ken debated inside his head as he watched this teenage kid transform in front of his eyes into a real terrorist operative. *Who is to blame here—Abdur Rahman or Russell?* Ken anxiously wondered. *Maybe Russell is so gung ho for his next promotion that he'd do anything to get this kid to act out?* Ken wondered cynically. But he pushed aside his doubt, knowing Russell was not the first FBI agent to pretend to be a co-conspirator in criminal activity. *I'm probably just being paranoid,* Ken chided himself.

"So it's impossible!" Russell let out an exacerbated sigh as he leaned on the Formica tabletop.

"Impossible to enter with a suicide vest, or an automatic rifle," Abdur Rahman corrected Russell with a gleam in his eye, "but not impossible to carry out an effective attack."

"How so?" Ken asked, leaning forward as well, becoming curious. *Maybe Abdur Rahman is a monster?*

"The way to kill many of the Senators is to somehow get them to come out of the building all at once," Abdur Rahman explained his face growing cold. "To create a diversion."

"I want you to help me make pipe bombs to plant on the streets outside the Capitol, at all the exits but one. The guards inside will have to evacuate the Senators through the one clear entrance," Abdur Rahman explained with a cold look in his steely brown eyes.

"And I'll be there—outside on the street, waiting for them—with an automatic rifle hidden inside my coat and a suicide vest around my chest. It will be a killing spree no one will ever forget!"[52]

Ken stared in horror at the kid who called himself Abdur Rahman. *Just a kid. Some mother's son who had swallowed the jihadi poison.*

Worrying Signs

"Look at this," Ken said showing Cathy a printout of Sophie's activities. "This young lady has declared herself an ISIS supporter. She's also been talking shit at her neighborhood church about making America pay for the airstrikes in Iraq, *and* she's been endorsing sites that talk about taking hijra to Iraq."

"Sounds serious," Cathy remarked looking at the photo Ken had found of Sophie prior to covering herself. "She's pretty," Cathy mused. "And so young."

"She's changed her name to Halima, and she lists her job on her Facebook page as Slave to Allah," Ken explained, "although she is actually a nurse's aide working in an eldercare facility. And she commented next to a video she posted that American women dress like sluts."[53]

"Ha! That's funny, but hardly dangerous," Cathy remarked as laughter filled her voice.

"Yeah but, like I said, she gets serious elsewhere," Ken continued. "On al-Awlaki's death by drone strike she posted: 'May Allah accept his martyrdom,' and she posted on her Google Plus account, 'When there are so few mujahideen, is it not our duty to fight regardless of our country of birth and/or residence?'"[54]

"Looks like somebody is looking for an adventure," Cathy commented.

"Yeah maybe becoming an ISIS warrior is a bit more glamorous than changing bedpans," Ken remarked. "I've read all her Facebook and Twitter posts and she knows how to shoot. Her daddy is former military. He taught her and she's been to the shooting range quite a few times—before she converted. And from her own reports, she's a good shot."

"From bedpans to the battlefield," Cathy commented. "But does she know how to get there? Have any serious contacts yet?"

"That's what I don't know," Ken answered. As he answered Cathy wondered, *How do we ever really know the people around us—who they really are? How do I know you won't be just like Matt and turn out to be a player as well, breaking my heart once more into tiny little pieces, now when I'm a mother and can least afford it?*

"You okay?" Ken asked reading her face.

"Yeah, I'm fine," Cathy said shaking herself out of her reverie. "I think it's time for a talk, what do you think?" Cathy asked. "You want to come along?"

"Count me in," Ken answered his face reflecting concern—either for Sophie or herself, Cathy wasn't sure. "Now?"

"No better time than the present," Cathy said going for her coat.

Snowflakes flitted lightly through the chilly air as Cathy and Ken stepped carefully on a snow packed parking lot to get the agency car. Cathy's heart felt as bleak as the gray skies while she thought of going to pay a visit to this mixed up teenager bent on ruining her life. Feeling chilled over Sophie's violent path, Cathy set her thoughts to thinking what she could say to possibly change Sophie's mind.

Assassin

"Hamid, I read about al-Awlaki's son. Those American pigs killed him. I cried for days," Sophie told her Tunisian boyfriend over Skype.

"Yes, a sickening and useless tragedy. Someday you will have a wonderful son like he was," Hamid replied, his hardened face turning soft at the thought.

"I'm looking into how to carry out a VIP assassination," Sophie bragged about how she'd like to fight back. "I'm studying," she told him as she held up the book, *Al-Qaida's Doctrine for Insurgency: Abd Al-Aziz Al-Muqrin's A Practical Course for Guerilla War.* "I'm willing to die as a shahida if necessary." [55]

"Masha'Allah! You are a brave and good woman, a lioness for Allah!" Hamid roared in approval. "Our brothers in Sham and Iraq will be so proud of you my little bird!"

Sophie basked in his approval, momentarily speechless. *A lioness for Allah.* Sophie repeated Hamid's words over and over like warm sunshine flowing from the outside in. How kind and sweet this man of Allah was who made her forget all of the ugliness of her existence. She would do anything for him! Sophie thought, as her body filled with a warm excitement.

"You can kill the American President," he added as his eyes suddenly shone with admiration. "Make them pay for the children they are killing here in their satanic airstrikes."

"No, he's way too hard to get close to," Sophie answered. "But I could maybe take out the Governor or a Senator here in Colorado," she explained. "I don't know though. They seem pretty well guarded as well."

"Allah will show you the path," Hamid encouraged. "He will guide your steps, Insha'Allah, my purest light of love."

Sophie nodded in agreement her body quivering with excitement, *Yes Allah will shine the light and illumine my path,* she thought as a feeling of euphoria suddenly filled her chest and spread throughout her body making her feeling suddenly light headed and giddy.

"I will die in the path of Allah," she announced, her face beaming as a feeling of bliss spread throughout her body.[56] "But Hamid, sadly enough no one here, except my parents, will ever miss me."

"Subhan'Allah, my dear pure dove," Hamid answered his face filled with admiration. "You will be a pure martyr rising to paradise. And that is all that matters. And I will miss you, my sweet beauty!"

A Word of Warning

"Ma'am can we have a word with you?" Ken asked as he and Cathy came alongside of Sophie as she was walking toward her nursing home job. They'd been waiting for her in their car and quickly caught up to her walking along the snowy sidewalk, after she came off the bus.

"We're FBI," Cathy added, flashing her badge.

"What do you want?" Sophie asked, alarm filling her voice. She was wearing her niqab so they could only see her green eyes widening underneath it. *The American authorities—always picking on the Muslims*, Sophie thought to herself. *The kafir infidels.* "What do you want with me?" she asked again.

"We just want to ask you a few questions," Ken explained. "Perhaps you could take a seat in our car? It's parked back down the street," he asked.

"Do I have a choice? I've got to be to work in a few minutes," Sophie answered with doubt lacing her voice. "I'd really rather not. I have nothing to say to you." *I don't want to sit in your infidel car,* Sophie thought as fear rose up in her chest.

"This will only take a few minutes," Ken assured her as he took her elbow and the threesome doubled back to their car. *Don't touch me!* Sophie wanted to scream but a numb paralysis was filling her arms and legs and chest. Her body was shutting down with the memory of Colin's hands forcing her into things she didn't want to do. Sophie briefly thought of making a run for it.

She was glad the FBI man was not alone. She didn't want to get into the car alone with him—it flashed up memories of when she went with Colin in his car, and she'd never forget how that ended.

Seated inside the car, Cathy began, "We have a report that you've been hanging around the premises and saying threatening things to the members of Faith Land Congregation."

"Those church people hate Muslims," Sophie answered. "They

followed me around and harassed *me!*"

"Our report states that you told them you want Americans to pay for the airstrikes in Iraq," Cathy pressed on.

"The American airstrikes are an act of Satan," Sophie hissed from beneath her niqab, although her eyes were wide with fright. The combined emotions of terror and anger were at war inside her chest and the anger made her feel like she'd be okay—that she'd get back out of this car without anyone hurting her again, like Colin had.

"An act of Satan?" Cathy repeated as laughter filled her face. "Are you serious?"

"American bombs are killing innocent women and children in Iraq!" Sophie insisted trying to hold herself together.

"You've been endorsing Anwar al-Awlaki and ISIS videos on your Facebook page," Ken commented. "Are you an ISIS follower?"

"Anwar al-Awlaki is a pure martyr, killed by the evil Americans," Sophie spat back at him. She felt terrified seated in the car with him and wanted to grab the door handle and bolt. "And Islamic State has brought back the Caliphate of the Prophet, Peace be Upon Him," Sophie added her eyes flashing hate at him.

Ken and Cathy exchanged glances, Cathy thinking, *This girl is a real handful!*

"So you would like to join ISIS?" Ken pushed onward.

"I didn't say that," Sophie answered, fear fighting with a steely look of determination in her eyes. *How can I get away from these people?* Sophie asked, while searching for her escape. *What are my rights? Do I have to sit here and answer their stupid questions? How long can they keep me prisoner in their kafir car?* Sophie's mind flashed to Hamid. He'd take them out. He'd pulverize that puny FBI man with one of his big fists in no time.

"You need to be careful what you get mixed up in," Cathy jumped in, warning. "These people are deceiving you and putting you on the wrong track—ending with you in a prison cell, or dead. You're young, Sophie, with a long life ahead of you." Cathy's mind moved to her own daughter. *How did this poor girl get mixed up in this mess?* Cathy wondered, her heart going out to the girl hidden behind the veil. *She looks terrified and infuriated—like a cornered animal,* Cathy reflected.

"I'd rather die than turn away from the true faith," Sophie answered, her voice hardening. "Are we finished here? I need to get to work."

"What's going on Sophie? You've got good parents, a nice home, friends. You want to talk about it?" Cathy asked as she leaned in toward Sophie with understanding softening her voice. She put her hand out to touch Sophie's burqa clad knee.

Sophie jumped back in alarm, knocking Cathy's hand from her knee. "Ha! Shows how much you know, big shot FBI lady. If you had just one clue what my life is actually like you would understand. But you don't really care. And my name is Halima—not Sophie. Now, just leave me alone. I have to get to work. And keep your hands off me," Sophie sputtered as she reached for the car door handle. "And thank you so much for your concern," she said with a sneer. It was taking all her self-control to not bolt out of the car and start running down the block. *Can they shoot me if I run?* Sophie wondered, her mind racing in panic and fear.

"Watch out, Sophie. Those people are very dangerous," Cathy warned. "And this hatred of the West is not what the real Islam teaches."

Sophie slammed the door behind her. Cathy jumped out and ran to catch up with Sophie. "Wait, Sophie!" Something about this girl tugged at Cathy's heart. She seemed so vulnerable beneath her anger and that ridiculous black garb.

Sophie stopped and looked back at Cathy running toward her. "Sophie, wait. Look, I'm a mom. Whatever is troubling you can be solved. Every problem in life can be solved. You can trust me," Cathy said breathing hard.

"You can't help me!" Sophie yelled back at her. "Leave me alone." Sophie pulled away and ran down the sidewalk finally giving into the urge to escape.

Cathy sighed, "Crap." She walked back to the car where Ken was standing outside of it waiting. "Oh no, I didn't mean for that to happen," Cathy moaned, as she and Ken watched Sophie depart down the street, a black shrouded, angry vision disappearing from their view.

"She stands out like a sore thumb in that garb," Ken said as they watched Sophie hurry down the street.

"I wonder what in the world is going on with her?" Cathy asked, her heart running after the girl who looked so scared.

"Let's find out," Ken said opening the passenger door as Cathy took the driver's seat.

Something has hurt her, Cathy thought. She could sense it. *Something's hurt her badly. But does that translate into dangerousness?* Cathy wondered silently.

"She's hell on wheels," Ken remarked, whistling between his teeth as Cathy started up the car.

"You know, in our day it was joining a neighborhood gang to make up for messed up families and missing parents. Now we have girls looking for acceptance and love in foreign terrorist groups," Cathy remarked.

"Yeah, and they have no damn clue about what they're getting into," Ken answered.

Family Visit

"Let's go talk to her parents," Cathy suggested. "Maybe they can get through to her?" Seeing Ken's nod of approval she opened a file folder she'd brought with her and put their address into the GPS.

Sophie's mother, Sarah sat in front of her laptop, an open bottle of wine uncorked on the kitchen table and a glass poured, looking anxious and impatient as they described their concern over Sophie's extremist attitudes.

"That black raven outfit she wears with the niki thing," Sarah remarked as she glanced everywhere else but into the agent's faces. Her eyes fell to her laptop as though she'd like to disappear back into her work, "It won't last, kids and their fads."

Sophie's father at least made eye contact as he listened. Looking from one to the other as he spoke, Ken noted that the wine in the bottle was already lower than the label and Mrs. Lindsay looked as though she had floated off to another universe—probably departing before they had even arrived.

"It's just a phase," Jake protested angrily, his fist clenching from time to time. "She's been in this burqa get up for about nine months now, but at home she always takes it off. She's perfectly normal at home. I think it's some kind of weird rebellion. Jihadi cool, or something like that. Hell, who knows?"

"Do you have any idea why she would say the U.S. needs to pay for the airstrikes in Iraq and why she's been endorsing an awful lot of extremist websites lately on her Facebook account," Cathy asked. "Has anything happened to her lately? Some kind of trauma?"

"Hell no. If anybody's got trauma around here, it's us!" Jake said, running his hand through his hair. "She dropped out of high school last year," Jake explained, his voice rising in anger. "Straight A student and flushes her whole future down the drain on some crazy whim. Decided she wanted to be a nursing assistant and a Muslim! Frankly I've had it with her," Jake spat out in frustration.

"Sir," Cathy said, "Are you sure there's nothing wrong in her life that could be driving all of this?"

"Hell, how would we know? We're just the parents. Doesn't every kid think they have demons in their life? Isn't life just one great big hellhole to teenagers between the hormones bouncing off the walls, peer pressure and dealing with an uncertain future at this age? Come on! You obviously don't have teenagers," Jake said starting for the door. "Show me a teen who is not a major pain in the ass and I'll show you Jesus Christ."

Cathy and Ken exchanged glances across the room. *What the hell did that mean?* It was clear that they weren't going to make any inroads here.

"Okay, thanks for your time," Ken said wrapping up the interview. "Here's my card," he added handing over his Fusion Center business card to Jake. "Please call us if anything comes up that is of concern, and *please* keep an eye on your daughter." Ken said.

"Mr. and Mrs. Lindsay, we are seeing an awful lot of American girls looking for love and acceptance in all the wrong places," Cathy warned before they left. "These terrorist groups are nothing to take lightly. We have arrested some girls already trying to get to the Middle East to help jihadis. The stories are very ugly. And…"

"*Please.* Our Sophie is not one of those. I should know. I'm her father. I was in the military you know. I'm not some kind of damned fool. Now thank you for your concern and goodnight," Jake protested as he opened the door signaling their time was used up.

"FBI. Can you damn believe it?" Jake said turning to his wife after they left. "Accusing Sophie of leaning toward terrorism. You'd think they had enough to do instead of cooking up stories like that and worrying parents for nothing."

"Uh huh," Sarah said while taking a long pull on her wine glass.

***

When Sophie walked in the door later that night, Jake was sitting there waiting for her, a beer in hand.

"The FBI were here tonight," he said his voice filled with anger. "They were asking if you're a terrorist."

"Why would they say that?" Sophie asked as she took off her niqab and wrapped her arms around herself, hugging her billowing black burqa around her waist. *Why didn't those kafir pigs just leave her the hell alone?* Sophie thought as she waited for him to break the cold silence building between them.

"Sophie, I think it's time you moved out, got a place of your own," Jake said, his voice filled with an icy resolve. "You're making a mess of your life and it's not something I'm enjoying watching anymore."

"Move out?" Sophie asked, gasping in surprise. She wasn't sure her salary could cover the rent anywhere safe to live. "Okay," Sophie said gulping and staring at him. "When do you want me to move out?"

"I don't know. I need to talk to your mother, but as far as I'm concerned, the sooner the better," Jake answered standing and exiting the room.

Love Story

"The FBI came and hassled me," Sophie told Hamid the next time they met over Skype. "Can you believe it? I told them to leave me alone," she said anxiously biting her lip. *Should she also tell him that her own father wanted her to move out?* She knew conservative, unmarried Muslim women didn't normally live away from their family homes. *What would he think?*

"The FBI? That's serious isn't it?" Hamid asked, his eyes mirroring her concern. "What does hassle mean?" he asked his face showing confusion.

"Oh, they just asked me about my Facebook comments and some things I said at our neighborhood church," Sophie answered, tossing her long blonde hair over her shoulders. "It's a free country—I can say what I want."

"Just be careful my beautiful little sparrow," Hamid warned. "Maybe you need to hide your true feelings a bit more, not let them catch onto you. These are our enemies, you must remember."

"Yes, the kafir infidels of the West!" Sophie parroted, as Hamid nodded his approval.

"I've been thinking about what you said," Sophie said, her voice becoming soft as she changed the subject. She leaned into the screen wishing she could reach into it and caress Hamid as she continued, "If I come to you in Iraq as you suggested, I want to bring something with me—more skills than I have now. I'm thinking of joining the Army Explorers."[57]

"The Army!" Hamid gasped in alarm.

"It's not the Army," Sophie quickly answered. "It's the Explorers. They have a three-month long training course where they teach U.S. military combat skills. I would have to uncover to go, but I might be able to receive some valuable training." *And it would be a place to get away to until I figure out where I'm going to live on my own.*

"What Allah deems necessary is blessed," Hamid answered,

understanding her wishes and giving his full approval. "Although I'd prefer you come sooner. You have skills to share—you're a nurse. Here you could be a medic to the mujahideen. And I could use your comforts as a wife."

Sophie felt the floor disappear beneath her as he spoke. "Your wife!" she gasped, a warm euphoria filling her body.

"Yes my wife," Hamid answered. "Come and join the mujahideen, come and be my wife," he repeated, his bearded face breaking into a warm smile.

Oh my, Allah! Sweet, dear Allah! Now I have a place to go where I belong! Sophie thought as her heart sang with relief and her body filled with desire. *He wants me! Me, as his wife!*

With that Sophie discarded her fantasies of trying to gun down a politician. *It would never work and just get me killed with no result,* she reasoned. *In the Explorers I'll learn to fight like a soldier and I'll be useful to the mujahideen in Iraq. Hamid will be proud of me,* she thought as a thrill of excitement coursed through her body. *Or maybe I should go to him sooner?* She wondered, as she felt her body thrill to the thought of being with him.

Death was not as appealing to her when she imagined his arms holding her, his hands removing her headscarf, opening her burqa and the babies they'd make together.

I can give myself to him. He is good and kind, she told herself, excitement spreading through her body.

Equipping the "Martyr"

"**Y**ou don't feel bad about this at all?" Ken asked as he helped Russell load up a camouflage duffel bag full of explosives, a suicide vest and a long-range automatic rifle.

"Not in the least," Russell answered as he zipped it shut. "If we didn't get to him first, this scumbag was going to find someone else to equip him to kill Americans. It's good we got to him before others did. He wants to specifically target Senators! Senators, Ken! How is our country supposed to keep running if we let lowlifes like him figure out how to take out a group of U.S. Senators?"

"But do you honestly think he would have ever gotten this far without us coming alongside of him, encouraging him—equipping him?" Ken asked, incredulity filling his voice at he dubiously stared at the bag of equipment.

"Yes, I do," Russell answered, his voice taking on a hard edge. "He's ready to die for his God—this Allah he worships. And he wants to kill others so he can go to Paradise. I'm glad we found him before ISIS or al Qaeda did."

Ken and Russell walked out to Russell's official undercover car and loaded it up. Arriving at the safe house they met again with Abdur Rahman.

"I have what you need," Russell said as they sat at the table. "You won't be able to take it on a plane so we'll need to pack it up carefully and send it via UPS at an address I'm going to give you," Russell explained. Then writing an address on his tablet he ripped off the page and handed it to Abdur Rahman.

"This is the address of another safe house the brothers have in Anacostia, a neighborhood in Washington, D.C.," Russell explained. "I'm going to have another of the brothers meet you there. He will show you how to assemble the explosives and pray with you before you put on your suicide vest. He'll drive you to the Capitol.

"He'll call you after you land in Washington D.C., on this phone,"

Russell explained handing a disposable phone and charger across the table to Abdur Rahman.

"Masha'Allah!" Abdur Rahman exclaimed as he took it.

"Do you know how to operate an automatic rifle?" Russell asked unzipping the camouflage bag and taking the gun out from among the other items.

"No," Abdur Rahman admitted.

"Then we need to go to the firing range and practice before you leave," Russell answered.

What he didn't tell Abdur Rahman was that the explosives, gun and vest he would be receiving in Washington, D.C. were totally incapacitated—unable to hurt anyone.

Pangs of Guilt

"**H**ow did last night go? I tried to call you a few times," Cathy asked while she waited for Ken to grab his coat and briefcase from his cubicle. She'd just returned from all day meetings out of the office and Ken was the only one still left at work—he'd been waiting for her.

"It was pretty wild. Abdur Rahman is determined to blow something up but he doesn't know the first thing about explosives or guns. He's just a stupid kid," Ken turned off his computer and stepped toward Cathy in the hallway. "You want to go get dinner?" he asked, nervous that she'd say no.

"Sure, I'm starving!" she answered, a twinkle lighting up her eyes.

The two walked to the elevator and waited for it to come. "What are you hungry for?" Ken asked as he opened the building door to the parking garage. A cold blast hit them in the face reminding them of the coming snowstorm.

"Peking Duck sound okay?" Cathy asked. Ken nodded in agreement. They got into Ken's SUV and drove out onto the highway. By seven p.m. the rush hour traffic was clear. Blues was playing on the radio and several minutes passed without a word.

"So what's up? You're quiet tonight. You're usually into an excited explanation of the latest goings on with the Cubs of the Caliphate, as you like to call those young ISIS recruits[58]," Cathy commented.

"Yeah, Russell is so gung ho about Abdur Rahman, and I just don't feel good about it," Ken answered as he turned to gaze momentarily into Cathy's eyes before turning back to the highway. "I mean he's just a kid, you know? If he was an adult with experience with bomb making and blowing things up, if he knew how to even shoot a rifle for God's sake—I wouldn't doubt the operation," Ken drew his fingers through his sandy brown hair.

"If it wasn't you and Russell tuning him up for the attack, it'd be someone else in the Bureau—or God forbid, ISIS themselves. Abdur Rahman might be just a kid, but he is fully brainwashed and determined to cause serious damage," Cathy said her voice taking on a sharp edge. On this topic they always disagreed.

"I guess. He's just so damned young. Where's his mother? Is she wondering where he's at, what he's doing? Ugh, he's going to end up a lifer in prison," Ken grimaced in frustration.

"Somebody's got to stop him," Cathy answered as they pulled into the parking lot of the Peking Duck.

Inside, the restaurant was toasty warm and nicely lit with small candles on each of the tables. Gold dragons were emblazoned on the red wallpapered walls, and in the back, a large fish tank was filled with silver and copper colored carp that swam back and forth peacefully in the water.

"Anything new on the Sophie Lindsay case?" Cathy asked once they were seated at a table covered with a silky red tablecloth, a small candle flickering between them.

"No, she's been quiet now," Ken said shaking his head. "Nothing new posted on the Internet, no complaints from the church goers. Maybe we scared her off?" Ken said smiling at the thought.

"I hope so," Cathy answered, her brow furrowing in concern. "She sure seemed troubled by something, hurt in some way…"

Uncovering

Over time their Skype sessions became daily. Hamid called Sophie in her late morning—his early evening—before she went to her nursing assistant job. She was working fulltime now in the nursing home—changing bedpans mostly. Hamid didn't grasp that and glorified her work referring to her as if she were a battlefield medic.

"I need you here," Hamid coaxed when she spoke about taking the Army Explorers training. "You already have so much to offer my little bird," he said.

"And it's time to take off that headscarf when you speak with me," Hamid sweet-talked, "I want to see you uncovered, now that you've agreed to become my wife."

Smiling Sophie reached up as her fingers flittered around her tightly tied scarf. She felt terrified removing it in front of him and excited at the same time.

Will he like what he sees? she wondered. Carefully pulling the pins that held her scarf in place, one by one from her head she slowly worked her hijab free.

Can he see the stain I carry inside? she worried as she carefully pulled her headscarf down the back of her head and untying it completely, freed herself of it. Then reaching up, she let her hair fall loose from the hairclip holding it up in back of her head. Slowly she unfurled her long blonde hair over both her shoulders for him to see.

Hamid stared in silence at her as Sophie sat nervously waiting for him to speak. It took him a few moments.

"You are glorious!" Hamid cried. "Incredible! I am a very blessed man!"

Sophie breathed a sigh of relief. *He accepts me,* she thought as her heart sang with pure joy as her body erupted with a feeling of sexual excitement.

His words followed her into the nursing home where Sophie fluttered about in her black abaya, from room to room, like a night moth seeking light. She couldn't wear her niqab while caring for the patients—they became too frightened and disoriented seeing only her eyes peering out at them. So she left it in her cubby alongside her lunch. She figured these elderly men fell into the Qur'anic category of too feeble to matter and it was not a sin to show her face here among them.

Emptying their waste from their soiled bedpans and washing their wrinkled backsides, Sophie filled her mind with nobler dreams. She imagined herself stitching up the wounds of bearded men that had the courage to fight for what they believed. And as she conjured up the mujahideen, she reflected on the fact that Hamid was both fierce and gentle as his brown eyes stared at her through her screen, admiring her across all the time and space that separated them.

He knows what happened to me, but he loves me anyway, Sophie reflected letting her love for him grow steadily stronger inside her once decimated heart. She also began fantasizing about him—his big brawny arms wrapping around her soft naked body.

"I applied for my passport," she told him the next time they talked. "It should arrive in early April."

"I can't wait to hold you in my arms," he answered, his eyes showing their longing.

Sophie flushed with excitement. "I can't wait either," she said as a tingling of sexual excitement shot through her body and flushed her checks a bright red.

Thinking back to how she used to vomit all her meals and hide sugary treats under her bed and a bottle of vodka that she downed within a week's time in her underwear drawer, Sophie suddenly felt freed of all her addictions. Freed and validated as the beautiful woman she had wished to become. Her heart sang with newfound love and joy.

He doesn't hold what happened against me, she thought. *He loves me and he'll protect me. He's a man of honor. Allah has blessed me greatly.*

At the same time she also felt afraid of what it might mean to make love to Hamid. *Will I be able to keep the memories down when it's time to be with him?* she anxiously worried. *Has Colin ruined me completely?*

Proposal

"My passport came!" Sophie announced one morning as they talked on Skype.

"That's good news, my little bird," Hamid answered with a broad smile. "It's soon time for you to fly to me. But you must know that as a Muslim, I need to ask your father's permission to marry you," he explained.

"Okay," Sophie answered, biting her lower lip as she wondered how that would go down. But she also knew that he was right. In Islam a woman's father gives her in marriage. *But would her father agree?*

Just then, as if right on cue, her father walked into the kitchen where she was sitting at the table talking to Hamid on her laptop. Her dad was dressed in his usual casual button down shirt and khakis—and was working from home today.

"Dad, my boyfriend, Hamid wants to talk with you," Sophie said looking up from the screen with a soft smile and big doe eyes. "Can you come here and talk with Hamid?"

"What?" Jake answered, surprised to learn that Sophie had a boyfriend. He came around the table to see who she was talking about.

"Dad, I'd like you to meet Hamid," Sophie said with a shy smile as her dad bent over next to her. "Hamid, this is my father," Sophie continued, seemingly oblivious to the shock her father would feel finding out who Hamid really was.

Jake stared in stunned silence as he took in the bearded man staring back at him.

"Salaam Alaikum," Hamid greeted him, his face suddenly becoming very serious.

"Hamid is a Muslim brother living in Iraq, Dad," Sophie explained. "He's from Tunisia. He wants to ask you something."

Jake stared at the screen with a puzzled look on his face as the bearded stranger spoke, "Mr. Lindsay, I will get right to the point. I would like to ask your permission to marry your daughter Halima."

"Halima? Who's that?" Jake asked, shock covering his face.

"Your daughter," Hamid answered, his eyebrows rising in surprise.

"Marry Sophie?" Jake gasped in surprise. "Aren't you over in Iraq?" he asked anger creeping into his voice.

"He's one of the holy mujahideen battling the infidels," Sophie explained adoringly. "He wants me to join him in Iraq and become his wife,, help build the Islamic State," Sophie added, enveloped in a cloud of euphoria and completely oblivious to her father's shock.

"Are you out of your mind? No! That's out of the question!" Jake cried out as he rose abruptly from the table, his chair scraping loudly across the floor. "There's no way my daughter is going to join a bunch of fighters in Iraq." As he left the room, Jake ran his fingers through his hair messing it up all which ways. "Dammit Sophie! You are way over your head into this Islamic shit…"

"Dad, wait!" Sophie cried, as she stood to follow him. Then stopping in her tracks she realized, *It no longer matters what he thinks. Pleasing Hamid is my priority now. I'm making my own family with Hamid now no matter what he has to say about it. I can leave this family behind and all the pain that I've felt here, as well. I'm Hamid's woman now,* she thought feeling that now familiar thrill of sexual excitement and the euphoria of being in love coursing through her body.

***

"Sarah, you'll never believe it," Jake told his wife as soon as she returned home from the office. "Sophie is Skyping with a Tunisian in ISIS!"

"What?" Sarah answered. "That's crazy."

"Oh it gets worse," Jake continued as anger and alarm filled his voice. "Her ISIS boyfriend wants to marry her, and have her come join him in Iraq."

"You're joking," Sarah gasped. "That can't be true."

"She is really losing it," Jake said. "We need to watch her a lot more closely. Maybe those FBI folks were on to something?"

"No, not our Sophie," Sarah said as she began taking food out of the refrigerator to prepare dinner. "She can't be serious. She's just experimenting with new identities on the Internet. It will pass."

Jihadi Brides

Ken stepped out of his shower and flipped on the television to watch the morning news as he toweled off. Jessie O'Neil, the usual morning newscaster was doing a story on ISIS. Ken's ears pricked up as he listened, "The emergence of an ISIS wedding certificate that allows jihadi brides to carry out a suicide mission without the husband's permission suggests the terror group will be using more women to carry out their twisted attacks, a counter-terrorism expert has told our news team." Music drummed up in the background as the young announcer continued, "I'm Jessie O'Neil and we are going to be exploring this shocking news in our next segment for CNN." The television feed moved to pictures of twenty or so women in black burqas wielding Kalashnikov assault rifles, lined up as they trained for ISIS.

Ken snorted as he reached for his khakis and shirt. *CNN loves to play up any ISIS footage—especially of the women,* he cynically thought as his towel fell to the floor. He began dressing as he waited for the segment to play out, interrupted by what seemed like endless inane commercials.

Across town Cathy was already dressed and putting a bowl of Lucky Charms in front of Daniela. She poured milk into Daniela's pink plastic bowl as she flipped on the television to CNN.

"SpongeBob SquarePants!" Daniela shrieked, but Cathy shushed her as she watched a news camera zoom in on an Arabic wedding certificate as a reporter explained, "The document declares that the final decision over an ISIS bride's life—and death—rests with the Islamic State's leader, Abu Bakr al-Baghdadi. Under 'Conditions of Wife' it states, 'If the Prince of believers—Baghdadi—consents to her carrying out a suicide mission, then her husband should not prohibit her.'"[59]

"What does this ISIS wedding certificate actually mean?" Jessie O'Neil asked as she turned to her panel of talking heads. Dr. Samira Strang, a counter-terrorism expert and a Muslim herself, was the first to weigh in,

"This is the Islamic State's desperate attempt to force women to the battle-front to replace the hundreds of male soldiers being slain in bloody battles across Iraq and Syria."

"So are the ISIS leaders sending women into combat now?" Jessie asked turning to the next talking head, Dr. Amy Wilson, a professor from Georgetown University, Security Studies Center.

"Not yet," Dr. Wilson answered. "ISIS has in fact prevented women from taking combat roles, but they *have* trained them for security positions and security analysts believe that at least one woman, a Canadian who joined ISIS is working as a spy. We know this from the geo-locator data on her phone. Her phone at least—and probably she—travels all through Syria and Iraq crossing into and out of ISIS-held territory. That's why analysts think she's spying for ISIS—which wouldn't be hard for a woman wearing a burqa and niqab to do—she can travel pretty anonymously."

"But are ISIS women going to be joining the battleground and becoming suicide operatives at this point?" O'Neil pressed.

"The pattern we often see with conservative Islamic terrorist groups is that they don't use women as combatants in the beginning, but when the going gets tough, and they get hemmed in from every side, then they begin to consider using women as operatives. It looks like al-Baghdadi may now be preparing for this possibility."

"Why would they shift to using women if the going gets tough?" the newscaster asked, her blonde hair and glossed lips shimmering under the bright television lamps.

"It's because women have many advantages for terrorist groups," Dr. Wilson answered. "Women can hide bombs inside their burqas—feigning pregnancy. The Tamil Tigers even developed a bomb bra for their female cadres. And ISIS women can travel practically anonymously if they wear a niqab covering their faces. They don't raise suspicion the same way men do at checkpoints and they are rarely searched as thoroughly so they can get their suicide bombs through. And when they do manage to carry out an attack the press goes crazy. We are not used to the violence of women. In fact we have a societal myth that women are *not* violent—but that's not really the case. In the case of ISIS we are likely going to see women joining the battle soon, given this news. This is just the start of it."

"Thank you for that Dr. Wilson and Dr. Strang," Jessie O'Neil said as she turned away and carried on to the next story. "This news emerges amid the shocking reports that three teenage girls, perhaps the same three that ran away from their homes in London four months ago and are believed to have become ISIS brides, have reportedly fled ISIS from their stronghold in Mosul, Iraq. According to our source, these girls are currently being hunted down by the militants."[60]

Cathy wanted to watch more and lingered for a moment with the remote control in her hand as she stared at the screen, but she couldn't delay, as she needed to get Daniela to school on time. She switched off the television just as pictures of the three British girls who had become ISIS brides were flashed up on the screen, showing them moving through the airport in London.

"Come on honey, we have to go," Cathy said as she picked up Daniela's green canvas, Ninja Turtle's backpack and her matching lunchbox and guided her daughter to the door. "Let's go."

Once she'd confirmed that Daniela was in her seatbelt, she checked her rearview mirror as she backed out of the driveway. Pausing there, Cathy dialed Ken on her cell.

"Ken, did you catch CNN this morning?" Cathy said as she drove toward Daniela's school.

"Oh hell yeah! Unreal. See, it's happening. You on your way?"

"Be there shortly. Bye."

Plane Ticket to Utopia

"I've found an imam here that will stand in for your father," Hamid told Sophie in their next Skype chat. "Since your father is not a Muslim, our imam will give you in marriage and sign the nikah," Hamid explained.

"Oh, I knew you would find an answer," Sophie answered, delight spreading across her face.

A few days later they carried out the ceremony over Skype with Hamid's ISIS imam standing in for Sophie's father to sign the Islamic marriage contract—the nikah—giving Sophie in marriage to Hamid. Soon after, just as promised, Sophie received her electronic plane ticket via her e-mail. Taking her laptop to her Dad's home office, Sophie printed it out. It was a ticket originating from Denver International Airport to Ankara, Turkey—via Toronto and Istanbul. It was dated for the following Wednesday and written in her legal name—Sophie Lindsay.

"You must buy your Turkish visa when you land at the airport," Hamid coached her. "Tell them you are an American student of history and in Turkey for tourism. You should say that you are there to study culture, that you will be traveling around Turkey to see the ancient sights. Study ahead of time so you are prepared to tell them what you want to see. Then when you get to Ankara, you must take a bus to Karkamis where a sister will meet you and take you across the border into Syria," he explained.

"What should I bring with me?" Sophie asked breathlessly.

"Bring your phone and make sure you have international service," he instructed. "And be sure you have nothing that can cause suspicion on your phone—remove any links to jihad. Wear strong walking shoes. Your clothes that you wear here in Sham and Iraq must be Islamic and cover you fully," he added. "But what you wear at home with me can be beautiful—pleasing to your husband—particularly your intimate items," he added, chuckling softly. "Bring the most beautiful underwear," he repeated, his eyes glistening with excitement. "You know in marriage any sex act is permitted. You are my bride and should please me."

Sophie smiled in pleasure, her body lighting on fire with desire.

"And bring whatever you can of value—gold, jewelry, cash, anything to help the brothers," Hamid answered. "And whatever you can fit in your suitcase to make our home comfortable—things that are important to you."

"While you travel, tell everyone you are Christian, and your name is Sophie—not Halima, until you cross into Syria. In this case you must uncover and travel in Western clothes until you're ready to cross the border so as not to raise suspicion. It is for the cause of Allah," Hamid instructed.

After they signed off, Sophie excitedly printed out multiple copies of her ticket and went to her bedroom to find her passport.

It was missing.

Showdown

"**Y**ou are not going to go to a warzone to marry a Tunisian you've never met!" Jake shouted, the vein on the side of his neck bulging as he spoke. "And you are *not* getting your passport back."

"It's not *your* decision," Sophie cried throwing her hands up in despair.

"I know what's right and wrong, and no daughter of mine is going to join ISIS," Jake stormed back.

"Dad do you know how many children have been killed by U.S. bombardments?" Sophie pleaded as helpless tears clouded her eyes. "Do you watch any other news than what's on the network and cable channels? Ever watched a video of a mother whose children were burned up in a drone strike?"

"You're still not going," Jake answered, gesturing wildly with his hands. "This whole Islamic thing is so deluded. Do you realize how lucky you are that you live in a democracy? Those Muslim countries are all corrupt," he answered softening his voice, hoping to reach her closed mind.

"Not the Islamic State," Sophie countered. "They are living according to the Prophet's laws, Peace be Upon Him. They are constructing the only place in the world where a woman can live protected. Do you know the kind of things that happen to young girls *here?*" she asked choking briefly on her words as they touched the painful memories buried deep inside. "Do you know Dad?"

"What are you talking about?" Jake replied, frustration and anger filling his face. "You've been the most protected girl in America! We've given you everything you could possibly need."

"You don't understand, Dad," Sophie answered, as her face hardened. "I'll find the way to go, passport or not. I thought I could trust you. But you're just like the rest." And with that she stormed out of the room.

Change of Plans

"My father took my passport," Sophie told Hamid on their Skype session the next morning. "I can apply for another one, but it will take months," she moaned. "And I don't know if the FBI is on to me. Remember they came and talked to me *and* my parents a few weeks ago," Sophie explained. "So I might not be able to get a new one. I don't know if they can block me from applying or not?"

"We need a change of plan," Hamid said his voice serious and his face clouding in disappointment. "How about the Army Explorers? Maybe you should enroll now—take off your scarf and pretend to be one of them again. You can deceive them into thinking you've given up being a Muslim…"

"You mean take the training as we originally planned?" Sophie asked, her eyes widening in surprise at this change in plans, her voice heavy with gloom.

"Yes, take off your Islamic clothes and tell them you gave up Islam," Hamid coached her. "Sometimes in evil times, Allah ordains that Muslims must practice deception. It's called taqiyya. Tell them you want to join the Army, but you are going to start with the Explorers. Gain your skills and in the meantime apply for a new passport. When it comes, you'll be ready to fly."

"Oh yes, I will do it all, and Allah willing, I will be with you in a matter of months," Sophie cried.

"I'll cancel your plane ticket for now," Hamid answered. "And when you are ready, I'll send a new one, Insha'Allah," Hamid answered. "By the way the brothers are giving the married fighters homes they've taken from the kafirs. We will have a big house in which to start our new family my beautiful jewel!"

"Our own home?" Sophie gasped in surprise.

"Yes my jewel, our own home," Hamid confirmed his big smile

lighting up his face. "The Islamic State wants to reward the fighters who marry and begin families. We will start our family there, my little bird."

Insha'Allah, Sophie mused. It was a big word that covered all the uncertainty she was facing now in going forward.

Army Explorers

In the next week Sophie put away her abaya and niqab. It was hard for her, but she knew Hamid was right. If she wanted to get her passport back from her Dad and get the FBI off her back—so she could get a new one if need be, she needed to convince both parties that she was giving it all up. She was part of a larger cause now and needed to engage in taqiyya—the Islamic practice of deception while living among unbelievers. And she needed to stay offline. No more listening from her laptop to Anwar al-Awlaki speaking in his soothing cadences, no more Skype sessions with Hamid from home. It all had to go underground. And she needed to be willing to give them all up—her parents, her former life, everything—to become one of the holy warriors with Hamid.

She still chatted with Hamid most mornings—although she did it now, sitting uncovered, using the library computer masking her activities under their IP address. She listened to Hamid through earphones and typed in her responses so no one could overhear their conversations.

I opened a new e-mail account, Sophie typed. It's littlebird777777@gmail.com Some of the brothers on the Internet wrote that it's the best way to communicate without being detected—for us write e-mails that we never send. We don't send what we write, and just read each other's e-mails in the draft folder. It's very hard to trace that way. You can get into our account with our password, AllahisRighteous.

"Masha'Allah, you are already a skilled operator," Hamid roared, laughing heartily through his thick beard. "My little bird, the spy. I will write you a letter tonight on the new e-mail account."

I applied for my new passport as well. I'm taking all these precautions just in case the FBI is watching me, Sophie typed. I don't know if I can get my passport back from my Dad and if not, I don't want the FBI to block me getting another one, or put me on a no fly list. I read that's what happens to some of the brothers that fall under suspicion.

"Hopefully you will be on your way soon to me," Hamid sighed softly. "I hate to think everyone there is enjoying your glorious beauty and not me."

***

"I'm going to join the Army Explorers," Sophie announced to Jake at breakfast the next day. "I'm done with being a Muslim. I might even apply to college now and enroll in ROTC," Sophie added watching her father's face as she lied into it.

"That's great news," Jake answered his face lighting up in a big smile. "I didn't think that black raven look suited you at all," he continued.

"Dad, I still really respect Muslims," Sophie answered crossly but then she remembered her higher vision. *I need to lie, cheat, and hide my true feelings if I want to accomplish my true goal and fly away into Hamid's arms and join the mujahideen,* she reminded herself.

"Oh, ok," Jake quickly answered, softening his voice to try to smooth over the rift that had suddenly opened again between them.

"Don't worry Dad," I'm done with the burqa now. "I'm thinking ROTC now," she said smiling cheerily.

"That's great Soph," Jake replied, his face filled with relief and joy. His daughter was back! "I always knew you'd do great in the military and it's a great way to pay for college too," Jake said getting excited just thinking about it.

"You don't happen to want to pay my enrollment and uniform fee for the Explorers, do you Dad? I'm going to start with that before I start applying to colleges," Sophie asked, breaking out her charming, sweet obedient daughter smile that often won him over.

"How much is it?" Jake asked, his voice exuberant, his face smiling back.

"Two hundred and twenty-five dollars to enroll and get the uniform, and thirty-five dollars for their monthly training fees," Sophie answered. "I can handle the monthly fees but the upfront costs are a bit steep for me."

"I've got you covered," Jake answered, his face lit up with pleasure. "You can use my Visa card to enroll. How's that?"

"It's great," Sophie said as she smiled back at him thinking, *He's got no idea how much I hate this country and our military, but I guess it's necessary to keep him in the dark if I'm going to achieve my objectives for Allah. Sad,* she thought gazing into his trusting eyes.

Later, using his Visa card, Sophie felt a small twinge of guilt as she used his money to enroll for the first monthly training session scheduled in five weeks time. It would be on patrol ambush training. Pushing away guilt, she reminded herself of her higher goal—to get to the mujahideen and hopefully bring something of value with her—this training for instance. Even if she used his money to accomplish it maybe in the end he'd understand. *If the veil ever falls from his eyes and he finally sees what a great and glorious religion Islam is and that the call to jihad is the greatest and most glorious calling!* Sophie thought as she overcame her pangs of conscience.

And I will never be that powerless victim again! She reminded herself as she signed up for courses to equip her to become a holy warrior. Looking ahead, Sophie saw that the following month featured emergency first aid training. Judging from the photos on the Explorers website Sophie concluded, *this might just be useful information to learn for the battlefield in Iraq.*

Terror Attack

"**A** foiled terrorist plot aimed at the U.S. Capitol was stopped today," Ken said as he popped his head into Cathy's office. "Come and watch the news," he said leading her back out to the break room.

"The terrorist has been identified as nineteen-year-old Sammy Stillman, a Muslim convert from the Federal Heights area of Denver, Colorado," the newscaster announced as a picture of Abdur Rahman flashed up on the screen. His flimsy beard looked even thinner on the television monitor.

"It's our man," Ken said, his face looking pale and sickened with the news.

"FBI agents stopped the man as he headed up to Capitol Hill armed with three pipe bombs that he planned to detonate at the entrances of the Capitol, trying to force an evacuation of the Senate which was in session today," the newscaster explained as images of the Capitol in Washington, D.C. and the pipe bombs filled the screen. "The terrorist was armed with an automatic rifle and suicide vest that he planned to use to kill as many Senators as possible as they fled the building."[61]

"He wasn't armed," Ken sidelined to Cathy as the segment finished. "His suicide vest was fake, as were the pipe bombs and his rifle couldn't fire," Ken explained, his voice weary for that time of day. "It was all a set-up to see how far he'd take it."

"He's still a killer," Cathy said, placing her hands on her hips. In this regard they held very different opinions. "If they hadn't been fake, he would have used them."

"But he would have never gotten to that point if it weren't for me and Russell," Ken answered glancing at the television ruefully.

"Ken he was as ready and willing as he could be," Cathy said, her voice growing sharp. "Do you really think if real jihadists had gotten to him first, he wouldn't have agreed to work with them? It just so happened that you and Russell got to him first, thank God. Really, you've got to let go of this thinking that we entrap these terrorists," Cathy said, her voice rising in frustration tinged with anger. All she could think of when they discussed this case was some unemployed, local creep soaking up the ISIS crap over the Internet and planting a bomb in Denver that hurt Daniela. "He needed to be stopped and stopped now," Cathy added. "And how it happened is beside the point!"

"But still, Cath. He's some mother's son," Ken said surprised to see her so angry. She'd never been mad at him before.

"Your point? He's a potential killer, a murderer in the name of his crazy religion that teaches violence against women and children. You can't save these kids. It's too late for them. All we can do is stop them before they wreak terror on innocents," Cathy said as she felt her anger towards anyone who would kill innocent people rising up in her throat. Realizing it was better to walk away than say more, she turned and walked from the room. "Maybe you should have been a defense lawyer instead of working for Homeland Security," she added as she departed. It was a low shot but somehow she couldn't resist. *Maybe it was for Daniela?*

"That's not fair!" Ken answered as she swung out the door. *Fuck!* he thought as she disappeared down the hallway. *Way to score points with the girl you can't stop thinking about. Fuck!*

Stay & Act in Place—In More Ways Than One

"**D**id you hear what just happened in Canada?" Ken asked as he poked his head into Cathy's office the next day, near the end of their workday. He had noticed how she had assiduously avoided him all day. She had arrived early, made the coffee, and disappeared into her office with the door closed. Only Russell had been seen going in, and he had closed the door and stayed for a good forty-five minutes. It boiled Ken's blood. *Forty-seven minutes to be precise,* Ken reminded himself. He'd clocked all forty-seven of them.

"There's been an active shooter at their Parliament," he said, hoping she'd invite him to come sit down, like she'd obviously invited Russell in.

"Nope, I missed it," Cathy answered a little smile erupting across her face at seeing him. "Do you ever give this stuff a rest?" she complained, though the hint of a smile lingered on her face.

"I can't let it go," Ken answered, his voice intense. "It's going to happen here too. Everyone thinks the Tsarnaev brothers were a one-off, but the truth is, they are just the beginning of an upward trend."

"So what happened in Canada today?" Cathy asked, although she didn't invite him to sit as he had hoped. Instead her mind wandered off toward terrain she had put on a shelf long ago, deciding that after Matt she would swear-off men—go on a man diet, maybe forever. Lately when Ken talked to her about ISIS, terrorism, homegrown extremists, and whatever else, Cathy felt pulled more strongly toward emotions she had ignored and stuffed down for so long—except for when they'd argued yesterday.

Now breathing in the scent of him, the aftershave he always used filled her senses. *Very masculine...and he has the guts to come around after we argued, He's loyal—like a sheepdog. Matt was never like that,* Cathy reflected, forgetting all about how angry she'd been at him yesterday.

"Remember that driver that ran over two soldiers in Ottawa for ISIS?" Ken began hoping he could catch her attention and she'd forget being angry with him.

Cathy nodded as she looked up into Ken's face as he spoke to her, noticing his animated expressions as he told the story, his hands gesturing to make his point. *He's so passionate about his work, life, everything. I love his laugh,* she thought as he talked.

"Well today this new guy, Michael Zehaf-Bibeau—a bit of a mental case who had his passport pulled because he was trying to go over to Syria probably to join ISIS—apparently got frustrated that he was stopped by the authorities, so he took a rifle concealed under his coat into the Canadian Parliament where they were holding a session with nearly everyone present. Amazingly, he managed to get inside the building and started shooting. He tried to massacre as many as possible," Ken said, pleased that he'd managed to regain her positive attention.[62]

"Geez, I guess I've really been out of it working on these files these last hours," Cathy commented as she gathered her things to leave the office.

Is she still angry? Ken wondered as she prepared to leave.

"Luckily an armed guard took him out and he didn't kill any of the Parliamentarians, but one of the policemen was killed," Ken explained. "This guy was basically trying to finish off what the Toronto 18 had started."[63]

"Who's the Toronto 18 again?" Cathy asked they walked toward the elevators. She pulled out her hairclip as they waited and let her long, red hair fall in lazy waves, shaking off the formality of the office. Ken felt exhilarated breathing in the after scent of her flowery shampoo and looking at how the waves of her hair crested down over her shoulders. *She's a knock out,* he thought gazing sideways at her, captivated by her beauty.

"They're the guys who were plotting to put truck bombs around Toronto and here too—in Washington, D.C.," Ken rattled off, desperate to keep her interested. "They also wanted to storm the Parliament and behead their Prime Minister. But they didn't succeed because the Canadians had an undercover agent, a former extremist—Mubin Shaikh—who infiltrated their group," he said noticing she was listening intently. "But now this new guy has come along and tried what they plotted! I don't know how we can stop all of these homegrown types—we can't track them fast enough and insert undercover agents everywhere,"[64] he finished, hoping she wouldn't walk away yet.

"Well, that's where your work tracking them on the Internet is so important," Cathy commented. She'd reverted a bit to her former cold self—the one that was still angry with him for thinking the Abdur Rahman case might have involved entrapment. *How could he think that? Wasn't he concerned with the safety of ordinary, innocent people and children—like Daniela?*

"You're parked next to me right?" Ken asked as he pushed level P3. *Don't be mad at me Cath,* he begged inside his head.

"Uh-huh," she answered. *He always looks out for me,* Cathy thought. *Matt never did that.*

In the garage, Ken stopped in front of her car. Looking up into his face, Cathy suddenly didn't want him to go. His lips were full, the bottom one a little more so than the top. She couldn't stop staring at his lips and his scent kept wafting through her nose, setting the embers that had begun in her thoughts to slowly escalate.

Cath, why are you afraid of trusting him when he's nothing like Matt? It doesn't make sense. Ken is not a self-centered, bad-mannered, egotistical slob like Matt was, she thought as she stood in front of him gazing up at his mesmerizing blue eyes, suddenly not wanting to say goodbye. *I can't stay mad at him,* she realized, smiling softly.

"Umm," Ken chuckled. "Uh, do I have spinach in my teeth or something?" he asked as he laughed nervously. *Wouldn't that top it all off, what a turn off?* He thought imagining himself as repulsive to her. *She said she thought I should have been a human rights lawyer instead of an analyst!* Ken reminded himself remembering her look of disgust as she'd made that parting comment yesterday.

"No. Not at all," She said softly and slowly. "I'm just thinking what a kind man you are."

"And?" Ken asked looking uneasy as he waited for her reply. *Don't be mad at me anymore,* he thought as he stared back into her eyes.

Cathy suddenly got on her tiptoes and pressed her lips softly, almost imperceptibly, to his. When their lips parted, she smiled up into his face.

"Wow! Do that again," Ken said, his face breaking into a huge smile, as he took her face in both of his hands and bent down to meet her waiting mouth. This time he kissed her fully on the mouth, hungrily.

Cathy avidly kissed him back as Ken pulled her closer.

"Wow!" Ken whispered when they finally broke apart, his hands still tenderly holding her. Then after a moment of silence he said, "I have a question."

"I may have an answer," Cathy smiled with her eyes still closed, languishing in the afterglow of their kiss.

"What got into you all of a sudden? I've been flirting with you for months."

"I guess your sweetness and the time we've had together got me to thinking. I've never experienced such a kind, smart and funny guy that also seems to get me," Cathy said, as she slowly opened her eyes to gaze into the peaceful blue of his.

"I enjoy spending time with you Cathy, you're really smart and tough. It's a rare combination. I've never been afraid of powerful women, although I hated when you were angry with me," Ken confessed.

"Well, with you I can't stay mad," she said smiling. "To tell the truth, I keep thinking about the difference between you and my ex-husband. Trusting again has been a huge issue for me. I'm so terrified of hooking up with a jerk again. But the contrast between you and the Jerk opened my eyes these last days."

"How do you know I'm not a Mr. Jerk underneath it all?" Ken laughed as he touched her face and kissed her again. "But I'm really not. Really," he smiled.

"I somehow know that, I think. Maybe," Cathy said wincing at the memory of how she had been so wrong in the past.

"How about we take it slow? There's no rush. It's been ages since I've enjoyed being with a woman like you. Even as partners at work we're good together. Don't you agree?" Ken suggested.

"Yes, we make a good team," Cathy mused. "Good idea – take it slow. See what happens. But Ken, I can't afford to get hurt again. I have a daughter to consider now. And why haven't you been snatched up yet?"

"I was snatched up once, got burned and then buried myself in my work to forget it all."

"So you understand?"

"All too well," Ken whispered and took her face in his soft hands again and kissed her forehead, her eyelids and her nose. "C'mon, let's go get dinner together and then maybe we can carry on from there."

***

"I'm starved, actually. Scallops look good," Cathy said once they were seated in the small French style brassiere they'd chosen for their dinner. A small tea light candle flickered between them as their hands intertwined on the blue and white checked tablecloth.

"How late can you stay out?" Ken asked as he gazed over the menu. Cathy looked up at him and he gave her a sultry wink. The waitress set down the two white wines that they had already ordered and took their dinner orders.

"Mmm, wine is so great after a long day at work," Cathy said taking a sip. "As for most evenings, I'm like Cinderella. My carriage turns back into a pumpkin around midnight. With getting Daniela off to school I get up really early," she explained as she took another sip of her wine.

"I have an empty dresser drawer," Ken said, as he caressed her hand.

"Uh, the keyword is *slow*, remember?" She smiled, raising her eyebrows.

"No problem. Can't blame a guy for trying," Ken said sheepishly.

"My mother covers for me some nights—like when I go out really late on undercover jobs," Cathy offered.

"Oh yeah, your dates with Miltie," Ken cracked as he changed the subject, "So we never finished talking about the Parliament shooter earlier…"

"Oh those guys," Cathy noted smiling peacefully. "Yeah, I remember—barely."

"Yeah, I kind of forgot too," Ken said as he picked up his glass and held it in mid-air. "I'm talking shop again, sorry. Must be nerves and that I need to take my mind off how badly I regret agreeing to taking it slow in the parking garage," he laughed.

"Don't be," Cathy said with an amused look lighting up her face. "It's our work!"

"What happened in Canada is going to come here too," Ken said. "We need to be ready, and stop them before they act in place."

"I hope you're wrong," Cathy said, her face turning serious. "Maybe the Muslims in Canada don't have it as good as American Muslims?"

"I don't know if it's always about real grievances," Ken said, happily getting sidetracked into territory where he was more comfortable. "ISIS is a hateful group with a twisted ideology that seems able to take an individual's anger over their life circumstances and focus it into anger over geopolitics with an apocalyptic religious spin. We've seen al Qaeda get their tentacles into Americans like the Tsarnaevs and many others so I think ISIS can succeed as well. It seems to me that these groups are really getting good at attracting youth from the West into their clutches, to join their battles, and fight in vain, even give their lives for their ridiculous causes. Like that Abdur Rahman—he's just a kid, for God's sake," Ken shook his head. "There's got to be a better way to stop all this madness without entrapping and putting kids like him in prison."

"You still think it's entrapment?" Cathy commented, her voice toughening and eyebrows arching. She suddenly remembered how angry he had made her. "If he's drunk the Kool-Aid as you always say, then he's become a poisonous viper and someone's got to stamp him out before he figures out how to carry out a real attack," she said rallying for another argument.

Then softening her tone she continued, "Ken, I see how much you care about everyone, but you have to step back sometimes from the ones that can't be saved. And you can't work all the time. You have to keep your life in perspective or you're going to burn out. I've seen it happen."

Cathy nodded to the waitress as she offered to bring another glass of wine. Ken reordered as well.

Waiting until the waitress departed, Ken slid his hand again across the table and took Cathy's in his. "You're right," he said. "I need a diversion. Will you and Daniela be my leisure pursuit…slowly of course?" He grinned.

Cathy smiled wide, "Sure. You got it."

Shocking News

A few weeks later Sophie was again at the library. She logged into her Skype account and texted to Hamid that she was online, following their usual morning routine. When he didn't answer she went to their shared littlebird e-mail account to look for his letter. Sometimes when Hamid couldn't be present he left her a letter explaining. Sophie loved his letters. They were always very romantic and flattering to her.

Opening the drafts file she found two e-mails. Excited she clicked on the first one.

Halima, my lovely jewel. I had to travel but I have good news. The house the brothers have given us in Raqqa is beautiful—two stories, five bedrooms and a swimming pool—just for our new family and us. Please remember to bring beautiful lingerie when you come because we are going to have very good and long nights my beauty. I am going to make love to you and you will be pregnant and carrying my child in no time. You have given me a reason to live. Come soon to me little bird. And always remember my love, our real goal is jannah where we will live united forever. Your warrior for Allah, Hamid.

Sophie's breath caught in her throat as she read it. She couldn't decide which was more exiting having their own beautiful home in which to start a family or Hamid's words of love. Colin and the rape seemed so far away now. Soon she would be reveling in Hamid's arms, protected, cherished, and loved. It was like being in a fairytale. She just needed her new passport to arrive.

Moving back to the drafts file Sophie excitedly clicked on the second e-mail. Her loins contracted in pleasure as she imagined a second love note. *Two in one day!*

But opening it she suddenly realized it wasn't written by Hamid, but by one of his "brothers." Hamid had told her he had shared their password with them in case anything happened. Sophie gasped in horror as she read the terrible missive:

I regret to inform you that Hamid along with five other brothers died in battle last night, it began.

"No! It's not possible!" Sophie cried aloud, forgetting she was in the library.

Struggling for breath she reread the first line. Whoever had written it knew to leave the unsent mail in the draft folder.

He was a lion of Islam, the message continued, and he is surely in Paradise already, having died a martyr's death at the hands of the infidel dogs, may they rot in hell forever.

Sophie read and reread it, while sickening bile rose up burning her throat. Sophie ran her fingers across the screen trying vainly to reach Hamid through her fingertips. Wasn't it just yesterday morning that his face had illuminated this screen, that his warm, manly voice had filled her ears with his strength and love?

Hamid, my love, Sophie moaned as she stared at the words that were making their way into her heart, freezing it into a hard knot.

"No, it can't be true," Sophie cried aloud again as she pounded the table and put her head down on her arms sobbing softly. "It's a trick…" she moaned as she grasped at straws.

"Miss, are you all right?" a kind voice coming up from behind her asked, as a soft hand touched her shoulder. Startled, Sophie jumped to her feet to see the librarian leaning over her, looking concerned. The librarian's eyes gazed into her face and then shifted to look at the screen.

"Sorry, yeah I'm fine," Sophie answered. "Just some bad news," she added as she quickly hit the log out button on their shared e-mail account and flicked off the computer screen. Sophie wiped her hand under her running nose and used her sleeve to dry her eyes as she turned to pick up her things and stood to exit the computer area.

Gazing around her, Sophie felt dizzy and disoriented, but somehow she made it home where she collapsed at the kitchen table sobbing into her arms.

After some time, her father walked into the kitchen and found her there still sobbing softly. "Sophie, what's wrong?" he asked gently as he wrapped his arms around her. "What happened?"

"It's Hamid," Sophie cried, letting her father's warm embrace encircle her. "He was killed last night."

"Hamid?" Jake asked in confusion, suddenly letting go and backing away. "Are you still in touch with him?" he asked, anger lacing his voice, his jaw flexing in sudden fury.

Sophie put her head back in her arms and sobbed some more.

"Sophie—are you really that stupid?" Jake shouted at her. "Those people are crazy! They are duping you into thinking what's happening in Syria and Iraq is all our fault. Don't you see, they're terrorists and they just want to use you!" he said through gritted teeth.

"No Dad, I don't see," Sophie cried out, raising her tear streaked face and pulling away from his touch. "I loved Hamid and I would have gladly died in his place!"

Jake stared at her in alarm. *What the hell is wrong with her anyway?* he asked.

"You don't know anything about me!" Sophie shrieked, as she backed away from him. "You have no idea how I feel about this country and the things we do to innocents all around the world!"

"Damn it Sophie!" Jake said taking a step toward her.

"No Dad," she screamed in rage. "I hate this country, I hate our murderous military and I hate you if you are on their side!"

Jake stared in shock, too speechless to reply.

Meanwhile, Sophie turned away and ran down the stairs to her room, where she threw herself on her bed and beat the mattress as she cried and screamed into her pillow until she finally exhausted herself and fell into a dreamless, troubled sleep. Even Colin's groping hands couldn't find her in this deep, black vortex into which she had suddenly tumbled.

Mission

I will avenge his death, please help me, Sophie wrote to the brothers in Iraq as she sat at the library computer again, glancing around her to be sure no one could see what she was writing. She remembered all that had happened to her, Colin's cruel hands pinning her to the lounge chair, his body pummeling into hers, his cruel words about being all grown-up.

Well now I am grown-up and I can decide for myself how I'll punish evildoers, Sophie bitterly thought as she continued her missive. I am willing to die in the path of Allah, she wrote. I don't have my passport yet, so traveling is difficult, but I am willing to carry out any action here. I am a good shot. She left the letter unsent in the drafts folder of her littlebird account hoping one of the brothers would soon discover and read it.

At work Sophie took care of the elderly patients in a haze of grief. All she could remember is Hamid's kind smile, his excitement over her beauty and his warm promises of making a family together and the lovemaking they would enjoy. *It's all ruined,* Sophie thought as she dumped the shit from some old man's bedpan into the toilet and came back to wash off his backside. *This is all that's left of my life—shit, literal shit day in and day out,* she thought as hot tears dripped down her face.

"Are you crying?" the elderly man asked.

"No, just allergies," Sophie answered, turning away from him and dropping the soiled wet wipes into the garbage can. "I'll be back soon," she said excusing herself from his room.

How can I go on? Sophie thought as she holed up in the ladies room, wiping the tears that wouldn't stop coming and blowing her nose until it was rubbed raw.

"I'm not feeling well today," Sophie told her supervisor. "I need to go home."

At home Sophie sat in her basement room and stared at the walls. Anwar al-Awlaki's kindly eyes stared out at her. *He's dead too,* Sophie thought dejectedly. *If only I could join them both in jannah!*

The next day, Sophie's hands shook as she sat at the library computer and clicked on the reply.

I am Hamid's brother, one of the brothers wrote. My name is Samir, and I know he was waiting anxiously for you to arrive. He had the house and everything ready for you in Raqqa. Are you sure you don't want to come and join the brothers here? He wrote. There are many mujahideen who need wives.

No, I want to avenge his death. I want to strike inside the belly of the beast, Sophie wrote back. And I can't travel anyway, as I don't have my passport. Help me please, she answered, anxiously hoping for a reply.

The next morning there was another letter. Buy a disposable phone and text your new number to this number 703-571-2246 when you have it in hand. I am Jamal and I'm here in the States, the e-mail sitting in her drafts folder read.

In the next weeks Jamal and Sophie texted back and forth by phone, as he helped her to make a plan. Jamal liked her original assassination plan— to strike her state's Senator to punish him for voting for the airstrikes in Iraq, although they bandied around other targets as well.

***

At home Jake wasn't sure how to approach his daughter anymore. Walking into her room one night he asked, "Who are all these Arab men on your walls?"

"Warriors of Allah," Sophie answered coldly as she stared him down. "Great men of God, all killed by the evil American drones. Something to be proud of Dad," she added sarcastically.

"Soph, are you still going to join ROTC?" Jake asked hopefully, thinking that this is what she desperately needed to straighten herself out.

"No, Dad, that's never going to happen," she answered, her eyes boring coldly into him.

Flustered by a daughter that had rarely stood up to him over the years, now seeming totally unfazed by his disapproval, Jake backed away and went back upstairs. He figured it was better to let her cool off and circle back on the ROTC plan later.

Who is this person my daughter has turned into? he wondered silently. *Am I to blame?*

***

Are you brave enough for this mission, sister? Jamal asked her via text.

Yes, I am so ready to join Hamid in Paradise, Sophie texted back, her face resolute, her heart racing with resolve. *I can't wait to exit this dirty world and join Hamid,* a desperate voice inside cried out.

Then, if you are sure, I will send a brother with a suicide vest for you, Jamal texted to Sophie's new phone. You must wear the clothing of the infidels and hide your weapon under your clothing and then get very close to him. The brother I am sending to you will show you how to detonate it. Wait till the last moment—when you get as close as possible—then you send him to hell and buy your ticket to paradise.

As Sophie waited for her "package" to arrive she began joining family meals again after work. Looking at her mother who spent half her suppers with her laptop open at the table, drinking glass after glass of wine and her father who seemed so lonely, Sophie felt a well of pity for them arising in her heart. *They'll never know the joys of jannah,* she thought silently as she watched them. *Soon I'll be drinking milk and honey in paradise with Hamid.*

They have no idea, she thought. *But I will earn them entrance to Paradise,* she reminded herself, thinking of the hadiths she had learned about the rewards of martyrdom. Dying a martyr would earn her the ability to bypass the final Day of Judgment and gain immediate entrance to Paradise, and then upon their deaths she could win favor from Allah for seventy of her relatives who could also bypass the Day of Judgment and be able to join her there. *Then they will understand,* Sophie reminded herself.

Meanwhile Sophie pushed away the constant fears that entered her mind of what it would be like to put on a bomb belt and explode herself. Instead she focused on becoming a martyr and instantly purified. *I'm ready to exit this dirty world,* Sophie reflected as she thought of moving instantly at the push of a button into a new reality—Paradise—where Hamid was already waiting for her.

Strangely, contemplating taking her own life—while murdering the infidel Senator—made her feel a sense of drugged out bliss. And as she imagined herself bypassing death and carrying on straight to Paradise to meet Hamid again she felt a growing sense of euphoria buoying her up. Sophie was about to meet her maker—and she felt only ecstasy.[65]

Ecstasy Delivered

He's going to meet you outside of Denver, Jamal texted. Can you drive to Estes Park? He's staying at the Stanley Hotel, and has the package for you there. Room 302.

Yes, of course, Sophie texted back. When?

Tomorrow, the answer flashed on her phone.

Senator Durham was scheduled to give a speech three days from today. If everything went according to plan, Sophie would be in Paradise very soon. Her heart fluttered with excitement as she went to look in the mirror.

I'll be with you in three more days, Hamid, she promised. *Then we will hold our wedding party in Paradise. That is if you are not too busy with the virgins.* That was the only thought that disturbed her—would they marry in Paradise? She'd waited so long for Hamid.

The next day Sophie called in sick to work. "I've got a fever and can't stop puking," she lied to her boss. "I don't want to spread this around, especially to our elderly folks. I think I'll be out for the rest of the week." *He bought it,* Sophie thought with satisfaction after hanging up.

Then she sat down and wrote her last will and testament. Dear Mom and Dad, Sophie wrote. At the time you read this I'll already be in Paradise. I will have punished those who kill innocents in Iraq. Please don't mourn for me; I am with Allah and in perfect peace. And I have rejoined Hamid. Please Mom and Dad, listen to my plea. You need to convert to Islam. Through my actions, I will make a way for you to Paradise, but you must convert. I hope you understand I had to stand up against the evils in this world and the terrible attacks on Muslims in Iraq. I'm sorry I wasn't the daughter you always wanted. Please forgive me. I'll see you in the afterlife. Love, Halima

Sealing it in a letter addressed to her father, Sophie took it out to the mailbox and plunked it in. *Should arrive a day or two after I'm in Paradise,* Sophie thought as she walked back to the house. *I hope they'll eventually understand and be proud of me.*

Next, Sophie packed a small bag and then headed out on the I-25 toward Estes Park. About forty-five minutes out of town, after passing Boulder, the Rocky Mountains came into view—snow covered blue peaks lining the sky. She knew all their names—the tallest was Longs Peak and beside it was the pristine Storm Peak. Her father had taken her hiking there as a child. As Sophie looked up at the snowy peaks she felt her soul rising up and mingling among them. Contemplating ending her life as a "martyr" was filling her mind with a strange euphoria that made it seem like she was barely in her body anymore, but instead floating above it blissfully, *about to depart for Paradise.* The ecstasy of leaving this dirty world behind and becoming totally pure was filling her with an exultation she didn't fully understand.

Perhaps it is a gift from Allah to help me be brave in fulfilling my mission? Sophie thought as she basked in what seemed to be the religious elation of her soon to be "martyrdom."

Sophie briefly remembered how she'd floated out of her body when Colin had raped her, how she had watched from above, momentarily detached from her senses as he tore into her body causing her overwhelming physical and emotional pain. This was completely different. Now she was floating above her body in total ecstasy—ready to depart, to join Hamid, to carry out her mission. It was a religiously imbued ecstasy, the euphoric blessedness of a soon to be "martyr," surely delivered to her as a gift from her all-knowing and merciful Allah. Now, she felt like she was hardly inhabiting her body, but it wasn't out of a sense of terror or shame. It was because she was nearly there—one step out of this world, the next into Paradise with Hamid.

Driving into Estes Park, Sophie used the GPS on her phone to locate the Stanley Hotel. Pulling her car into the parking lot, Sophie saw that the hotel was a grand, old massive building with immaculate white siding and a red tile roof. The American flag flew above it atop a white cupola and five

American flags waves waved to her from flagpoles above the colonnaded porch. Smirking at them, Sophie thought, *You won't wave so proudly after I finish my mission.*

Parking her car, Sophie walked up the wide stairs into the plush lobby and without asking directions, went searching to find room 302. It turned out to be down a long, plush red-carpeted hallway. Sophie felt like a disembodied ghost already, floating down it. Raising her hand she tapped on the door.

A handsome Mediterranean, bearded face opened the door. "You are Halima?' the young man asked.

"Yes, I am here to receive a package," Sophie answered smiling into his warm brown eyes.

"Come in," the man said, furtively looking up and down the hallway as he opened the door for her. Passing by him Sophie caught the scent of musky cologne and noticed his strong build. "I am Yousef," he said gently smiling down at her as Sophie noticed the antique table and chairs and gold plush pillows and bedspread covering the king size bed in the luxurious suite he was staying in. "Alhamdulillah! You are more beautiful than Hamid shared with us," he added as he closed the door behind him.

Sophie felt a thrill and also a sense of alarm. "Don't worry I won't lay a hand on a sister," Yousef reassured her, reading her thoughts although he continued to look her up and down. "You are pure as the snow on the mountains, as beautiful as our Prophet's young wife, Fatima," he said as he gazed appreciatively at her.

Sophie's heart leapt suddenly as his compliments and gentle, poetic way of speaking reminded her of Hamid. For a slight moment, she felt as if he was Hamid.

As Yousef continued speaking, Sophie barely heard what he was saying. She was here, but not really present. She felt as though making this decision to become a "martyr" had already taken her away. She was here in body only. Her soul had already disembarked on its way to Hamid.

From what seemed a great distance she heard Yousef say, "Let's get to work," as he turned into the room and began laying out the equipment to use in their attack. The next hours Yousef spent explaining how to get close to the Senator and showing Sophie how to operate her suicide vest. "These are the wires that activate the detonator, Yousef said as he showed Sophie how the wires were disconnected and how they would later be fitted into a detonating device when she was ready to activate. "We'll connect them like this—when you are ready for your mission," Yousef told her as he showed how she should connect them and activate the detonating device in the end—just before she approached her target.

"Now you should try it on," Yousef instructed.

Sophie took the vest from his hands, her own hands shaking as she placed her arms into it and let Yousef wrap it around her body. Suddenly the euphoria she'd been feeling all this time jolted up to a whole other level, flooding her brain and body a hundred times more powerfully with pure joy and ecstasy. Despite knowing her feet were still on the ground, Sophie now felt her spirit soaring way high above and out of her body. While it was the same disembodied feeling she had experienced in the rape—this time it was pleasure-filled, banishing any and all fear of dying in this way.

"I feel like I'm in Paradise already," Sophie gasped as she turned her enraptured face to Yousef.

"You are a holy warrior now, my sister. All things are possible for you," Yousef answered, mirroring her excitement.

"Yes, I know!" Sophie answered bursting into tears of joy.

Sophie also felt a sudden rush of power move through her body as she looked down at the explosive vest encapsulating her. She was suddenly an empowered force—like a force of nature—that nothing could stop. Smiling with the explosive vest strapped around her, she spun around in a circle.

"Let's be careful with this," Yousef said as he carefully unwrapped and removed the vest from her body as Sophie smiled again in pure pleasure. *Nothing will stop me now!* Sophie thought as she knew now, for certain, she would carry out her mission.

"You know all your sins are instantly forgiven when you martyr yourself," Yousef explained, his voice turning suddenly into a wheedling tone, as he rested his hands gently on her shoulders, running one of them along her long, flowing blonde hair.

"You are so beautiful—too beautiful to die a virgin," he added wistfully, as he kissed her neck gently. Sophie flinched and moved away from his hands. But somehow the tenderness of his touch and his physical admiration caught at something deep inside—painful emotions she could still access, despite the euphoria. He reminded her so much of Hamid that she felt torn in the face of his approval.

"I'm not a virgin," Sophie answered as her voice caught in a sob. "I was raped as a young girl."

Suddenly all the sordid images flooded her mind again. Colin pushing her down hard on the lounge chair, the wooden arm of it digging into her flesh, Colin's hands tearing at her clothes and her body, hurting her, and she unable to escape, Colin's hard voice telling her this is what it is to be *all grown-up.* Then her mind flashed to the pints of Ben & Jerry's and the acrid smell of vomit, the vodka shots and the horrible shame and terror of waking up at the party and finding her panties missing with no memory of what had happened. Suddenly, Sophie felt flooded again with shame, horror and self-loathing.

"To hell with the infidels," Yousef said pulling her close to his body, wrapping his arms gently around her. "That was before you took Islam, right?"

Sophie nodded while she let his arms enfold her. It felt safe to share her shame—as she had imagined it would be with Hamid. *These people accept and protect me,* Sophie thought as she let Yousef hold her while tears streamed down her cheeks. *This is how it was supposed to be with Hamid,* she realized, enjoying the comfort Yousef provided.

"All is forgiven when you come to Allah," Yousef crooned as he softly petted her blonde hair. "Oh my beautiful martyr," Yousef said pulling her hand gently, "come sit with me on the bed."

Sophie felt like a zombie as she let him lead her over to the bed. Yousef began kissing her again while Sophie felt dazed and confused by his attention.

Am I a slut or beautiful martyr? Who am I? she questioned, but no answers came. Without protesting she let Yousef part her lips and explore her mouth with his tongue. Meanwhile his hands went to her breasts, touching them gently through her clothes. It felt good but confusing.

This was supposed to be Hamid, Sophie thought from a million miles away.

"I don't think we should be doing this" Sophie said as she pulled away again while his hands were already exploring her body. Her voice felt far away from the body he was running his hands over.

She'd waited so long to be in Hamid's arms and now Yousef was offering himself to her. The way he was touching her, his gentle kisses, his moans of desire—it awoke something inside that she'd tried to keep buried for so long. All her longing and grief for Hamid suddenly awoke. Confusion, grief and dizziness all collided as her resistance waned. Sophie wanted and willed Yousef to be Hamid as she realized she wanted to be kissed, embraced and touched passionately—something she had not allowed anyone to do for so long.

"All is forgiven to the martyr," Yousef intoned as he continued kissing her neck, hands and arms. "You are so beautiful, my jewel!"

Yousef's attention and his gentleness felt so good, yet somewhere inside the haze of her crazy, conflicted emotions Sophie knew it wasn't right. She wasn't drunk. She had no excuse for this. Yet she didn't protest as she let him slowly begin to remove her clothing, making his way down her neck to her breasts and belly and finally reaching her underwear. Gently he pulled them off. Sophie made no protest as she floated above it all, now watching from above.

"Let me make love to you as you deserve my beautiful martyr, my hero for Allah. You know that the mujahideen need comfort too my sister. To give comfort to me now is to show your love for Allah," Yousef pleaded as his breath came ragged now with desire.

In her bliss-filled state of mind, completely absorbed with the fact that she was about destroy the very body he was begging to make love to, Sophie felt a detached absence of feelings. Letting him push her gently back on the bed, Sophie made no protest while she allowed Yousef's hands to move along her legs and inside her thighs.

Normally, she would have been terrified of a man's hands upon her—she'd even worried about being with Hamid—if she could stay present as he made love to her, but now Sophie felt nothing. It seemed his request was of no real consequence, given that she was about to strap on a bomb and explode herself. Suddenly nothing felt wrong or scary anymore.

Sophie felt only a very far removed delight as she allowed Yousef to duck his head between her thighs and expertly pleasure her, sending tingles running throughout her body. Suddenly Sophie's back arched with her first orgasm as she felt again that she was back, inside her body. She involuntarily let out a long moan of pleasure.

So this is what it's supposed to be like? She thought as thrilling undulations coursed through her limbs and up her spine.

Am I wrong to let him do this? she pondered from a very detached place in her head. *I'll soon be exiting this world anyway,* she thought. *No. Nothing matters anymore—nothing and no one. My sins will all be forgiven and I will soon be in Paradise for my martyrdom…*

Sophie was determined. Only one fact remained. She would carry out her mission and pour out her anger at the world injustices and humiliations in one final act of rage and then she was going to be with Hamid in jannah.

Let Yousef take his pleasure with my body—it isn't long for this world, she rationalized from thoughts that hardly felt like her own anymore.

Yousef didn't stop at one orgasm. Delighted with his success, he pleasured her again and again before finally asking her, "May I enter you now, sister?"

"Yes!" Sophie whispered. Her mind was so far away at this point she had no real idea what she was doing.

Hamid! She whispered as he entered her gently. *Hamid, I'm coming to you.*

Zombie Zone

The next morning Yousef begged Sophie for sex again—and again she allowed him to use her body as he wished while she experienced it all from a very detached vantage point. As the day before he was careful to pleasure her before taking his own pleasure, and again she imagined it was not Yousef, but Hamid making love to her.

What does it matter what I do with this body before destroying it? Sophie thought as Yousef came inside her. Yet, despite her total detachment from her body, deep inside something felt wrong—*this can't be okay,* Sophie realized when the rare, rational thought entered her already numbed-out and bliss-filled mind.

It's okay, another voice argued as she submitted to him—*I'm offering comfort to the brothers—our holy warriors.*

Finishing, Yousef rose from the bed and ordered breakfast to the room as they began to plan their attack.

"He's coming to a rally at the Civic Center park in Denver tomorrow," Sophie explained when they finished their breakfast of pancakes piled high in strawberries and cream. She showed Yousef what she had learned, while together they studied websites they pulled up on his laptop.

"If I get there early and get a spot right in the front, I should be able to approach him after his speech," Sophie explained. "They usually let some of the participants get near him—but the time will be short before he departs."

"You are so brave," Yousef praised her, although he no longer met her eyes as he had the day before—some shame at using her body lingered on his face as well, making it impossible for him to look directly into her eyes. "But what a pity to lose such a beauty," he said brushing his hand through her hair. He was fascinated with her long blonde hair.

Sophie pushed the compliment away. She couldn't afford to let herself become attached to Yousef. *I'm leaving this dirty world,* Sophie reminded herself.

"What about security? Can I pass through a metal detector with this vest?" Sophie asked, ignoring his hand running through her hair. *I've got to finish this—join Hamid.*

"There is very little metal in it, but if you must go through a metal detector you should have some distractions to throw them off," Yousef answered, his eyes narrowing as he became serious, focusing again on their mission. "It would be good if your clothing has non-removable metal parts so if you buzz, they will attribute it to that—perhaps a shirt and pants with metal ornaments sewn into it? And you must wear bulky enough clothes so that if they pat you down they can't feel it underneath," Yousef warned.

"I'll go out and buy a corset today with metal hooks and eyes. I can wear that over the vest and a thick cable knit sweater over that. I'll find one with metal loops sewn in around the waist," Sophie answered.

"Wear metal hair clips and metal in your boots as well," Yousef added. "It will confuse them completely if you don't pass the metal detectors. They won't be able to know what it is, as you take things off and it still buzzes—I've seen that work already."

"And if they catch me?" Sophie asked.

"Then you must detonate prematurely," Yousef answered, his face suddenly solemn. "Even if you don't hit our target, it will all be in the service of Allah. And it will still strike fear in their hearts."

D-Day

The next morning Sophie rose early for first prayers, leaving Yousef lying in the bed beside her. Washing herself carefully she prepared to pray for the last time of her life. Standing in her plush white hotel bathrobe before Allah, on the bath mat she used for a prayer rug, she thought before beginning her prayers, *Hamid, I come to you today.*

Although in truth, Hamid had faded a bit from memory and was confused now with Yousef. Finishing her prayers, Sophie thought back with a smile to how Yousef had held her close throughout the night. *It was a sin,* Sophie thought, *but after today all my sins are gone,* she told herself as she gazed at her face in the bathroom mirror. *Finally, I'll be purified—entering Paradise.*

Sophie padded across the carpet to the bed and gently woke Yousef by shaking him lightly. "It's time," she said softly.

Yousef sat up and stretched, then rose naked from the king bed and went to the bathroom to shower. Emerging in his white hotel robe and slippers he went to the chest of drawers and pulled the explosive vest out from its hiding place behind Sophie's clothes. He carefully unwrapped it as Sophie readied her clothing.

Standing in her underwear he strapped it carefully on her body. "Stand still, my beauty," Yousef said as he worked. Then Sophie pulled her new corset up over her thighs and began hooking it shut over the explosive vest wrapped around her lower waist. *I'm wearing the sexy lingerie you asked for, Hamid,* Sophie thought as she carefully fastened the line of hook and eyes that led straight up to her lacy brassiere. The explosives made her look heavier than usual but were easily concealed inside her new corset.

"Wait," Yousef said, remembering to thread the wires to the detonating device through one of the gaps between the hooks that he reopened. Then Sophie pulled her turtleneck sweater over her head and carefully pulled it in place over the corset and down over her leggings. Patting herself carefully, Sophie checked to be sure there were no protrusions. Yousef did the same.

"I need to thread the wires down your sleeve," Yousef said, lifting her sweater again. Seeing her breasts exposed above her bra, he gazed first at them admiringly. "You are very brave and painfully beautiful," he said as he carefully threaded the wires from the opening in her corset up under her arm and back down the sleeve of the turtleneck sweater where he carefully fastened the first of them to the detonating device. Checking to be sure it was in the inactive position, Yousef broke out into a cold sweat as he fastened the second wire. Then, sighing in relief that he had done everything right, he carefully tucked the plastic detonating device inside the sleeve of Sophie's sweater.

"There, you can pull it out and put it in your hand when you are ready," he explained. "You see how to slide the switch to active mode?" he asked pulling it back out to show her. "And this button is for detonating. You remember? But you have to switch it on first," he instructed as a look of concern crossed his face.

"Yes," Sophie answered solemnly. She felt dizzy contemplating it and very far away from the room right now, lost in the euphoric bliss again.

"Here," Yousef said handing her the long pullover sweater that she had bought the day before. It had an attached metal link belt sewn into the sweater along the waistline. Yousef helped her pull it over her head and down over her body. "This will throw off *any* metal detector," Yousef commented. "They'll be so confused by it all," he added, standing back to view his work.

Taking a high-heeled pair of leather boots out of her closet—also new, Sophie pulled them up over her leggings, knowing they would distract any security guards as well. Placing a scarf around her neck, large sunglasses on her face, gloves on her hands and a coat atop it all she and Yousef left the hotel room and walked silently out to her car.

It was a sunny cloudless day and Sophie felt the ecstasy spreading to every cell in her body. With every breath of the crisp spring air she felt it enter her, flooding her mind and leaving her tingling down to her fingers and toes. "Be brave," Yousef said as he held the door for her. They didn't embrace as Sophie nodded. She she sat zombie-like in the driver's seat and Yousef closed the door behind her.

"Goodbye," Sophie softly said as she waved through the window. Sophie could hardly concentrate on the road as she headed back toward Denver. It seemed her spirit was already soaring upward, leaving her body spilling out on the road behind her. Looking around her she noticed again the huge rock formations rising up behind the hotel, the blue foothills beyond that, all of it surrounding her as she sped off toward her target. It seemed to Sophie as she drove through the valley, and saw far in the distance the snow covered peaks along the skyline, that they were also reaching for the heavens, rising up as she soon would, to praise Allah. Their majesty mirrored her lifted spirits.

After a few hours, according to plan, Sophie arrived at the Civic Center Park early and was one of the first of those assembled waiting to enter the rally before the Senator arrived.

Hamid, I will come to you today, Sophie thought as she walked in her black, high heeled boots toward the park, happy that her act today would erase all her wrong doings, purifying her for her celestial journey to join her intended husband.

Honey Trap

"Holy shit!" Ken exclaimed staring at his monitor. His eyes zipped across the screen as he read once more the e-mail just arriving across the classified SIPRNet. It was from headquarters and warned about a potential, imminent attack against a Senator. Jumping up from his desk, Ken raced over to find Cathy and her team.

"We've got a situation," Ken exclaimed. "It just came in—a warning about an active suicide attack against a U.S. Senator."

"Oh that's great—there's only a hundred of them," Russell quipped.

"Where does it originate from?" Cathy asked seeing how serious Ken's face was. "How reliable is it?"

"The Intel was picked up from the Syrians. They used a honey trap," Ken answered.

"Syria?" Cathy asked, her voice rising in doubt.

"Yes, Syria. It's an intercept, but I think it's reliable," Ken answered. "The ISIS guys are looking for wives. Well, the Syrians got smart and started tweeting from fake accounts and putting up fake Facebook sites, pretending to be women interested in becoming jihadi brides. Then they started chatting with the ISIS guys and when it got far enough along, the ISIS cadres predictably asked for a photo."

"The fake account set up by the Syrians sent out a sexy photo, but the Syrians included malware along with it that lifted everything from the guy's phone, the minute he opened the picture," Ken explained. "Well one of these lifts picked up plans about a suicide bomber here in the States, ready to attack. And the target is a U.S. Senator—someone who voted for bombing ISIS. I think this is serious and reliable Intel."

"Holy shit," Russell commented, breaking out into a wicked smile. "That is an awesome move. The honey trap of all traps!"

"Okay, knowing that he voted for the airstrikes in Iraq narrows it down a bit," Cathy commented, moving to her monitor. "Let's check how our Senators voted." After a few minutes of checking her screen, Cathy lifted her head and reported, "Bad news, both our Senators voted in favor of the airstrikes."

"Okay so both our Senator's are potential targets," Ken commented. "Let's find out where they are right now and let's up their security."

Cathy and Russell went back to their desks and starting calling the Denver police to find out where they were and to alert them of a potential attack. Operation Noble Defense was rolling into motion.

A Father's Concern

"Is this Mr. Follett?" Ken heard on the other end of the line. "I'm Sophie Lindsay's father."

"Yes, I'm Ken Follett," Ken answered wondering what had given Mr. Lindsay the occasion to call. Since his daughter had reverted back from her crazy obsession with Islam and stopped wearing her abaya and niqab, and posting in support of pro-ISIS sites, she had fallen off Ken's radar.

"You said I should call if I'm ever concerned about Sophie..." Jake said, hesitating for a few moments, his head swirling in a cloud of confusion.

"Yeah, is anything wrong?" Ken asked.

"Well, I thought she was through with that Muslim bit," Jake faltered. Then his voice broke into sobs.

"Mr. Lindsay?" Ken spoke into the phone. "What is it?"

"It's Sophie," Jake said. "I think she's going to explode herself," he said, his voice choking with emotion.

"What?" Ken asked.

"She wrote us a letter and it says that she is going to 'martyr' herself and that she's going to Paradise," Jake explained, his voice breaking in pain. "I don't think she's going to Iraq anymore—her boyfriend was killed. I think she's going to do something here. Oh God," Jake moaned.

"Mr. Lindsay, are you at home?" Ken asked.

"Yes," Jake answered.

"I'm sending a car around for you," Ken explained. "Bring that letter with you. Thank you for calling. We'll help you save your daughter."

Hanging up the phone, Ken stood and started shouting to his colleagues in the Fusion Center. "Sophie Lindsay, the white Muslim convert we were following is potentially on a suicide mission. Does anyone know where Senator Durham and Senator Thomas are today?"

"Senator Thomas is in Washington, D.C., but Senator Durham is scheduled this afternoon for a political rally at Civic Center Park in Denver," Cathy answered. "He's going to take the podium in the next twenty minutes actually."

"We need to stop him," Ken shouted. "We've got a live one!"

"Let's go," Cathy shouted to her partner. "Ken, you coming?" she called as they made their way to their unmarked FBI car. Ken grabbed his coat and ran to catch up with them as Cathy began dialing the Denver police force that was responsible for protecting the Senator. "There's a possible suicide attack on Senator Durham. You need to get him to safety now!"

Meanwhile, Ken opened his phone and taking an old "uncovered" photo from Sophie Lindsay's Facebook page sent it out to the Denver police to create an all points bulletin of the suspected terrorist. Next, he called the driver picking up Sophie's father and told him, "Bring Mr. Lindsay to the rally..."

End Game

Sophie joined a short line of people as she approached the entrance to the outdoor political rally. Looking ahead she saw that there was a security tent set up at the entrance with metal detectors and guards searching purses and the bodies of those who set off the detectors. A wave of fear spread over her body as she stopped in her tracks looking at the security set up. *What if they find my bomb?* Then forcing the terror out of her mind Sophie reminded herself of the power she held strapped to her body.

Taking a deep breath she accessed the bliss again. *Hamid, I'm coming to you,* she thought as she stepped forward. Taking a deep breath and calming herself, Sophie opened her purse and quickly, before she reached the checkpoint, grabbed for some change to put in the pockets of her sweater to create even more diversions. Then numbing her emotions, she stepped forward. Sophie looked at the guard, trying to keep fear out of her eyes and face as she placed her open purse on the folding table for the guards to search. *It's just like the airport,* she reminded herself as she passed through the scanner. It buzzed.

"Please step back, ma'am," the guard instructed.

"Oh, it must have been these coins," Sophie said emptying her sweater pockets and placing the coins on the table near her purse. Her heart started beating faster as she stepped again through the detector.

It buzzed again. Sophie gasped and felt her knees go weak. "You think it could be my hair clips?" Sophie asked as she tried to suppress the shaking in her voice as she unfastened the two metal clips she had put into her hair to confuse things. She laid them down beside the coins. As she did so, she tossed her long blonde hair free over her shoulders and asked, "Should I go through again?" looking toward the metal detector.

"No," the guard answered picking up a wand. Starting at her head he ran the wand down her body. It buzzed near her bra where the wires were and at the waist where the metal belt was sewn in to the sweater and again when he came to her boots that were adorned with a thick metal zippers and metal coated toes. "You've got a lot of metal on your clothing," he commented.

"Yeah, could be my underwire bra too," Sophie volunteered as she fought back the terror filling her stomach and rising up to her chest. She forced her hands not to shake as she purposely readjusted her bra and looked him in his eyes, smiling innocently.

"You're good," the guard said, blushing as he motioned her forward with his wand, turning to the next person to pass through the detector.

Sophie's heart pounded hard as she moved ahead.

***

"Senators don't have body guards when they're away from the Capitol, do they?" Ken asked from the passenger seat, as Cathy steered their unmarked car out of the parking lot, into traffic. A Denver police escort screeched alongside and overtook them, its lights flashing and siren blaring as Cathy pulled their FBI car up behind it and together they began racing at top speeds toward the park.

"No, they don't," Russell answered with his usual know-it-all voice booming from the backseat. "Although some of them have started wearing concealed weapons. Let's just hope his aides are packing something, or we get there in time!"

Ken and Cathy exchanged worried glances as they sped along behind the Denver police car, sirens blaring and forcing all the cars in their path to the sides. Looking in the rearview mirror, Ken noticed they'd picked up another police car from behind.

***

Sophie could feel the blood whooshing in her ears and her legs felt like they could give out beneath her as she walked up to the front and staked out a space near the stage. The fear was climbing up her shoulders now and spreading down her arms as well. Her head felt heavy and everything seemed far away.

Hamid, I'm coming to you, Sophie recited inside her mind as she forced herself into the calm numbness and again felt the bliss pushing the terror back down that had been rising from the pit of her stomach. *I'll be joining you in Paradise soon...*

Slowly the crowds filled in and Sophie saw that the Senator had also arrived. Flanked by two aides, he walked up and took the podium where he gave a big smile and started thanking some of the other dignitaries on the platform before launching into his speech. As he spoke Sophie edged closer and brought her hands together. With her left hand she reached into her right sleeve, her hands visibly shaking now, and drew the detonator switch down into her right hand.

***

Racing through traffic Cathy felt frustration as the police sirens and flashing lights cleared traffic out of the way. "We're not going fast enough," she complained as her foot twitched over the accelerator. "We're not going to get there in time," she said glancing over to Ken.

"Why don't those stupid aides answer their phones?" Russell cried out from the back as he again dialed all the numbers they had for the Senator and his entourage.

"She's going to do it," Ken suddenly said, his voice somber as his eyes met Cathy's.

"No, she can't," Cathy gasped in disbelief. "She a troubled kid, not a killer!" Yet deep inside Cathy realized overwhelming pain could often translate into dangerousness—like an animal beaten and cornered can suddenly lash out. She'd seen it before in other criminals. Hurt people reaching a breaking point and suddenly striking out at others. *Was Sophie one of them?*

Can't these guys go any faster? Cathy wondered as she listened to the police feed coming over the radios. *Why don't the Senator's aides answer their phones?*

Maddeningly the police car in front of them slowed at a red light as he waited for traffic to pull over. Ken took the opportunity to reach over to hold Cathy's hand.

As traffic cleared, she realized he was squeezing her hand so hard it hurt.

Unstoppable

It was time for questions. "Senator! Senator!" the voices around her rang out. Reporters nearby vied for position, jostling Sophie as they competed for the Senator's attention.

The time had come. A surge of energy passed through her as Sophie also rushed forward with her left arm raised. Waving, she shouted at the top of her lungs, "Senator Durham!" Her voice seemed detached, disembodied.

"Why?" came the unfamiliar bark from her throat. "Why did you vote for the airstrikes in Iraq?"

Sophie felt the stares around her, the bodies moving back to give her a little more space, just as they did when she was wearing her black burqa and niqab—looking like a threatening raven. She realized she was unstoppable. A force of nature. And they—a part of her was suddenly aware—felt her power as much as she did.

The Senator stepped forward and turned in her direction to answer. Brows furrowed, he looked into her face and opened his mouth to answer.

Sirens.

The Senator looked up in their direction, confused. The audience also turned to witness ten or more police cars suddenly screeching into the park area. Policemen piled out of the cars and started running toward the Senator, shouting as they ran. Sophie saw that among them were the two FBI agents who had questioned her earlier, also running and shouting. The man was slower, but the woman was sprinting. Her hair, falling loose from its hair clip, trailed like a red streak behind her. Pistol in one hand, her eyes scanned the crowd as she ran.

Sophie watched as the red haired FBI agent suddenly spotted her. Locking eyes for a second, Sophie felt a moment of fear rush down to her feet, freezing her in place. Then she turned away, back to her target knowing she was strong and unstoppable.

No one, not even this FBI lady, can stop me now, Sophie thought, her mind steadfast, as she edged closer with steely determination toward the Senator. *This is my day to enter Paradise, and no one can stop me now.*

With an almost imperceptible movement, Sophie opened her right hand. She took a split second to look downward, just enough to see the sliding switch.

Using her thumbnail she slid it into activated mode.

***

Don't do it, Cathy thought as she raced toward Sophie. No longer in her niqab, Cathy easily recognized Sophie from her Facebook photos, although her face looked deathly pale now as she moved toward the Senator.

You're just a scared kid, Cathy thought as she weighed her options, considered if she could take a shot. *No, there are way too many people surrounding her to take her out that way,* Cathy realized as she ran toward Sophie.

I'm going to have to throw myself on her and hope she can't detonate before I disarm her.

***

I'm almost there Hamid, Sophie thought as her ears were filled with the sound of police sirens wailing in the distance. Her right hand trembled as she held the detonator ready. Her heart was beating hard inside her ribcage and her breath became shallow as she pushed forward toward the Senator.

Glancing back to the FBI lady and the police running toward them Sophie was shocked to see her father getting out of a car and running toward her as well.

Dad? Sophie thought as she turned back in numb confusion to the Senator and her reason for being here.

"Get down! Get the Senator down. Get down!" Sophie heard the female FBI agent screaming in the distance.

Sophie saw out of the corner of her eye that policemen were closing in on them as the Senator still stood on the stage with his aides, looks of fear and consternation filling their faces. People around Sophie had started to turn and run away. One of his aides began pulling on the arm of his suit coat. Some of the people began screaming and the crowd was thinning as most ran from the stage.

***

Running at top speed Cathy sprinted across the field separating them. *Daniela!* she gasped inside her head, knowing what she needed to do. *I'm sorry, so sorry Daniela…*

Cathy's heart contracted in pain as she ran—not from the physical effort but from the possibility of leaving her daughter in this way. It was the risk of the job, the cost of providing security for all, although Cathy recognized she did this job for Daniela, more than any other child.

And this girl she longed to shoot right now, but knew she couldn't risk doing so, seemed like another Daniela, although hurt, confused—and now lethal. Cathy's lungs burned as she pushed her legs to run faster toward her target. Realizing she might not make it in time, Cathy raised her pistol in the air and fired warning shots as she shouted, "No, Sophie, stop!"

Milk and Honey

Everything moved in slow motion. From far away she heard the warning shots and the FBI lady screaming.

Suddenly a lifetime of events flashed through her mind as Sophie took her final steps. The images were disjointed, big Technicolor pictures flashing up on the movie screen inside her head. *Colin's face, as he smiled at the bar, asking if she wanted a drink. Perching on the swing as a little girl begging her mother, "Higher Mommy! Push me higher! Her little legs pumping as she floated up into the sky. Her father's face—a mix of disappointment, anger and contempt. The vodka bottles, undigested puke in the toilet, Colin's semen inside her, the smell and shame of it all.*

A final picture flashed into Sophie's mind—*unveiling herself for Hamid and his look and words of pleasure as she unfurled her hair and showed him herself—naked, in a way ,to her very soul. And he'd accepted her.*

A calm descended on her.

Hamid. *I'm coming to you, Hamid…*

"AllahuAkbar!" Sophie screamed as she pushed down hard on the detonator.

Fury

Ken ran behind Cathy trying to keep up with her, but he was no match for her adrenalin surging sprint. Scanning the crowd he saw Sophie too, uncovered now. She was the blonde, lithe, desirable looking Sophie he knew from Facebook. He ran watching her, knowing he was powerless to stop Sophie as he saw her pushing toward the Senator.

"No! Don't do it!" he yelled in a ragged voice above the murmurs and screams of the crowds that were already turning in panic, their faces filled with horror as some of them ran helter-skelter away from the stage and toward the police who were closing in on the Senator.

Ken turned his eyes back to Cathy, her red hair streaking out behind her as she ran toward Sophie. He pumped his legs to try to catch up to her. Cathy had her pistol drawn, but even he knew there was no way she could take a shot.

He'd studied it a million times: the only and best way to take out a suicide bomber was to shoot them in the head so they'd be totally and completely incapacitated and couldn't still detonate once downed. Cathy would never risk it here with Sophie still surrounded by crowds of panicked people.

No! She's going to throw herself on the girl, Ken suddenly realized as he saw Cathy gaining on Sophie. A sudden burst of energy spurted to his legs as he ran faster toward Cathy.

Don't do it! he screamed inside his head. *Don't throw yourself on her!*

***

In the next instant a blast of light and a roaring wave of sound. *Cathy! No! Cathy!* Ken cried.

A surge of raw energy ripped through the air carrying with it bits of flying, razor sharp metal, nails, bolts, broken glass and shrapnel. It slashed at lightning speed through flesh—piercing hearts and faces and separating limbs from bodies, flesh from bone. In its wake, a ball of fire erupted.

Somewhere in the chaos, the Senator and his aides lay in torn up fragments; their clothing ripped into pieces—some that were now on fire.

Near him, amidst the destruction, Sophie's corpse lay broken in pieces on the ground, her head ripped from her torso.

Screams filled the air along with the anguished moans of the injured as Ken ran frantically through the scene of destruction. He had only one thought—Cathy.

Not noticing, he ran past Sophie's father, Jake, lying bleeding and broken on the grass, knocked out by the explosion. His legs were still angled in his futile attempt to stop his daughter.

Ken hardly saw the burning bodies, dangerous debris, Sophie, or the Senator.

Cathy! his mind screamed. Then he was calling her name aloud. Shouting it, bellowing it from the depths of his being, his own anguished voice unfamiliar, his ears deafened from the bomb blast, as he desperately searched among the remains for her.

Body surging with frantic energy, he pushed past others hysterically searching through the corpses of the fallen, their faces shocked, looking like pale mirrors of death. Their anguished screams and the sirens roaring around him were all muted by a roaring silence reverberating inside his head.

"Cathy!" Ken cried out as he ran between the bloodied and torn bodies lying on the ground.

Then he saw her.

Cathy's form knocked down from the blast lay twisted to one side, her red hair splayed out around her bleeding face, flames on the ground licking at her clothing. Collapsing to his knees beside her, Ken saw that she was in shock, but still alive. Picking her up, Ken stood slowly and moved with her in his arms away from the others as he kicked at the flames nearby to extinguish them. Holding Cathy close, he looked around at all the carnage and sobbed as he stared down into her ghostly, pale white face—unconscious, yet still breathing. "Thank God, you're alive," he sobbed.

Cathy lay lifeless in his arms and all that Ken heard around him were the wails of the injured, but not yet dead. Then he saw it—a floating stream of white ash rising up from the fireball. The cloud of white smoke ascended like a pathway to paradise into the clear blue sky—the ashen white smoke separated the living from the dead as it rose upward, as though making a sacrificial offering to an unseen God. Although he couldn't make it out, he almost felt like he could hear voices murmuring within the cloud.

Looking up at it Ken felt fury rushing through his body knowing one thing was certain as he vowed inside his head, *I'll find you! Whoever planned this—whoever took this young, mixed up girl and made her into a killer—by God, I'll find you,"* Ken vowed.

Cathy will survive, Ken told himself as his mind raced in panic at the possibility of her internal injuries. *You'll be okay,* he softly said to her as a feeling of dread filled his chest while looking at her pale, white bleeding face.

Eyes blurry, ears ringing, he knew whether Cathy lived or died, he would never be the same. "You were right. You were right," he murmured softly to her. "We have to stop them early, before they hurt others. I'm so sorry."

Tears streaking down his face, Ken held Cathy's nearly lifeless body in his arms as he made his way slowly and with steely determination, through the chaos around him, toward the just arriving medics and first responders.

We'll make them pay for this! he promised. *The two of us—we'll hunt them down!*

Author's Note

Bride of ISIS is a work of fiction. However the book was *inspired* by a composite of real cases. The idea to write this book arose from reading about Shannon Conley, a Colorado teenager who converted to Islam, took the niqab, and who ultimately ended up in the clutches of ISIS. Conley was arrested in April 2014 while trying to board a flight to Turkey with the alleged goal of traveling to Syria to join and marry an extremist she had met online. When questioned by authorities Conley admitted that she wanted to use her American training in the Army Explorers to aide ISIS as they waged jihad on the United States.[66] Many would ask why would a "normal" American teen convert to Islam and then transition into terrorism? This book is an attempt to answer that question with one of many possible explanations.

Other real cases also inspired characters in the book. Abdur Rahman and the debate between Ken, Russell and Cathy over whether the sting operation moving him along the terrorist trajectory was entrapment is based on a combination of two real cases, one involving a sting operation, and both aimed at killing Senators.[67] Thus far U.S. courts have ruled in cases similar to the one described in this book that they *were not* entrapment, but others have argued otherwise.

The idea of volunteering for a suicide mission to revenge the death of one's lover comes also from a real case. Palestinian Arin Ahmed, who I interviewed while she was still in Israeli prison is an example of this. According to Arin, an Israeli missile assassinated her militant boyfriend. Within weeks she abandoned her academic studies and plan to become a banker in Kuwait and volunteered herself to Hamas for a suicide mission to avenge his death. She, like Sophie, dressed in Western clothes to carry her bomb into a crowded area. Ahmed was driven by her sender with another young male bomber into to a crowded Israeli area to create a series of deadly explosions. The male bomber detonated but Arin seeing a young baby suddenly had a pang of conscience that she described as realizing that "only Allah gives life and only Allah can take life." She called her sender asking to be taken home and was arrested shortly thereafter. In prison Arin came to the realization that the terrorist group had been more than willing to take advantage of her posttraumatic grief and bereavement over the death of her boyfriend and had no actual care for her.[68]

Likewise the Internet radicalization of a young woman is based on a real case. In 2010, Roshonara Choudhry, a top King's College student completely derailed her life and education by attempting to assassinate British MP Stephen Timms. Choudhry admitted to interrogators right after the attack that she had radicalized over a period of months after downloading and watching over a hundred hours of al-Awlaki videos during the months leading up to her attack. Her Internet mentor, Anwar al-Awlaki, who she had never met or communicated directly with, convinced her that it was her duty to take part in militant jihad and that if she could not come to the battleground then she needed to attack at home. Roshonara was the first al-Qaeda sympathizer to attempt an assassination in Britain. Completely changed by her immersion in extremism, the once successful student told her interrogators, "I wanted to die. I wanted to be a martyr."[69]

My research interviews with over four hundred actual terrorists, or in the case of those who have committed suicide—their hostages, family members and close associates, has shown that the lethal cocktail of terrorism consists of four ingredients: a group that has decided to use terrorism to try to promote it's political cause; an ideology that wrongly justifies the targeting of civilians to achieve that cause; social support—which is these days easily found over the Internet; and individual vulnerabilities.[70] In writing *Bride of ISIS* the goal was to explore the character of a young, seemingly "normal" American woman who joins ISIS—to explore what might cause her to convert and want to hide her body under an abaya and niqab and also to look at the powerful pull of the ISIS ideology (built largely upon the al-Qaeda one preceding it) and the captivating power of the Caliphate currently declared in Iraq and Syria.

The allure of the militant jihadi ideology and the way in which "martyrdom" operations can act as short-term psychological fixes for those who have psychological vulnerabilities and who suffer from posttraumatic stress disorder (PTSD) is also extremely real and based on many actual cases from the author's research.[71] While there is no evidence that Shannon Conley suffered *any* traumas in her life, the fictional character of Sophie is put on the terrorist trajectory as she grapples with trying to overcome her traumatic responses to rape. Estimates in the U.S. are that one out of six women has been the victim of an attempted or completed rape, and in one out of ten rapes, the victim is male. Children of all ages and both genders are also sexually molested at startling rates.[72] Rape and sexual abuse, as well as many other traumas occurring both inside and outside of conflict zones create real vulnerabilities that can create an opening for an individual to resonate to an ideology and a group that promises purity, empowers victims and offers a means of channeling anger into so called "righteous" causes. Of course most victims of rape will not ever encounter a terrorist ideology nor be drawn into terrorism, but sexual assault is a trauma that can create a powerful set of vulnerabilities to act out rage later in life.

Today's terrorism, particularly ISIS related terrorism builds on the teachings of Anwar al-Awlaki who also features prominently in the book as a real character. Al-Awlaki amazingly continues to inspire terrorism worldwide from beyond the grave—living on and inspiring lost individuals via the Internet into the militant jihadi ideology and then on to virulent acts of terrorism. His power to inspire even after death is explored as Sophie finds and begins to follow him into death.

Law enforcement officials today face great difficulty in battling homegrown terrorism. They are faced with thousands of what the FBI Director, James Comey calls "mouthrunners"—individuals who brag about being jihadis and who show extremist tendencies in their social media profiles, and even when interviewed. Yet, despite their bravado, only a few of them will actually take it to the next level and find a group to equip and encourage them or the means to self-activate. This creates a quandary for law enforcement as shown by Ken, Russell and Cathy as they try to identify the real threats among the thousands of possibilities and grapple as fictionalized in the case of Abdur Rahman and Sophie Lindsay, with how far they can go in pursuing the ones who appear serious.

The United States has not yet seen a homegrown suicide bomber slip through the law enforcement net. But it's clear that although ISIS has not yet sanctioned the use of female combatants, they will likely attempt to do so in the future. As reported in the book, ISIS recently announced that women who marry in their movement do not need permission of their husbands to become suicide bombers. Many terrorist movements who begin to use female operatives do so when needs dictate. That will likely be the next iteration for ISIS—using women as "martyrs" when they are hemmed in on all sides. Females have many advantages for terrorist groups—they can often pass security checkpoints more successfully and they garner more media attention for their attacks. This gives the terrorist group a double dividend for using women: greater chances for a successful attack and media amplification of its effects. Al Qaeda in Iraq, the precursor movement to ISIS, began to use female suicide terrorists when the going got rough for them. It's likely the same will occur with ISIS.[73]

Throughout the book there are endnotes that point out where events in the book were inspired by, or link to, actual cases. In the real case of Shannon Conley, she, like the fictional character of Sophie, changed her name to Halima after converting. Shannon Conley posted on social media under that name revealing some of what she was thinking as she delved deeper into extremism. For instance she listed her job on her Facebook page as "Slave to Allah." She also remarked on social media platforms, "But you prefer the worldly life while the hereafter is better and more enduring."

In the months leading up to her arrest Conley asked in March of 2014 on her Google+ account "when there are so few mujahideen, is it not our duty to fight regardless of our country of birth and/or residence?" She also posted the words "Caravan of Martyrs" on her homepage likely referencing how al Qaeda refers to those who give their lives for jihad. In April 2014 she posted "American women dress like sl**s." [74] She also appears to have been upset by "Israeli occupation of Palestine" and what she saw as apartheid. She frequently reposted pro-Palestinian posts including one that read, "Israel occupies Palestine for 47 years and no-one bats an eye. Russia occupies Crimea for a week and everybody loses their minds." [75]

After she converted, Conley is reported to have set up a dating profile as Halima95 on the website singlemuslim.com where she claimed to already be living in Morocco, eating halal, and stating that she wants to marry within the year. [76] According to court documents Shannon Conley began communicating online with a thirty-two-year-old Tunisian man known to her as Y.M. who claimed to be an ISIS fighter. He wanted to marry and help her come to join ISIS in Syria. [77]

The FBI became aware of Shannon Conley's radicalization as a result of complaints in November 2013 from the Faith Bible Church in Arvada, Colorado, the site of a 2007 shooting that left two missionaries dead. Conley's wandering about the church campus in a burqa taking notes caused suspicion and the church alerted authorities. When an FBI agent and Arvada policeman spoke to Conley she allegedly told the investigators that she "hated those people." [78] She also told them, "If they think I'm a terrorist, I'll give them something to think I am." [79]

Federal agents repeatedly contacted Shannon Conley and her parents trying to deter her progression on the terrorist trajectory. In December of 2013, Conley naively admitted to an FBI agent that she had signed up for the U.S. Army Explorers to train in military tactics and firearms hoping to transmit her knowledge to jihadi fighters. She also said that she would be ready to wage jihad in a year's time. In a court affidavit a federal agent wrote, "Conley stated she wanted to wage Jihad and would like to go overseas to fight," but if she were prevented as a woman from fighting she would use her medical training, as a licensed nurse's aide, to assist jihadi fighters. She stated that she would rather go to prison than turn away from jihad. [80]

Conley reportedly believed "defensive jihad" against Westerners was acceptable and that legitimate targets of attack include military facilities and personnel, government facilities and personnel, and public officials." She also included law enforcement as a legitimate target "because police enforce man-made laws that are not grounded in God's law. Conley stated targets to be avoided include women, children, and the elderly," the affidavit said. [81] In an affidavit about the case an FBI agent reported, "To Conley, it is okay to harm innocents if they are part of a target. She felt that if wives, children, and chaplains visiting a military base are killed during an attack, it is acceptable because they should not have been at a legitimate target. She repeatedly referred to US military bases as 'targets.'" She also was reported to have said government employees and law enforcement were fair game to be killed. [82]

In one interview with the FBI, Conley showed them a book she was studying: *Al-Qaida's Doctrine for Insurgency: Abd Al-Aziz Al-Muqrin's A Practical Course for Guerilla War.* She had underlined passages about carrying out a motorcade attack and waging guerilla warfare but told the agents that she had given up on that idea because security in the U.S. was too good. She bragged that she thought she could plan, but not carry out, such an attack. Conley also told agents that she liked the idea of 'guerrilla warfare because she could do it alone.' [83]

Conley also detailed to FBI agents her plans to travel to Syria to use her training as a nurse's aid to help the ISIS cause. She rejected federal agents' suggestions of diverting her passions to humanitarian use of her nursing skills—perhaps working for the Red Crescent, rather than devoting herself to militant jihad. [84] According to court documents, "Conley stated she has no interest in doing humanitarian work. Conley felt that Jihad is the only answer to correct the wrongs against the Muslim world. Conley said she preferred to wage Jihad overseas so she could be with Jihadist fighters." [85]

When the FBI became aware of her communications with an ISIS fighter they intervened and spoke again with both Shannon and her parents. John Conley was surprised to hear the FBI concerns saying that his daughter had told him that jihad involved "struggles to help the oppressed or the poor." Her parents also alerted the FBI that they owned guns and that Shannon and a friend had taken one of their rifles to practice marksmanship at a shooting range. [86] When they understood the seriousness of the threat, John and Ana Conley tried to dissuade their daughter from a path to destruction. Their daughter however, reportedly, refused all interventions. [87]

Conley was apparently an al-Awlaki devotee—she had CDs and DVDs in her possession labeled in his name. Referring on her social media pages to al-Awlaki who was killed in a U.S. drone strike, she wrote: "May Allah accept his martyrdom." [88]

Unlike the fictional character, Sophie, Shannon Conley did *not* carry out an actual terrorist attack. Instead she headed to the airport to travel to Syria to join ISIS and was thwarted by her father alerting the FBI. Conley was arrested April 8, 2014 as she attempted to leave the country to join Y.M. She pled guilty in September 2014 and was convicted of conspiring to provide material support to a foreign terrorist organization. She was sentenced to four years in prison with an additional three years, after release, under supervision. [89]

The fact that Shannon's parents, in the end, understood the seriousness of what she was doing and thwarted her plans to join ISIS by alerting the FBI is something that authorities must find a way to encourage. In many countries, while parents have made difficult phone calls to law enforcement in attempts to save their children from joining terrorist groups, others may be less inclined in the face of stiff prison sentences. Governments should look to make such calls easier—perhaps by offering hotlines with real help from psychologists and imams for those that call.

Shannon Conley is not the only American woman to fall into extremism and be seduced into a relationship with a male terrorist over the Internet. Colleen LaRose, the so-called "Jihad Jane" from Pennsylvania and Jamie Paulin-Ramirez, the so-called "Jihad Jamie" from Leadville, Colorado were also seduced into traveling, or planning to travel, to take part in jihad. In their cases, they plotted to kill Lars Vilks, a Swedish cartoonist, who had drawn disrespectful images of the Prophet Mohammed.[90]

There is no publicly available information as to why Shannon Conley was motivated to convert and then fell into extremist violence. She did tell the FBI that she had wanted to serve in the U.S. military, but gave up that desire after converting, believing the military would not accept her with her religious beliefs and wearing a niqab.[91]

While this story is inspired by Ms. Conley and her desire to join ISIS after converting, radicalizing and falling in love with an ISIS fighter, her personal background other than what is noted here in the author's note and by endnotes throughout the texts is unknown. I contacted her attorney requesting an interview with Conley and her parents but, not surprisingly, was refused. Her personal and sexual history and her family dynamics are all unknowns. There is no evidence that Shannon Conley was ever sexual assaulted, or the victim of any trauma of any sort, and this fictionalized account does not in any way aim to imply that she was. The character of Sophie Lindsay has been *inspired* by the open source press and court reports of Shannon Conley but it is purely fictional and bears no resemblance to Shannon Conley's actual history other than by coincidence or where it is clearly marked as having been drawn upon reports of Conley's story.

Likewise, John and Ana Conley are not public figures and little is publicly available about them. The parents depicted in this book are purely fictional, imagined figures and should not be confused in any way with Shannon Conley's actual parents. The *only* similarity in this book was that Shannon's father told the FBI that he walked into a Skype session in which his daughter was talking with Y.M. and that he ultimately turned her in to the FBI. At the time of their Skype session, Shannon invited Mr. Conley to join their conversation during which Y.M. asked Mr. Conley for his blessing for Shannon to relocate to Syria to marry him as soon as possible. John Conley told the FBI that he denied both these requests and that his daughter and her Tunisian boyfriend seemed surprised. [92]

Both Shannon's parents are reported to have informed her that they did *not* support her relationship to militant jihad or her plans to relocate to Syria. Evidently Conley agreed to marry her Tunisian boyfriend, as her father learned later that she had a one way plan ticket to Turkey in her possession. He then called the FBI who stopped her before she could leave the country. [93] Other than mirroring her father having been invited to give his blessing to their marriage and trying to stop his daughter from flying to Syria, the professions and proclivities of Sophie's parents are purely fictional and have no bearing whatsoever, other than coincidence, to Shannon Conley's actual parents.

While *Bride of ISIS* is a work of fiction, ISIS is not. ISIS is currently propagating an extremely virulent ideology and encouraging Muslims the world over to make "hijra"—that is come and travel to Syria and Iraq to join their jihad—and even more chillingly to "stay and act in place." This is a fictionalized story of the latter. Thankfully, it is still only fiction. I pray that it remains so.

Please Like this Book on Amazon!

Readers like to know how other readers like a book they are considering buying. If you found *Bride of ISIS* a good read, please give it some good words and loads of stars on Amazon, Barnes & Noble, or wherever you purchase your books. Thanks for your time in doing so!

Other Books by, or coauthored by, Anne Speckhard, Ph.D.

Talking to Terrorists: Understanding the Psycho-Social Motivations of Militant Jihadi Terrorists, Mass Hostage Takers, Suicide Bombers and "Martyrs",

Undercover Jihadi: Inside the Toronto 18—Al Qaeda Inspired, Homegrown Terrorism in the West

Warrior Princess: A U.S. Navy SEAL's Journey to Coming out Transgender

Fetal Abduction: The True Story of Multiple Personalities and Murder,

Beyond the Pale: A Story of Love and Friendship from the Minsk Ghetto and Holocaust in Belarus (forthcoming)

Timothy Tottle's Terrific Dream

Acknowledgements

A special thanks to my esteemed colleagues and friends for reviewing and commenting on the book: Dr. Max Abrams; Major General HRH Princess Aisha Bint Al Hussein; Dr. Laurence Brooks; Kylie Bull; Rita Cosby; Joe Charlaff; Dr. Alistair Edgar; Laurie Fenstermacher; Ambassador Alberto Fernandez; Carol Rollie Flynn; Dr. Rohan Gunaratna; Peter Knoope; Dr. Robert Lambert; Dr. Allison McDowell-Smith; Amanda Ohlke; Dr. Jerrold Post; Dr. David Rapoport; Ken Reidy; Dr. Marc Sageman; Mubin Shaikh; Dr. Stephen Sloan and Dr. Lorenzo Vidino. Many of you know your work over the years has influenced and helped me grow as an academic and a counter-terrorism expert.

Thank-you also to my colleague, Mubin Shaikh who helped write the glossary of Islamic terms. Thanks to T. and L., both FBI analysts who were kind enough to read an earlier version of the book and give inputs about how agents and analysts work together and how undercover missions and the Fusion Center would likely run. Thank you so very much to Jilly Prather, developmental editor for her suggestions to craft the book; to Maya Sloan who helped breathe life into the text; and to Vanessa Veazie, copy editor, for her painstaking work making sure things were done right! Thank you all for your thoughtful insights, great job editing, hours of support and valuable advice throughout the process of writing this book. Thank you also to Ellin Sanger of Sanger Blackman Media Solutions for her work as my publicist. Thanks to Sourabh Aryabhatta for the layout and book design of all of the various digital versions of this book. Thank you to Madison Campe for modeling for the cover. And kudos to my daughter and artist, Jessica Speckhard for her creative vision for the cover artwork.

Thank you to my family for supporting me as I research, write and work on issues of terrorism and Daniel who always tells me don't worry about the money—follow your heart. Daniel, Jessica, Danny and Leah, you have all put up with me when I've traveled into dangerous territories, prison cells and ghettos to talk to nefarious folks and always supported me as I prepared, went and returned from such trips even when it took time and care away from our family to do so. And Katarina you keep me remembering what a pure and clean heart looks like and you make me laugh even when the world is in a sorry and sad state.

Lastly, thanks to all the analysts and agents in the FBI, Homeland Security, Fusion Centers, Intelligence Services and our military who risk their lives and work tirelessly to detect, prevent and combat terrorism and keep our country secure. I hope I've represented well your passion, care, diligence and the risks you take daily to keep the rest of us safe.

About the Author

Anne Speckhard, Ph.D. is Adjunct Associate Professor of Psychiatry and of Security Studies in the School of Medicine and the School of Foreign Service at Georgetown University. Dr. Speckhard has been working in the field of posttraumatic stress disorder (PTSD) since the 1980's and has extensive experience working in Europe, the Middle East and the former Soviet Union. She was the chair of the <u>NATO Human Factors & Medicine Research and Technology Experts Group (HFM-140/RTG) on the Psychosocial, Cultural and Organizational Aspects of Terrorism</u>, served as the co-chair of the <u>NATO-Russia Human Factors & Medicine Research Task Group on Social Sciences Support to Military Personnel Engaged in Counter-Insurgency and Counter-Terrorism Operations</u> and served on the <u>NATO Human Factors & Medicine Research Task Group Moral Dilemmas and Military Mental Health Outcomes</u>. She is a member of the United Nations Roster of Experts for the Terrorism Prevention Branch Office on Drugs and Crime and was previously awarded a Public Health Service Fellowship in the United States Department of Health & Human Services where she served as a Research Fellow.

She has provided expert consultation to European and Middle Eastern governments as well as the U.S. Department of Defense regarding programs for prevention and rehabilitation of individuals committed to political violence and militant jihad. In 2006-2007 she worked with the U.S. Department of Defense to design and pilot test the Detainee Rehabilitation Program in Iraq. In 2002, she interviewed hostages taken in the Moscow Dubrovka Theater about their psychological responses and observations of the suicidal terrorists and did the same in 2005 with surviving hostages from the Beslan school take-over. Since 2002, she has collected more than four hundred research interviews of family members, friends, close associates and hostages of terrorists and militant jihadi extremists in Palestine, Israel, Iraq, Lebanon, Jordan, Morocco, Russia, Chechnya,Canada, the United States, Belarus, Netherlands, United Kingdom, Belgium and France.

Dr. Speckhard is the director of the <u>Holocaust Survivors Oral Histories Project – Belarus,</u> a project constructing the history of the Minsk Ghetto and Holocaust in Belarus through oral histories and archival research.

She also researched traumatic stress issues in survivors of the Chernobyl disaster and has written about stress responses to toxic disasters. Dr. Speckhard worked with American expatriates after 9-11 (at SHAPE, NATO, the U.S. Embassy to Belgium and Mission to the EU) and conducted research on acute stress responses to terrorism in this population. She also studies psychological resilience to terrorism in various populations including American civilians, military and diplomats serving in Iraq under high threat security conditions. Dr. Speckhard co-directed the NATO Advanced Research Workshops - Ideologies of Terrorism: Understanding and Predicting the Social, Psychological and Political Underpinnings of Terrorism and Understanding and Addressing the Root Causes of Radicalization among Groups with an Immigrant Heritage in Europe and served on the NATO/Russia Counter-Terrorism Advisory Group.

Dr. Speckhard has consulted to NATO, OSCE, foreign governments and the U.S. Departments of State, Defense, Justice, Homeland Security, Health & Human Services, CIA and FBI. She is a sought after expert on the subject of terrorism frequently appearing on CNN, BBC, NPR, Fox News, MSNBC, CTV, and quoted in Time Magazine, New York Post, London Times and many other publications. She frequently lectures on subjects related to her books and research studies. She is the author of Talking to Terrorists: Understanding the Psycho-Social Motivations of Militant Jihadi Terrorists, Mass Hostage Takers, Suicide Bombers and "Martyrs", Fetal Abduction: The True Story of Multiple Personalities and Murder, Beyond the Pale: A Story of Love and Friendship from the Minsk Ghetto and Holocaust in Belarus (forthcoming), and Timothy Tottle's Terrific Dream and co-author of Undercover Jihadi: Inside the Toronto 18—Al Qaeda Inspired, Homegrown Terrorism in the West and Warrior Princess: A U.S. Navy SEAL's Journey to Coming out Transgender.

Website: www.AnneSpeckhard.com

Glossary

AllahuAkbar – "Allah is Greater." Can be used in exclamation of anything positive.

Alhamdulillah – "All praise is due to Allah." Used primarily in thanks and gratitude.

Al Qaeda – Normally understood to be the group headed by the late Osama Bin Laden that declared war on the West. Better illustrated in the statement of al Qaeda ideologue al-Suri: It is a system and methodology, not a group per se. Al Qaeda has many affiliates under various names.

Bid'ah – A word that literally means innovation, but that in Islamic terms connotes new heretical doctrines, ways and carrying out actions that displease Allah and his messenger.

Burqa – An outer garment that envelopes the head, face and whole body, used by some Islamic women to cover themselves in public.

Caliph – A spiritual leader of Islam, claiming succession from Muhammad.

Caliphate – The rank, jurisdiction, or government of a caliph.

Deen – The way of life believed by Muslims to be laid out according to divine law in the Qur'an that Muslims are obligated to follow.

Fard Al Ayn – Individual obligation in Islam, such as the five daily prayers.

Hadith – A traditional account of things said or done by the Prophet Muhammad or his companions.

Hijab – A traditional scarf worn by Muslim women to cover the hair and neck.

Islam – The religious faith of Muslims, based on the words and religious system founded by the prophet Muhammad and taught by the Qur'an, the basic principle of which is absolute submission to a unique and personal god, Allah.

ISIS – "Islamic State in Iraq and Syria." A modern day terrorist group that originated in Iraq and crossed into Syria in defiance of al Qaeda's orders to make war upon the mujahideen fighting in Syria and returned back to Iraq to continue their insurgency. In June 2014, their leader Abu Bakr al-Baghdadi unilaterally declared himself to be the Caliph of the entire Muslim world.

Imam – The title for a Muslim religious leader or anyone who leads prayer.

Insha'Allah – "If Allah wills it." Usually said in response to a request or desire.

Sometimes cynically described as a polite way of saying, "No."

Innovation – (see Bid'ah) A new way or action that is displeasing to Allah and his messenger, a heresy.

Islam – The religious faith of Muslims, based on the Qur'an (the speech of Allah) and the Sunnah (the life example of the Prophet Muhammad.

Jihad – There are two forms of jihad—the inner struggle every Muslim makes to attempt a life of morality and a second form that involves fighting as a militant for the defense of Muslim lands, people and honor.

Kafir/Kuffar – Technically: one who knows the truth but conceals it. Falsely made synonymous with "infidel," a Judeo-Christian concept describing a person unfaithful to God.

Masha'Allah – "What Allah desires is done." Used in exclamation when something is affirmed or achieved.

Martyr – Someone who has died carrying out jihad, in the military expansion of Islam or carrying out a religious commandment.

Militant Jihadi – An Islamic fundamentalist who participates in or supports jihad, especially armed and violent confrontation.

Mujahid – One who participates in Jihad. Plural: Mujahideen

Niqab – A traditional head, face and shoulder covering worn by Islamic women that shows only the eyes, if that. It is debated by some, but generally believed to be nonobligatory to cover the face in Islam.

Qur'an – The holy scriptures of Islam.

Radicalization – Very simply, the process by which an individual comes to support non-traditional political views. "Violent Radicalization" refers to a process whereby an individual comes to support violent political views. "Violent Extremism" refers to a state of being where an individual acts out their violent thoughts in support of particular political extremist groups. Terrorism is thus a type of violent extremism. These terms apply equally to Muslim and non-Muslim extremists and can include ultranationalists, white supremacists and even street gangs.

Shahid/Shahida – Originates from the Arabic root that means "witness". Denotes a martyr, someone who has died in jihad or in the military expansion of Islam or carrying out a religious commandment.

Subhan'Allah – "Glory be to Allah." Can be used in exclamation as well as when receiving negative news.

SIPRNet – The Secret Internet Protocol Router Network of the U.S. government used to transmit U.S. Department of State and U.S. Department of Defense classified information, up to and including information classified SECRET, through a system of interconnected computer networks.

Taqiyya – when a Muslim is permitted to lie to non-believers to escape persecution, guard against a danger, or to advance the cause of Islam, sometimes by gaining the trust of non-believers in order to draw out their vulnerability and defeat them.

Ummah – "The Muslim Nation." The term used by the Prophet to describe his people and his followers who coexist as a singular entity, whether a spiritual community, a political community, or a mix of the two. The Hadith states, "The Ummah is like a body, if one part hurts, the whole body hurts" has frequently been used to suggest a transnational identity of Muslims in which the suffering of a Muslim in one place, creates a fard al ayn (obligation) upon another Muslim in some other place, to respond to that suffering. This reasoning is widely accepted by radicalized individuals, as a framework in which ideology and moral grievance/outrage narratives are constructed in behalf of Muslims in faraway lands.

Endnotes

1   CBS News. (June 29, 2014). ISIS declares creation of Mideast caliphate across Iraq and Syria. http://www.cbsnews.com/news/isis-declares-creation-of-mideast-caliphate/

2   Speckhard, A. (2015). The militant jihadi message propagated by ISIS is a contagiously virulent meme in the West—the Ebola of terrorism. Multi-Method Assessment of ISIL. https://www.researchgate.net/publication/271195840_The_Militant_Jihadi_Message_Propagated_by_ISIS_is_a_Contagiously_Virulent_Meme_in_the_Westthe_Ebola_of_Terrorism

3   According to FBI Director James Comey it is very hard to estimate how Americans have actually gone over to join ISIS. See: CBS News. (September 10, 2014). Colorado teen Shannon Conley's support of ISIS raises alarm about American jihadists. Retrieved from: http://www.cbsnews.com/news/colorado-teen-shannon-conleys-support-of-isis-raises-alarm-about-american-jihadists/

4   According to FBI Director James Comey, FBI agents try to distinguish between people only chatting about their extremist views—individuals he called "mouthrunners" and those who are actively taking steps to engage in terrorism. He said in August of 2014, ""This is a great country with lots of traditions of protecting mouth-running," he said. "We should continue that. But those who are inclined to cross the line, I've got to focus on them." See: CBS News. (September 10, 2014). Colorado teen Shannon Conley's support of ISIS raises alarm about American jihadists. Retrieved from: http://www.cbsnews.com/news/colorado-teen-shannon-conleys-support-of-isis-raises-alarm-about-american-jihadists/

5   Speckhard, A. (January 9, 2015). The Isis 'attack and stay in place' meme and the 'why' behind the Charlie Hebdo attacks. Huffington Post. http://www.huffingtonpost.co.uk/anne-speckhard/charlie-hebdo_b_6440146.html

6   Speckhard, A., & Shaikh, M. (June 3, 2014). End Times Brewing: An Apocalyptic View on al-Baghdadi's Declaration of a Caliphate in Iraq and the Flow of Foreign Fighters Coming from the West. Huffington Post. http://www.huffingtonpost.co.uk/anne-speckhard/isis-iraq_b_5541693.html

7   Bleier, E. (April 4, 2015). CIA and NSA analysts who spend all day watching ISIS beheadings, brutal attacks and hard core child pornography are treated by specialist psychologists. Daily Mail. Retrieved from: http://www.dailymail.co.uk/news/article-3025771/CIA-NSA-analysts-treated-specialist-psychologists-help-cope-watching-graphic-videos.

html#ixzz3bwPrSDGm

8   Traumatic flashbacks are a feature of posttraumatic stress disorder and
occur after experiencing an overwhelming, seemingly inescapable, life
threatening or highly terrifying event involving threat to or actual bodily
harm. Flashbacks entail serious time distortions and often feel to the
person experiencing them as if they are actually reliving the traumatic
event in full sensory detail.

9   See: Hall, E. (December 1, 2014). Teen ISIS bride From Britain blogs
about the death of her jihadi husband. BuzzFeedNews. http://www.
buzzfeed.com/ellievhall/teen-isis-bride-from-britain-blogs-about-the-
death-of-her-ji#.tp9eAYADdj and Hoyle, C., Bradford, A., & Frenett, R.
(2015). Becoming Mulan? Female Western migrants to ISIS. http://www.
strategicdialogue.org/ISDJ2969_Becoming_Mulan_01.15_WEB.PDF

10 I'll be first female executioner: Briton linked to IS vows to behead
British or US prisoner. (August 20, 2014). Mirror. Retrieved from:
http://www.mirror.co.uk/news/world-news/ill-first-female-executioner-
briton-4081514

11 I'll be first female executioner: Briton linked to IS vows to behead
British or US prisoner. (August 20, 2014). Mirror. Retrieved from:
http://www.mirror.co.uk/news/world-news/ill-first-female-executioner-
briton-4081514

12 Her Royal Highness, Princess Aisha of Jordan is an incredibly forward
thinking leader. She serves in her country's military and currently holds
the rank of Major General. She was one of the first Arab leaders to
understand and push successfully for women to be allowed into Special
Forces.

13 Hall, E. (September 17, 2014). An ISIS love story: "Till martyrdom do us
part". Retrieved from: http://www.buzzfeed.com/ellievhall/an-isis-love-
story-till-martyrdom-do-us-part#.qdoryEyjao

14 Hall, E. (September 17, 2014). An ISIS love story: "Till martyrdom do us
part". Retrieved from: http://www.buzzfeed.com/ellievhall/an-isis-love-
story-till-martyrdom-do-us-part#.qdoryEyjao

15 Hall, E. (September 11, 2014). Inside the chilling online world of the
women of ISIS. BuzzFeedNews. http://www.buzzfeed.com/ellievhall/
inside-the-online-world-of-the-women-of-isis#.jd1XZQZR6z

16 Hall, E. (September 11, 2014). Inside the chilling online world of the
women of ISIS. BuzzFeedNews. http://www.buzzfeed.com/ellievhall/
inside-the-online-world-of-the-women-of-isis#.jd1XZQZR6z

17 See: Speckhard, A. and K. Akhmedova (2006). Black Widows: The
Chechen Female Suicide Terrorists. Female Suicide Terrorists. Y.
Schweitzer. Tel Aviv, Jaffe Center Publication; Speckhard, A. and

K. Ahkmedova (2006). "The Making of a Martyr: Chechen Suicide Terrorism." Journal of Studies in Conflict and Terrorism 29(5): 429-492.; and Speckhard, A. and K. Akhmedova (2008). Black Widows and Beyond: Understanding the Motivations and Life Trajectories of Chechen Female Terrorists. Female Terrorism and Militancy: Agency, Utility and Organization: Agency, Utility and Organization C. Ness, Routledge.

18 See: Speckhard, A. (2008). "The Emergence of Female Suicide Terrorists." Studies in Conflict and Terrorism 31: 1-29; Speckhard, A. (2012). Talking to terrorists: Understanding the psycho-social motivations of militant jihadi terrorists, mass hostage takers, suicide bombers and "martyrs". McLean, VA, Advances Press.

19 Hoyle, C., Bradford, A., & Frenett, R. (2015). Becoming Mulan? Female Western migrants to ISIS. http://www.strategicdialogue.org/ISDJ2969_Becoming_Mulan_01.15_WEB.PDF

20 BBC News. 7 July bombings. http://news.bbc.co.uk/2/shared/spl/hi/uk/05/london_blasts/investigation/html/bombers.stmhttp://news.bbc.co.uk/2/shared/spl/hi/uk/05/london_blasts/investigation/html/bombers.stm

21 BBC News. (May 11, 2006). Profile: Germaine Lindsay. http://news.bbc.co.uk/2/hi/uk_news/4762591.stm

22 See: Speckhard, A. (2013). The Boston Marathon bombers: The lethal cocktail that turned troubled youth to terrorism. Perspectives on Terrorism.; and Tomlinson, S. (November 14, 2014). White Widow 'is alive and living with jihadist al-Qaeda husband in Somalia', Kenyan spies say. Daily Mail Online. http://www.dailymail.co.uk/news/article-2834673/White-Widow-alive-living-jihadist-al-Qaeda-husband-Somalia-Kenyan-spies-say.html

23 Berger, J. M. (September 9, 2011). Anwar al-Awlaki's links to the September 11 Hijackers. the Altantic. http://www.theatlantic.com/international/archive/2011/09/anwar-al-awlakis-links-to-the-september-11-hijackers/244796/ and Mazzetti, M., Savage, C., & Shane, S. (March 9, 2013). How a U.S. citizen came to be in America's cross hairs. New York Times. http://www.nytimes.com/2013/03/10/world/middleeast/anwar-al-awlaki-a-us-citizen-in-americas-cross-hairs.html?pagewanted=all&_r=0

24 al-Awlaki, A. Constants on the path of jihad. https://archive.org/details/Consta and Berger, J. M. (October 31, 2011). The enduring appeal of al-Awlaqi's "Constants on the Path of Jihad". https://www.ctc.usma.edu/posts/the-enduring-appeal-of-al-awlaqi's-"constants-on-the-path-of-jihad"

25 Speckhard, A., & Shaikh, M. (2014). Undercover Jihadi: Inside the Toronto 18--Al Qaeda inspired, homegrown terrorism in the West:

Advances Press, LLC.

26   See: BBC News. (November 12, 2009). Profile: Major Nidal Malik Hasan. http://news.bbc.co.uk/2/hi/8345944.stm and Blaze, T. (August 28, 2014). http://www.theblaze.com/stories/2014/08/28/fort-hood-shooter-nidal-hasan-writes-chilling-letter-to-islamic-state-leader/

27   See: Esposito, R., Vlasto, C., & Cuomo, C. (May 6, 2010). Sources: Shahzad had contact with Awlaki, Taliban chief, and Mumbai massacre mastermind. ABC News. http://abcnews.go.com/Blotter/faisal-shahzad-contact-awlaki-taliban-mumbai-massacre-mastermind/story?id=10575061 and Adams, L., & Nasir, A. (September 18, 2010). Inside the mind of the Times Square bomber. The Guardian. http://www.theguardian.com/world/2010/sep/19/times-square-bomber and

28   Dodd, V. (February 28, 2011). British Airways worker Rajib Karim convicted of terrorist plot. The Guardian. http://www.theguardian.com/uk/2011/feb/28/british-airways-bomb-guilty-karim

29   Dodd, V. (November 3, 2010). Roshonara Choudhry: I wanted to die..I wanted to be martyr. The Guardian. http://www.theguardian.com/uk/2010/nov/04/stephen-timms-attack-roshonara-choudhry

30   Speckhard, A. (2012). Talking to terrorists: Understanding the psycho-social motivations of militant jihadi terrorists, mass hostage takers, suicide bombers and "martyrs". McLean, VA: Advances Press.

31   Ellis, R. (October 22, 2014). Canadian police say man who ran down, killed soldier was 'radicalized'. CNN. http://www.cnn.com/2014/10/21/us/canada-soldiers-killed-officer-attack/index.html

32   Steinbach, M. (February 11, 2015). Statement before the House Committee on Homeland Security. Retrieved from: http://www.fbi.gov/news/testimony/the-urgent-threat-of-foreign-fighters-and-homegrown-terror

33   Steinbach, M. (February 11, 2015). Statement before the House Committee on Homeland Security. Retrieved from: http://www.fbi.gov/news/testimony/the-urgent-threat-of-foreign-fighters-and-homegrown-terror

34   Mr. Steinbach referenced the ISIL video release's actual date of January 2015 but we have taken editorial license and changed it to August 2014 to fit the timeline of this book.

35   This fictionalized individual is a composite based upon the real cases of Michael Robert Hoyt who had a history of mentally illness and who may also have been inspired to act in behalf of ISIS and of a Moroccan born, illegal immigrant, Amine El Khalifi who taken in by a sting operation in which he strapped on a fake suicide bomber's vest and walked up to the U.S. Capitol hoping to at least thirty individuals along

with himself. He was arrested at the foot of Capitol Hill. See: Horwitz, S., Wan, W., & Wilber, D. Q. (February 17, 2012). Federal agents arrest Amine El Khalifi; he allegedly planned to bomb Capitol. http://www. washingtonpost.com/world/national-security/federal-agents-arrest-man-who-allegedly-planned-suicide-bombing-on-us-capitol/2012/02/17/gIQAtYZ7JR_story.html; Michael Robert Hoyt: 5 Fast Facts You Need to Know. (January 13, 2015). Heavy. http://heavy.com/news/2015/01/michael-hoyt-john-boehner-bartender-assassination-poison-plot-ebola-jesus-devil/ and Pergram, C. (January 15, 2015). Murder, terror plots underscore security risks at US Capitol. Fox News. http://www.foxnews.com/politics/2015/01/15/murder-terror-plots-underscore-security-risks-at-us-capitol/

36   Speckhard, A. (2012). Talking to terrorists: Understanding the psycho-social motivations of militant jihadi terrorists, mass hostage takers, suicide bombers and "martyrs". McLean, VA, Advances Press.

37   The parts in Courier print in this chapter are quoted and paraphrased from http://www.iupui.edu/~msaiupui/qaradawistatus.html

38   http://www.islamreligion.com/articles/204/

39   See: Speckhard, A. and K. Akhmedova (2006). Black Widows: The Chechen Female Suicide Terrorists. Female Suicide Terrorists. Y. Schweitzer. Tel Aviv, Jaffe Center Publication; Speckhard, A. and K. Ahkmedova (2006). "The Making of a Martyr: Chechen Suicide Terrorism." Journal of Studies in Conflict and Terrorism 29(5): 429-492.; and Speckhard, A. and K. Akhmedova (2008). Black Widows and Beyond: Understanding the Motivations and Life Trajectories of Chechen Female Terrorists. Female Terrorism and Militancy: Agency, Utility and Organization: Agency, Utility and Organization C. Ness, Routledge; Speckhard, A. (2008). "The Emergence of Female Suicide Terrorists." Studies in Conflict and Terrorism 31: 1-29 and Speckhard, A. (2012). Talking to terrorists: Understanding the psycho-social motivations of militant jihadi terrorists, mass hostage takers, suicide bombers and "martyrs". McLean, VA, Advances Press.

40   al-Awlaki, A. Constants on the path of jihad. https://archive.org/details/Consta

41   For a transcript of the video that bounces around on locations on the web see: al-Awlaki, A. (april 25, 2010). The Transcript Of "A Call To Jihad" the Unjust Media. http://www.theunjustmedia.com/Islamic%20Perspectives/April10/The%20Transcript%20of%20A%20Call%20to%20Jihad%20by%20Imam%20Anwar%20al-Awlaki%20(may%20Allah%20protect%20him).htm

42   Mazzetti, M., Savage, C., & Shane, S. (March 9, 2013). How a U.S. citizen

came to be in America's cross hairs. New York Times. http://www.
nytimes.com/2013/03/10/world/middleeast/anwar-al-awlaki-a-us-citizen-
in-americas-cross-hairs.html?pagewanted=all&_r=0

43   Mazzetti, M., Savage, C., & Shane, S. (March 9, 2013). How a U.S. citizen
came to be in America's cross hairs. New York Times. http://www.
nytimes.com/2013/03/10/world/middleeast/anwar-al-awlaki-a-us-citizen-
in-americas-cross-hairs.html?pagewanted=all&_r=0

44   These are all things actually posted by Shannon Conley. See: Faberov, S.,
& Bates, D. (Jully 2, 2014). American nurse who was arrested for trying
to join ISIS set her Facebook profile to 'slave of Allah': Denver teen also
wrote that U.S. women dress like s****' after she was seduced by a Syrian
militant Daily Mail. http://www.dailymail.co.uk/news/article-2678662/
Denver-woman-19-charged-plotting-join-ISIS-militants-wage-jihad-U-S.
html

45   See: Friedersdorf, C. (October 24, 2012). How team Obama justifies the
killing of a 16-year-old American. the Altantic. Retrieved from: http://
www.theatlantic.com/politics/archive/2012/10/how-team-obama-
justifies-the-killing-of-a-16-year-old-american/264028/ and al-Awlaki,
N. (July 17, 2013). The drone that killed my grandson. New York Times.
Retrieved from: http://www.nytimes.com/2013/07/18/opinion/the-drone-
that-killed-my-grandson.html?_r=0

46   al-Awlaki, A. (May 1, 2009). 44 Ways of Supporting Jihad. the Unjust
Media. http://theunjustmedia.com/Islamic%20Perspectives/Jan09/44%20
Ways%20of%20Supporting%20Jihad.htm

47   al-Awlaki, A. (May 1, 2009). 44 Ways of Supporting Jihad. the Unjust
Media. http://theunjustmedia.com/Islamic%20Perspectives/Jan09/44%20
Ways%20of%20Supporting%20Jihad.htm

48   al-Awlaki, A. (May 1, 2009). 44 Ways of Supporting Jihad. the Unjust
Media. http://theunjustmedia.com/Islamic%20Perspectives/Jan09/44%20
Ways%20of%20Supporting%20Jihad.htm

49   Something similar to this occurred in the Shannon Conley case. She is
reported to have approached the Faith Church taking notes and when
challenged made less aggressive comments such as "Why is the church
worried about a terrorist attack?' and, that terrorists are "not allowed
to kill aging adults and little children." See: Gathright, A. (July 2, 2014).
19-year-old Arvada woman, Shannon Maureen Conley, charged with
aiding ISIS terror group, FBI says. ABC News - the Denver Channel.
http://www.thedenverchannel.com/news/local-news/19-year-old-
colorado-woman-shannon-maureen-conley-charged-with-aiding-
terrorist-group-fbi-says07022014

50   Human Rights Watch. (February 6, 2014). Iraq: Security forces

abusing women in detention. Retrieved from: http://www.hrw.org/news/2014/02/06/iraq-security-forces-abusing-women-detention

51   Council on Foreign Relations. The Sunni-Shia divide. Retrieved from: http://www.cfr.org/peace-conflict-and-human-rights/sunni-shia-divide/p33176#!/

52   This terror plot mirrors two real cases, one of Michael Robert Hoyt who had a history of mentally illness and who may also have been inspired to act in behalf of ISIS and secondly of Moroccan born, illegal immigrant, Amine El Khalifi who taken in by a sting operation in which he strapped on a fake suicide bomber's vest and walked up to the U.S. Capitol hoping to at least thirty individuals along with himself. He was arrested at the foot of Capitol Hill. See: Horwitz, S., Wan, W., & Wilber, D. Q. (February 17, 2012). Federal agents arrest Amine El Khalifi; he allegedly planned to bomb Capitol. http://www.washingtonpost.com/world/national-security/federal-agents-arrest-man-who-allegedly-planned-suicide-bombing-on-us-capitol/2012/02/17/gIQAtYZ7JR_story.html; Michael Robert Hoyt: 5 Fast Facts You Need to Know. (January 13, 2015). Heavy. http://heavy.com/news/2015/01/michael-hoyt-john-boehner-bartender-assassination-poison-plot-ebola-jesus-devil/ and Pergram, C. (January 15, 2015). Murder, terror plots underscore security risks at US Capitol. Fox News. http://www.foxnews.com/politics/2015/01/15/murder-terror-plots-underscore-security-risks-at-us-capitol/

53   This is something that Shannon Conley actually posted. See: Faberov, S., & Bates, D. (July 2, 2014). American nurse who was arrested for trying to join ISIS set her Facebook profile to 'slave of Allah': Denver teen also wrote that U.S. women dress like s****' after she was seduced by a Syrian militant Daily Mail. Retrieved from: http://www.dailymail.co.uk/news/article-2678662/Denver-woman-19-charged-plotting-join-ISIS-militants-wage-jihad-U-S.html

54   These are all things actually posted by Shannon Conley. See: Faberov, S., & Bates, D. (Jully 2, 2014). American nurse who was arrested for trying to join ISIS set her Facebook profile to 'slave of Allah': Denver teen also wrote that U.S. women dress like s****' after she was seduced by a Syrian militant Daily Mail. http://www.dailymail.co.uk/news/article-2678662/Denver-woman-19-charged-plotting-join-ISIS-militants-wage-jihad-U-S.html

55   Shannon Conley was also suspected of having contemplated an attack inside the U.S. according to her chats FBI agents and had underlined passages in the same book about undertaking motorcade attacks and waging guerilla warfare. See: Gathright, A. (July 2, 2014). 19-year-old Arvada woman, Shannon Maureen Conley, charged with aiding ISIS

terror group, FBI says. ABC News - the Denver Channel. http://www.
thedenverchannel.com/news/local-news/19-year-old-colorado-woman-
shannon-maureen-conley-charged-with-aiding-terrorist-group-fbi-
says07022014

56   This feeling of bliss, euphoria and empowerment is commonly reported
by would be "martyrs" and we also found it in a thought experiment
conducted with college students who were merely imagining putting
on a suicide vest. See: Speckhard, A. (2012). Talking to terrorists:
Understanding the psycho-social motivations of militant jihadi terrorists,
mass hostage takers, suicide bombers and "martyrs". McLean, VA:
Advances Press and Speckhard, A., Jacuch, B., & Vanrompay, V. (2012).
Taking on the persona of a suicide bomber: A thought experiment.
Perspectives on Terrorism, 6(2), 51-73. Retrieved from: http://www.
terrorismanalysts.com/pt/index.php/pot/article/view/speckhard-taking-
on-the-persona.

57   Shannon Conley actually did join the Army Explorers reportedly to
gain skills to take along with her into Syria where she planned to marry
her Tunisian boyfriend. See: Gathright, A. (July 2, 2014). 19-year-old
Arvada woman, Shannon Maureen Conley, charged with aiding ISIS
terror group, FBI says. ABC News - the Denver Channel. http://www.
thedenverchannel.com/news/local-news/19-year-old-colorado-woman-
shannon-maureen-conley-charged-with-aiding-terrorist-group-fbi-
says07022014

58   See: http://www.cnn.com/videos/world/2015/02/24/pkg-holmes-isis-
children-recruiting-tactics.cnn

59   This is true. See: Verkaik, R., & Akbar, J. (May 13, 2015). Is ISIS about
to send women to die on suicide missions? Daily Mail. Retrieved
from: http://www.dailymail.co.uk/news/article-3079857/Is-ISIS-send-
women-die-suicide-missions-Chilling-fanatic-wedding-certificate-
states-jihadi-brides-carry-bombings-without-husband-s-permission.
html#ixzz3aS3BKtfx

60   Although this story was reported in the news, it turned out to be a false
lead. See: Dodd, V. (May 14, 2015). Girls who 'escaped ISIS' not east
London teens, say families. The Guardian. Retrieved from: http://www.
theguardian.com/world/2015/may/14/girls-who-escaped-isis-not-east-
london-teens-say-families

61   This terror plot mirrors two real cases, one of Michael Robert Hoyt who
had a history of mentally illness and who may also have been inspired to
act in behalf of ISIS and secondly of Moroccan born, illegal immigrant,
Amine El Khalifi who taken in by a sting operation in which he strapped
on a fake suicide bomber's vest and walked up to the U.S. Capitol hoping

to at least thirty individuals along with himself. He was arrested at the foot of Capitol Hill. See: Horwitz, S., Wan, W., & Wilber, D. Q. (February 17, 2012). Federal agents arrest Amine El Khalifi; he allegedly planned to bomb Capitol. http://www.washingtonpost.com/world/national-security/federal-agents-arrest-man-who-allegedly-planned-suicide-bombing-on-us-capitol/2012/02/17/gIQAtYZ7JR_story.html; Michael Robert Hoyt: 5 Fast Facts You Need to Know. (January 13, 2015). Heavy. http://heavy.com/news/2015/01/michael-hoyt-john-boehner-bartender-assassination-poison-plot-ebola-jesus-devil/ and Pergram, C. (January 15, 2015). Murder, terror plots underscore security risks at US Capitol. Fox News. http://www.foxnews.com/politics/2015/01/15/murder-terror-plots-underscore-security-risks-at-us-capitol/

62   Ahmed, S., & Botelho, G. (October 23, 2014). Who is Michael Zehaf-Bibeau, the man behind the deadly Ottawa attack? CNN. Retrieved from: http://www.cnn.com/2014/10/22/world/canada-shooter/

63   Ahmed, S., & Botelho, G. (October 23, 2014). Who is Michael Zehaf-Bibeau, the man behind the deadly Ottawa attack? CNN. Retrieved from: http://www.cnn.com/2014/10/22/world/canada-shooter/

64   Speckhard, A., & Shaikh, M. (2014). Undercover Jihadi: Inside the Toronto 18--Al Qaeda inspired, homegrown terrorism in the West: Advances Press, LLC.

65   This feeling of bliss and euphoria in contemplating taking one's own life in a "martyrdom mission" is commonly reported by individuals who are thwarted in their plans. We also found it in a thought experiment conducted with college students who were merely imagining putting on a suicide vest. See: Speckhard, A. (2012). Talking to terrorists: Understanding the psycho-social motivations of militant jihadi terrorists, mass hostage takers, suicide bombers and "martyrs". McLean, VA: Advances Press and Speckhard, A., Jacuch, B., & Vanrompay, V. (2012). Taking on the persona of a suicide bomber: A thought experiment. Perspectives on Terrorism, 6(2), 51-73. Retrieved from: http://www.terrorismanalysts.com/pt/index.php/pot/article/view/speckhard-taking-on-the-persona.

66   Faberov, S., & Bates, D. (July 2, 2014). American nurse who was arrested for trying to join ISIS set her Facebook profile to 'slave of Allah': Denver teen also wrote that U.S. women dress like s****' after she was seduced by a Syrian militant Daily Mail. Retrieved from: http://www.dailymail.co.uk/news/article-2678662/Denver-woman-19-charged-plotting-join-ISIS-militants-wage-jihad-U-S.html

67   This fictionalized individual is a composite based upon the real cases of Michael Robert Hoyt who had a history of mentally illness and who

may also have been inspired to act in behalf of ISIS and of a Moroccan born, illegal immigrant, Amine El Khalifi who taken in by a sting operation in which he strapped on a fake suicide bomber's vest and walked up to the U.S. Capitol hoping to at least thirty individuals along with himself. He was arrested at the foot of Capitol Hill. See: Horwitz, S., Wan, W., & Wilber, D. Q. (February 17, 2012). Federal agents arrest Amine El Khalifi; he allegedly planned to bomb Capitol. http://www.washingtonpost.com/world/national-security/federal-agents-arrest-man-who-allegedly-planned-suicide-bombing-on-us-capitol/2012/02/17/gIQAtYZ7JR_story.html; Michael Robert Hoyt: 5 Fast Facts You Need to Know. (January 13, 2015). Heavy. http://heavy.com/news/2015/01/michael-hoyt-john-boehner-bartender-assassination-poison-plot-ebola-jesus-devil/ and Pergram, C. (January 15, 2015). Murder, terror plots underscore security risks at US Capitol. Fox News. http://www.foxnews.com/politics/2015/01/15/murder-terror-plots-underscore-security-risks-at-us-capitol/

68   Speckhard, A. (2012). Talking to terrorists: Understanding the psycho-social motivations of militant jihadi terrorists, mass hostage takers, suicide bombers and "martyrs". McLean, VA: Advances Press

69   Dodd, V. (November 3, 2010). Roshonara Choudhry: I wanted to die..I wanted to be martyr. The Guardian. Retrieved from: http://www.theguardian.com/uk/2010/nov/04/stephen-timms-attack-roshonara-choudhry

70   For in-depth analysis of real cases where that occurs see: Speckhard, A. (2012). Talking to terrorists: Understanding the psycho-social motivations of militant jihadi terrorists, mass hostage takers, suicide bombers and "martyrs". McLean, VA, Advances Press.

71   For in-depth analysis of real cases where that occurs see: Speckhard, A. (2012). Talking to terrorists: Understanding the psycho-social motivations of militant jihadi terrorists, mass hostage takers, suicide bombers and "martyrs". McLean, VA, Advances Press.

72   Rape Abuse & Incest National Network. Who are the victims? Retrieved from: https://www.rainn.org/get-information/statistics/sexual-assault-victims

73   See: Speckhard, A. (2008). The Emergence of Female Suicide Terrorists. Studies in Conflict and Terrorism, 31, 1-29; Speckhard, A. (2009). Female suicide bombers in Iraq. Democracy and Security, 5(1), 19-50.; and Speckhard, A. (May 4, 2015). Female terrorists in ISIS, al Qaeda and 21rst century terrorism. Trends Research. Retrieved from: https://www.academia.edu/12606010/Female_Terrorists_in_ISIS_al_Qaeda_and_21st_Century_Terrorism

74 Faberov, S., & Bates, D. (July 2, 2014). American nurse who was arrested for trying to join ISIS set her Facebook profile to 'slave of Allah': Denver teen also wrote that U.S. women dress like s****' after she was seduced by a Syrian militant Daily Mail. Retrieved from: http://www.dailymail.co.uk/news/article-2678662/Denver-woman-19-charged-plotting-join-ISIS-militants-wage-jihad-U-S.html

75 Faberov, S., & Bates, D. (July 2, 2014). American nurse who was arrested for trying to join ISIS set her Facebook profile to 'slave of Allah': Denver teen also wrote that U.S. women dress like s****' after she was seduced by a Syrian militant Daily Mail. Retrieved from: http://www.dailymail.co.uk/news/article-2678662/Denver-woman-19-charged-plotting-join-ISIS-militants-wage-jihad-U-S.html

76 Faberov, S., & Bates, D. (July 2, 2014). American nurse who was arrested for trying to join ISIS set her Facebook profile to 'slave of Allah': Denver teen also wrote that U.S. women dress like s****' after she was seduced by a Syrian militant Daily Mail. Retrieved from: http://www.dailymail.co.uk/news/article-2678662/Denver-woman-19-charged-plotting-join-ISIS-militants-wage-jihad-U-S.html

77 CBS News. (September 10, 2014). Colorado teen Shannon Conley's support of ISIS raises alarm about American jihadists. Retrieved from: http://www.cbsnews.com/news/colorado-teen-shannon-conleys-support-of-isis-raises-alarm-about-american-jihadists/

78 Faberov, S., & Bates, D. (July 2, 2014). American nurse who was arrested for trying to join ISIS set her Facebook profile to 'slave of Allah': Denver teen also wrote that U.S. women dress like s****' after she was seduced by a Syrian militant Daily Mail. Retrieved from: http://www.dailymail.co.uk/news/article-2678662/Denver-woman-19-charged-plotting-join-ISIS-militants-wage-jihad-U-S.html and Gathright, A. (July 2, 2014). 19-year-old Arvada woman, Shannon Maureen Conley, charged with aiding ISIS terror group, FBI says. ABC News - the Denver Channel. Retrieved from: http://www.thedenverchannel.com/news/local-news/19-year-old-colorado-woman-shannon-maureen-conley-charged-with-aiding-terrorist-group-fbi-says07022014

79 CBS News. (September 10, 2014). Colorado teen Shannon Conley's support of ISIS raises alarm about American jihadists. Retrieved from: http://www.cbsnews.com/news/colorado-teen-shannon-conleys-support-of-isis-raises-alarm-about-american-jihadists/

80 Gathright, A. (July 2, 2014). 19-year-old Arvada woman, Shannon Maureen Conley, charged with aiding ISIS terror group, FBI says. ABC News - the Denver Channel. Retrieved from: http://www.thedenverchannel.com/news/local-news/19-year-old-colorado-woman-

shannon-maureen-conley-charged-with-aiding-terrorist-group-fbi-
says07022014

81   Gathright, A. (July 2, 2014). 19-year-old Arvada woman, Shannon
      Maureen Conley, charged with aiding ISIS terror group, FBI says.
      ABC News - the Denver Channel. Retrieved from: http://www.
      thedenverchannel.com/news/local-news/19-year-old-colorado-woman-
      shannon-maureen-conley-charged-with-aiding-terrorist-group-fbi-
      says07022014

82   Faberov, S., & Bates, D. (July 2, 2014). American nurse who was arrested
      for trying to join ISIS set her Facebook profile to 'slave of Allah': Denver
      teen also wrote that U.S. women dress like s****' after she was seduced by
      a Syrian militant Daily Mail. Retrieved from: http://www.dailymail.co.uk/
      news/article-2678662/Denver-woman-19-charged-plotting-join-ISIS-
      militants-wage-jihad-U-S.html and Gathright, A. (July 2, 2014). 19-year-
      old Arvada woman, Shannon Maureen Conley, charged with aiding
      ISIS terror group, FBI says. ABC News - the Denver Channel. Retrieved
      from: http://www.thedenverchannel.com/news/local-news/19-year-
      old-colorado-woman-shannon-maureen-conley-charged-with-aiding-
      terrorist-group-fbi-says07022014

83   Gathright, A. (July 2, 2014). 19-year-old Arvada woman, Shannon
      Maureen Conley, charged with aiding ISIS terror group, FBI says.
      ABC News - the Denver Channel. Retrieved from: http://www.
      thedenverchannel.com/news/local-news/19-year-old-colorado-woman-
      shannon-maureen-conley-charged-with-aiding-terrorist-group-fbi-
      says07022014

84   Faberov, S., & Bates, D. (July 2, 2014). American nurse who was arrested
      for trying to join ISIS set her Facebook profile to 'slave of Allah': Denver
      teen also wrote that U.S. women dress like s****' after she was seduced by
      a Syrian militant Daily Mail. Retrieved from: http://www.dailymail.co.uk/
      news/article-2678662/Denver-woman-19-charged-plotting-join-ISIS-
      militants-wage-jihad-U-S.html

85   Gathright, A. (July 2, 2014). 19-year-old Arvada woman, Shannon
      Maureen Conley, charged with aiding ISIS terror group, FBI says.
      ABC News - the Denver Channel. Retrieved from: http://www.
      thedenverchannel.com/news/local-news/19-year-old-colorado-woman-
      shannon-maureen-conley-charged-with-aiding-terrorist-group-fbi-
      says07022014

86   Gathright, A. (July 2, 2014). 19-year-old Arvada woman, Shannon
      Maureen Conley, charged with aiding ISIS terror group, FBI says.
      ABC News - the Denver Channel. Retrieved from: http://www.
      thedenverchannel.com/news/local-news/19-year-old-colorado-woman-

shannon-maureen-conley-charged-with-aiding-terrorist-group-fbi-says07022014

87 Faberov, S., & Bates, D. (July 2, 2014). American nurse who was arrested for trying to join ISIS set her Facebook profile to 'slave of Allah': Denver teen also wrote that U.S. women dress like s****' after she was seduced by a Syrian militant Daily Mail. Retrieved from: http://www.dailymail.co.uk/news/article-2678662/Denver-woman-19-charged-plotting-join-ISIS-militants-wage-jihad-U-S.html

88 Faberov, S., & Bates, D. (July 2, 2014). American nurse who was arrested for trying to join ISIS set her Facebook profile to 'slave of Allah': Denver teen also wrote that U.S. women dress like s****' after she was seduced by a Syrian militant Daily Mail. Retrieved from: http://www.dailymail.co.uk/news/article-2678662/Denver-woman-19-charged-plotting-join-ISIS-militants-wage-jihad-U-S.html

89 CBS News. (September 10, 2014). Colorado teen Shannon Conley's support of ISIS raises alarm about American jihadists. Retrieved from: http://www.cbsnews.com/news/colorado-teen-shannon-conleys-support-of-isis-raises-alarm-about-american-jihadists/

90 CBS News. (September 10, 2014). Colorado teen Shannon Conley's support of ISIS raises alarm about American jihadists. Retrieved from: http://www.cbsnews.com/news/colorado-teen-shannon-conleys-support-of-isis-raises-alarm-about-american-jihadists/

91 Gathright, A. (July 2, 2014). 19-year-old Arvada woman, Shannon Maureen Conley, charged with aiding ISIS terror group, FBI says. ABC News - the Denver Channel. Retrieved from: http://www.thedenverchannel.com/news/local-news/19-year-old-colorado-woman-shannon-maureen-conley-charged-with-aiding-terrorist-group-fbi-says07022014

92 Gathright, A. (July 2, 2014). 19-year-old Arvada woman, Shannon Maureen Conley, charged with aiding ISIS terror group, FBI says. ABC News - the Denver Channel. Retrieved from: http://www.thedenverchannel.com/news/local-news/19-year-old-colorado-woman-shannon-maureen-conley-charged-with-aiding-terrorist-group-fbi-says07022014

93 Faberov, S., & Bates, D. (July 2, 2014). American nurse who was arrested for trying to join ISIS set her Facebook profile to 'slave of Allah': Denver teen also wrote that U.S. women dress like s****' after she was seduced by a Syrian militant Daily Mail. Retrieved from: http://www.dailymail.co.uk/news/article-2678662/Denver-woman-19-charged-plotting-join-ISIS-militants-wage-jihad-U-S.html

Index

CPSIA information can be obtained at www.ICGtesting.com
Printed in the USA
LVOW08*0400170715

446230LV00001B/4/P